AUTUMN
GRACE

AUTUMN GRACE

AMISH SEASONS
BOOK 2

Marianne Ellis

JOVE
New York

A JOVE BOOK
Published by Berkley
An imprint of Penguin Random House LLC
penguinrandomhouse.com

Copyright © 2013 by Parachute Publishing, LLC
Penguin Random House supports copyright. Copyright fuels creativity, encourages
diverse voices, promotes free speech, and creates a vibrant culture. Thank you for buying
an authorized edition of this book and for complying with copyright laws by not
reproducing, scanning, or distributing any part of it in any form without permission.
You are supporting writers and allowing Penguin Random House to continue to
publish books for every reader.

A JOVE BOOK, BERKLEY, and the BERKLEY & B colophon are registered
trademarks of Penguin Random House LLC.

ISBN: 9780593334898

Berkley hardcover edition / November 2013
Jove mass-market edition / August 2021

Printed in the United States of America
1   3   5   7   9   10   8   6   4   2

Book design by Laura K. Corless

For Jane, Cam, and Ellen
The best writing team ever!

One

༄

Ruth Schrock straightened up and brushed rich, black earth from her apron. She loved working in her family's vegetable garden, but summer had extended its heat and humidity into September. The sun beat down on her, and only her bare toes, curled into the earth, were cool. She pulled out a handkerchief and wiped her forehead and her nape beneath her *kapp*. She was looking forward to a soak in the tub tonight. That would help her sleep so she could finish harvesting tomorrow.

She picked green beans and placed them in the bucket with a late squash and the final tomatoes. Everything else, except for the pumpkins, was already canned. The pumpkins still needed a week or two before being cut from their wandering vines. Then, she would slice, peel, cook, and mash them. To some she would add nutmeg, ginger, and cinnamon, for desserts and sweet sauces. The rest would be canned without spice. *Daed* liked egg noodles, chicken, and stewed pumpkin after he finished the milking on a cold winter's night.

Ruth did most of the cooking now, because *Mamm* was going to have another *boppli* in early December. Ruth was the oldest of seven daughters, so her *mamm* was praying as hard for a boy as *Daed* was. All Ruth prayed for was that the *boppli* be healthy. It was her mother's tenth pregnancy, including a miscarriage and a stillborn son.

Ruth dropped the last beans in the bucket and glanced at the old, white farmhouse with porches on each side. *Gut!* *Mamm* wasn't in sight. Maybe she was resting, as the midwife had ordered. The barn behind the house was the same white, and the wide door to the upper story gaped open. *Daed* had finished chopping corn for the day, and the mules were in the pasture. By now, he would be starting evening chores.

The grass tickled her feet as she crossed the yard. One of her younger sisters would need to mow tomorrow. She couldn't remember if it was Maisie's or Ella's turn.

Climbing the steps to the mud porch set between the kitchen and the vacant *dawdi-haus*, she opened the screened kitchen door. She wasn't surprised to see *Mamm* by the table, mixing something in a bowl she had propped against her large stomach. A smudge of flour accented her turned-up nose that was so much like Ruth's. Her eyes were brown, and her light-brown hair glittered with gray. She wasn't very tall, unlike Ruth who towered over her. Now that *Mamm* was so round, she looked even shorter.

"*Mamm*, I thought you were going to sit," Ruth chided her gently.

"I tried, but I promised your sisters some ginger molasses cookies." *Mamm* smiled, but nothing could erase the fatigue on her face. "It's not in my nature to sit and do nothing all afternoon."

"I know." Ruth didn't bother to remind *Mamm* there were things she could do: mending, working on the *boppli*'s quilt, or making new clothes for the younger girls. But *Mamm* wasn't one for sitting. Neither was Ruth, which was why she loved working in the garden, even on a hot day. "Let me make supper tonight."

"*Ach*, that will be *gut*, Ruth."

"I'm going to wash up at the pump. I think I brought half the dirt from the garden with me."

Mamm laughed then put her hand to her stomach. "That was a big kick." She winced. "A very big one."

"Are you all right?" If her *mamm* went into labor early, the *boppli* might die. "Do I need to call the midwife?"

"No. I'm fine." She waved toward the door. "You worry too much. Go and wash up. Make sure Vera and Mattie wash, too. I saw them playing in the mud by the pump earlier."

Ruth set the bucket of vegetables in the sink, reminding *Mamm* to leave the cleaning to her. She planned the evening meal while going back outside to find her youngest sisters. *Mamm* had baked bread that morning, and Ruth

3

would make a stew with leftover chicken. That should be enough for the nine of them, with *Mamm*'s delicious cookies and pie for dessert.

If only Ruth could be as *gut* a cook as *Mamm* . . . She tried, but she found cooking traditional recipes boring. When she added a new ingredient and the meal came out tasting strange, *Mamm* laughed. "That's our Ruth. Always needing to do something different."

Daed wasn't so forgiving, especially when he didn't like Ruth's experiments. He was a stickler for tradition. Maybe that's why God had picked him to serve as the district's deacon, even though *Mamm* joked with her daughters that *Daed* needed an excuse to escape so many females. The mules were female, the cows were female, the hens were female, most of the barn cats were female, and he had seven daughters.

Now Ruth needed to find the two youngest. Vera was six and Mattie just four. It was *gut* that *Mamm* was having another *boppli*, because Mattie had been lonely since Vera began school two weeks ago. As far as Ruth could see, the two tried to compress a day's worth of mischief into the hours after school.

"Ruth! Ruth!" called Vera, breaking into Ruth's thoughts. "*Komm* and play with us."

Her youngest sisters rushed to her. Their bare legs were splattered with mud, and so were the hems of their burgundy dresses. Their brown hair, streaked with gold as light as Ruth's hair, stuck out in every direction from beneath their white, heart-shaped *kapps*.

"Play with two such dirty girls?" Ruth wrinkled her nose in feigned distaste. "Why would I want to do that?"

"We can't play snake with just two of us," Mattie explained.

"All right. One quick game, then we'll clean up and you can help me wash the vegetables for supper."

Taking each of her sisters by the hand, Ruth began to lead them across the yard in the snake game she had played when she was their age. They wound between the big maples and the towering oak, then around the trampoline, and back past the pump. Her sisters' giggles became excited squeals when Ruth spun them around, their bare feet flying behind them. She flipped Vera, then Mattie, over her arm, landing each on her feet. They bounced around her, begging her to do it again.

Laughing, she asked, "Do you know how silly you look?" She copied their motions, her long skirt flying up around her shins. Grabbing their hands again, she twirled them around until they were all giggling.

"Ruth Deborah Schrock!"

At *Daed*'s sharp voice, Ruth froze along with her sisters. They recognized the tight, restrained tone he used when he was furious.

He strode toward them. His light-blond beard, which reached down over his blue shirt, jutted toward them. That was a sure sign he was angry.

Not them, Ruth corrected herself when he told her younger sisters to go in the house. *He's angry at me.*

She quickly lowered her eyes. *Daed* didn't like to be

reminded that she was tall—an inch taller than he was, in fact. He blamed her height for her still-unmarried state at the age of twenty-two.

He put his hand on her shoulder and turned her toward the house. Neither of them spoke as they walked into the kitchen. Only *Mamm* was there, putting a tray of cookies into the oven.

Mamm glanced at them, then went to the sink, where she poured water into a bowl and began washing the beans Ruth had brought in. *Mamm* didn't interfere when *Daed* chastised them. It was the deacon's job to reprimand members of the district when they hadn't followed the *Ordnung*. He expected no less from his daughters than from the rest of the community. Ruth girded herself for what her father would say.

Daed took off his straw hat and hung it on the peg by the door, where eight everyday bonnets waited. Crossing to where Ruth stood, he demanded, "What if someone had seen you dancing like that?"

"*Daed*, we were shielded from the road." She looked into his eyes, that were the same deep blue as her own. "Nobody passing by would have seen us."

"I saw you from the barn. What if the bishop and the preachers had been meeting with me there?"

Ruth had no argument for that. She had let herself get caught up in the moment, enjoying the chance to play with her sisters. But now *Daed* was disappointed with her—again! She hung her head, knowing she'd been wrong.

"I am sorry, *Daed*," she whispered, as she had so many times before. Why was it easy for Martha, Ella, and Maisie to live up to *Daed*'s expectations? Martha was on her *rum-springa*, but never gave *Daed* a moment of concern. Her sisters seemed to instinctively know what behavior was perfect for a deacon's daughter. It wasn't that Ruth didn't know, but sometimes she got caught up in the moment.

As if she had spoken her thoughts out loud, *Daed* said, "Ruth, a deacon and his family must show esteemed behavior to the *Leit*." The *Leit* were the people of their district; her father seemed to measure every act in terms of how it would look to them.

When her *daed* was chosen as the district's deacon, *Mamm* had explained to Ruth and her sisters that a deacon and his wife were expected to follow the district's rules even more closely than other members. She had said nothing about a deacon's *kinder*, but *Daed* believed they must be exemplary, too.

And Ruth tried.

She really did.

Lord, you know how I long never to disappoint my daed *so he will be glad I am his daughter.*

How often had she prayed those words?

And how many times had she found herself bending the rules? Never breaking them, for she had agreed to live within the *Ordnung* when she was baptized.

But even so, she seemed to disappoint her *daed*. It never was anything outrageous . . . at least to her. Just last week, she had been walking along their farm lane and humming a song she had heard through the window of an *Englisch* neighbor's house. It was such a catchy tune that she hadn't even realized what she was doing until *Daed* overheard her.

But the scolding she received then was nothing compared to what she would hear now, if she were to judge by the stern fire in *Daed*'s eyes. "If you don't show exemplary behavior, how will your younger sisters know how they should act?" *Daed* asked. "You know your *mamm* and I depend on you to be a *gut* example for them. You aren't a *kind* any longer. You are a baptized member. You need to act as the other women do. You can't be cavorting about like a *kind*."

"I know, *Daed*," she replied as she stared at the mud dotting her bare toes.

"You must consider each decision you make with the greatest care and consider the consequences of that decision."

"I try."

"If I saw any effort on your part to change . . ." He sighed.

Pain cut through her. Did he have any idea how she wanted to please him? She tried, but she wasn't like the women her age because she wasn't married or even being courted. Most girls she had gone to school with had at least one *boppli* by now. It wasn't that she hadn't had offers for rides home from singings. She had taken buggy rides with several young men, but none ever touched her heart enough for her to consider that he was the one God intended her to spend the rest of her life with. She wanted to find a man she could love with all her heart, but was it God's will or her own that she wasn't ready to be a *fraa*?

She wanted to do something else first. What? She didn't know. But she felt that she had a calling, that there was some work that God meant for her to do. Last year, she'd assisted at the schoolhouse, and she had loved having time with the scholars, as they called the students. When the teacher left to have a *boppli*, Ruth prayed the job would be hers. That hope ended when the teacher decided she wanted to return to teaching. It wasn't unheard of for a married woman with a *kind* to teach, but it was unusual enough for Ruth to have gotten her hopes up. She couldn't remember when she had been so disappointed.

She prayed for God to show her what plans He had for her.

"Zeb." When *Mamm* spoke, Ruth wasn't sure if it was she or *Daed* who was more surprised. "What Ruth did was no different from what I did with our *kinder* when they were young. I appreciate Ruth helping them use up their energy. Especially now." She placed her hand on her full belly.

All bluster vanished from *Daed*. Even though he ruled their home, Ruth and her sisters had long ago discovered that *Mamm* ruled *him* with the gentle warmth she showed to everyone. *Mamm* and *Daed* loved each other so much that they respected each other's opinions and needs.

That was what Ruth wanted in a marriage.

But she also wanted her *kinder* to have a *daed* who was both stern and loving. Once, her *daed* had been that way, but when he became the district's deacon, he had set aside everything but strictness. She missed the *daed* she recalled from her childhood: the man she could go to with any concern, the man who held her and comforted her over a skinned knee, the *daed* she adored. She still respected her *daed*, and she loved him, but it sometimes felt more like a duty.

While *Daed* put his arm around *Mamm* and walked her into the living room, Ruth finished washing the vegetables. She heard their muted voices, but concentrated on her task. By the time *Daed* returned to the kitchen, she was chopping vegetables into the stew pot. Her eyes met his, and she saw his anger was gone, but not his disappointment in her. She quickly lowered her eyes as she blinked back tears.

"I'm sorry, *Daed*," she said as she stared into the pot. "I wouldn't do anything that would bring shame on you or this family."

"Gut." He added nothing more as he walked out, letting the screen door slam shut behind him.

Mamm came back to remove fragrant cookies from the oven. "Ruth, God gave you a joyous spirit. I've known that since you were as young as this one." She patted her belly. "But your *daed* worries that your unconventional ways will catch the attention of Bishop Abram." She reached for the bowl with the dough, and began spooning more cookies onto another cookie sheet.

"I know. But there's something within me that won't be stilled."

Mamm nodded. "You never were still then, and you aren't now. You always follow your heart, and leap before you look. Maybe once in a while you should look?"

In spite of her dismay, Ruth smiled. "I think I can manage once in a while, and maybe that once in a while will become a habit."

"Maybe." *Mamm* laughed, the sound as warm as the

heat from the oven as she opened it to put in the other tray of cookies.

A knock sounded on the back door as Ruth was helping Maisie clear the supper table. She glanced over her shoulder and saw a familiar face.

Bishop Abram wasn't a young man. His beard was gray, and his shoulders stooped from years of working as a blacksmith. He always had a kind word, but took his duties as their spiritual adviser very seriously.

"I hope we're not interrupting," the bishop said in his booming voice.

Daed stood and gestured for him to come in. He was followed by two men Ruth didn't recognize. That astonished her. She knew everyone in their district.

"*Wilkomm*, Abram," *Daed* said. "If you and your companions haven't eaten, we would be honored to have you join us at our table. My Deborah always enjoys sharing her baking with our neighbors."

Bishop Abram nodded. *Mamm* and Ruth got cups and plates for their guests while ten-year-old Naomi pulled up two more chairs.

The bishop introduced the men as Joseph Hooley and Paul Beiler, adding that they lived in a district about fifteen miles away.

"That is a long distance to come at this hour," *Daed* said. "Which district is it?"

"We're in Bishop John's district, north of Bird-in-Hand," Joseph replied with a smile.

"I read in *The Budget* about a district over that way where a farm stand burned recently. Is that the one?"

Paul nodded. "*Ja*, the Stony Field Farm Stand. It's now rebuilt and better than ever, or so my *fraa* tells me. You'll probably read about that in *The Budget*, too."

The men chuckled, and *Mamm* smiled along with Ruth. The weekly newspaper was written by hundreds of correspondents from Amish and Mennonite communities, and it kept its readers up to date on all the births, marriages, deaths, and other events in the various districts.

Bishop Abram sat at the table but didn't explain why he had brought two strangers to the Schrock farm. Instead, the men sat and talked about the heat wave and asked *Daed* how much more corn he had left to chop while Ruth placed plates with *Mamm*'s *snitz* pie in front of each man, the delicious scent of baked apples wafting over them.

"Let me do that," Ruth murmured to halt her *mamm* from lifting the heavy kettle off the stove. "You sit and rest your feet."

"*Danki*. My ankles are swelling tonight." With a grateful smile, *Mamm* lowered herself onto a chair. Her distended belly almost bumped the table, and the men grasped their pie plates.

Finally Bishop Abram rested his fork on his empty plate. "Excellent, as always, Deborah."

"I'd be glad to send a few pies to your house, Abram, on our next baking day."

He patted his belly. "You know I won't insult you by saying no."

Everyone laughed, but Ruth shifted her gaze from the bishop's companions to *Daed* and back. His uncertainty matched her own. Why were these strangers here, and why did they keep looking at her?

"You're blessed to have so many daughters to help you, Deborah," Bishop Abram went on.

"Ja," Mamm said. "I don't know what I would do without them. Ruth oversaw all the canning this year."

"My *fraa* would have gladly given anyone else the job of canning."

Ruth smiled, glad to hear Bishop Abram speak easily of his late wife. She had died from lung cancer two years ago. They had been married for over forty years, and he mourned her deeply.

At last, even *Daed*'s pie was done and the *kaffi* finished. Bishop Abram pushed himself back a few inches from the table and clasped his fingers over his stomach.

"We are grateful for your hospitality," he said, "but Joseph and Paul have a long trip home, so it's time to get to the business that brought us here tonight." His gaze focused on *Daed*. "Zeb, we're here to speak with your oldest, if that's all right with you."

Daed shot a glare at Ruth. She saw the question in his eyes. What had she done to upset Bishop Abram, as well as men from another district?

She wanted to tell him that she couldn't imagine that the bishop and the other men would be upset because she had played with her sisters. There couldn't be any complaint about her behavior the last time she went into Lancaster.

She had accompanied *Mamm* to the Central Market and delivered pies to be sold by *Mamm*'s friend who had a booth there. They had sold the pies and come home.

Daed looked at the bishop and the other men. "If my daughter has done anything that reached your ears—"

"That's exactly why we're here," Joseph said with a smile.

Ruth's heart sank. *Mamm* appeared as shocked and dismayed as Ruth. Her sisters were exchanging anxious glances.

Joseph must not have noticed because he continued, "It has reached our district that your daughter Ruth has taught in your school."

"*Ja*, she has," *Mamm* said when *Daed* seemed at a loss for words. "Both when she was a scholar and last year, when our teacher had to leave for family reasons." She looked down at her own full belly.

Paul smiled more broadly. "Losing a teacher sounds too familiar. Joseph and I are members of our school board," he explained, "and the teacher we hired suddenly decided to jump the fence and marry an *Englischer*. We hear they now live in Baltimore."

Ruth silenced her gasp. To have a teacher choose to marry an *Englischer* and leave their district must have been a huge shock.

Joseph grew serious. "Even if she had remained nearby, we decided her behavior wasn't appropriate for what we wanted in a teacher."

"I can understand that," *Daed* said. "But why are you looking for a new teacher now? School started here more than two weeks ago."

"As it should have in our district," Paul replied. "We looked without success in our district and in our bishop's other district for the right person. We came up empty. Then Sadie Lambright suggested we come to speak to your oldest daughter because she has experience teaching but isn't teaching this year."

Mamm smiled. "How are Sadie and Mervin? I seldom get to see my sister and her family."

"They are doing well," Paul said before looking back at *Daed*. "Zeb, after we heard about your oldest from Sadie, we hoped Ruth would be the answer to our prayers."

This time Ruth was unable to hold back her gasp of astonishment. *She* was the answer to someone's prayers? That seemed as unlikely as the moon landing in their cornfield. Her eye caught Bishop Abram's, and he gave her a quick wink.

Or had he? Maybe she had only imagined it. Everything seemed out of kilter.

"Are you asking me to teach at your school?" Her clasped hands tightened until her knuckles were white.

She longed to see more of the world than their district and the Central Market. Teaching fifteen miles from her home was the opportunity she'd been praying for. She could do a job she loved and prove to *Daed* that she was worthy of an important position like teaching.

"We know it's short notice," said Joseph. "But when we heard you've done some teaching, we thought you might be willing to help us this year. Your aunt and uncle said they would be happy to have you live with them."

Every inch of Ruth wanted to agree, but she looked to

her parents. As long as she lived beneath their roof, such a decision would be theirs.

Daed leaned back in his chair and tapped his first two fingers together. "Your *mamm* may need you now."

"Mamm?" she asked quietly.

Mamm reached across the table and squeezed Ruth's hand. "If you want to go, go. I've got plenty of help here." She glanced at her other daughters. "If it's all right with you, Zeb."

"If you are willing to let her go, so am I."

Guilt pinched Ruth's heart. Maybe she should say no. After all, if she went and Mamm had trouble with her pregnancy . . . No, she wouldn't think of that. She had prayed for God to open a path before her, and He had. She must trust in His will.

"Ja," she said with a smile as she looked from one school board member to the other. "I would be very happy to accept your offer to teach at your school."

Two

❧

As he strode across the Lambrights' yard, Levi Yoder listened to the excited *kinder* playing on the sprawling farmhouse's porch. Their voices filled the evening with laughter as they planned to catch lightning bugs once dusk fell. They were using a screwdriver and a hammer to drive holes in the lids of mayonnaise jars.

He liked visiting the Lambrights' home. His own house, where he lived alone now that his *gross-mammi*, his grandmother, had joined her husband in heaven, was quiet. So quiet that he heard the animals moving about in the barn.

To others, that might be a lonely sound, but not for Levi. Whether he heard the cows lowing or a whicker from a horse or the more feral noise made by the wild animals he nursed to health, the noises were like a prayer. He couldn't help thinking of an *Englisch* hymn he had heard during his brief *rumspringa*. The gentle melody played through his mind:

"All things bright and beautiful,
All creatures great and small,
All things wise and wonderful,
The Lord God made them all."

Levi felt closest to his Lord when he brought wounded animals into his barn and tended to them until they could be free again. The chance to watch an animal heal seemed like a miracle each time.

Truth be told, he found it easier to be around animals than people. He didn't have to worry about saying the wrong thing to animals. They simply accepted him as a provider of food and care.

At the Lambrights', he was comfortable with the patriarch, Mervin. The Lambrights' eldest, Samuel, was Levi's *gut* friend. Here, Levi didn't have to weigh every word to be sure it wouldn't bring shame on his grandparents' memory or his parents'.

Opening the back door, Levi walked into the bright kitchen. It had been two years since Bishop John decided they could put solar panels on their roofs. The electricity gathered in the batteries was used only for lamps. The Lambrights had been among the first to install panels and purchase lights. Levi preferred the softer glow of kerosene lamps, but he never would have admitted that to his friends. Mervin and his *fraa*, Sadie, were excited to have the bright light.

"Sit down," Mervin called from the head of the table where he had been reading *The Budget* aloud while Sadie washed the supper dishes. Folding the newspaper, he motioned to their oldest daughter, Esther, to bring Levi a cup of *kaffi.* "So, do you have news of our horse? Do you know why Bonnie went lame?"

Levi sat and smiled his thanks when Esther set a cup in front of him on the long oak table. "Bonnie picked up a piece of glass in her hoof. I cleaned it and put some peroxide on it. Once it's dry, I'll put on a poultice of honey. You'll need to change it twice a day, but she should be fine."

His friend Samuel walked into the kitchen. "Sounds *gut.*"

Black-haired Samuel was tall and slim with the broad shoulders that drew the eyes of the *maedels* eager for a husband. Levi suspected his friend had already selected a girl to court. Maybe he was already courting her. Such matters were kept quiet, even among the best of friends, until an engagement was published during the church service two weeks before the wedding.

After Samuel poured himself some *kaffi* and sat down at the table, Levi said, "Don't be stingy with the honey, Mervin. It cleans bacteria from the wound."

"How long should we keep the poultice on Bonnie's hoof?" Mervin asked.

"Until the wound is healed." Levi nodded his thanks as Sadie set slices of apple pie in front of them. "Better to put the honey on too long than for too short a time. Stopping too soon risks infection. If you see any pus, call the veterinarian fast."

"Or we could call you," Samuel said with a chuckle. "You do as *gut* a job, and you don't charge more than a piece of pie."

"Maybe two." Levi leaned one elbow on the table. "But if you see infection, call Dr. Hopkins. Bonnie is a fine horse. I would hate to see you have to put her down."

"I agree," Mervin said. "If we aren't sure about her hoof—"

"Call me." Levi grinned. "And *I* will call Dr. Hopkins."

Levi let the conversation flow around him while he enjoyed Sadie's pie. Though he had learned to cook after his *gross-mamm* became an invalid, he had never mastered baking. Maybe he should buy a propane stove like the Lambrights and get rid of his temperamental, old woodstove.

He scraped up the last crumbs from his pie, and Esther slid another piece on his plate. She looked like her *mamm*, with brown hair and eyes. "How are you, Esther?"

"How do you think I am?" she asked playfully as she sat beside him. "I can't wait to turn sixteen in a few weeks. Or have you forgotten?"

"I remember," he replied.

"Do you know what I want to do first?"

Samuel groaned. "Esther, Levi doesn't want to hear about plans for your *rumspringa*."

"What first?" Levi asked, eager to let Esther become the focus of the conversation. Now that he wasn't talking about animals, the words didn't come easily, even with friends.

Esther had no chance to say anything, because headlights flashed through the kitchen windows. The bright light coming up the country lane silenced everyone.

Sadie wiped her hands on a dish towel. "Who's coming at this hour in a car?"

While she went to the window, Levi carried his dishes

to the sink. The Plain people hired Mennonite drivers when the distances were too great for a buggy—to go to the market or the doctor or to visit a faraway friend. Or in an emergency, which was what Sadie obviously feared.

Steps sounded on the porch.

"It's my sister Deborah's husband. At last!" Sadie threw open the door. "Zeb! *Komm* in! *Komm* in! I'm so glad you're here. When it got so late, I guessed you wouldn't be coming tonight." She hugged the man then embraced the tall, young woman who stood just a few steps behind him. "Ruth, look at what a pretty woman you've become! I haven't seen you since Cousin Myron's wedding three years ago."

Levi remained by the sink, not wanting to intrude. From there he had a *gut* view of Ruth. He had to agree with Sadie. Ruth was pretty. Her golden hair was pulled neatly back beneath her *kapp*, offering him an excellent view of her high cheekbones and full lips. Sparkling blue eyes grew even brighter as she returned Sadie's hug.

He found himself wondering how it would feel to have those slender arms around him. He put a halt to that thought immediately. In spite of the veiled hints from Sadie about how lonely he must be in that big house, and the outright prodding from Samuel, he still hadn't gotten around to looking for a *fraa*. Up until his *gross-mammi*'s death two years ago, he hadn't had time to join other young people at singings or frolics. He had been too busy taking care of his grandmother when she could no longer take care of herself.

He owed her and *Dawdi* for rearing him after his parents died. Even if there wasn't that debt, he would have done everything he could for *Mammi*, as he called his grand-mother. No one in the district was surprised when he set aside a young man's pleasures to nurse her until God took her home. It was what a *gut* grandson did, and he'd proved himself by obeying his grandparents in all but their request that he stop bringing injured animals into the barn to heal them.

"The beasts of the field and the air live according to God's will, just as we do," *Dawdi* had said more than once. "If it's their time to die, then we should let them."

"But what if it's God's will that I nurse them back to health?" Levi had argued with a *kind*'s logic. "Doesn't the Bible tell us every creature is *gut*?"

Dawdi had given his most indulgent chuckle. Whether or not he agreed, *Dawdi* was always pleased when Levi stood up for what was in his heart.

At a laugh much lighter than his *dawdi*'s, Levi's eyes were drawn to Ruth Schrock. He shouldn't stare. Not many women were as tall as she was, but she didn't seem both-ered by her height as she towered over Sadie and Esther. As other members of the Lambright family—except the twins, Lewis and Ray, who were sick with a stomach bug—rushed into the kitchen to see who was calling, she greeted each one warmly. Then she began to tell them how the Menno-nite car they'd come in drove so fast that it had to swerve to miss a deer.

Samuel sidled up next to Levi and grinned. "My cousin is pretty, don't you think?"

"She's pretty talkative," Levi said as he watched Ruth

illustrate her story with lively gestures. Her young cousins listened, rapt.

"Everyone is talkative compared to you," Samuel said with a laugh. "Unless you're going on and on about animals, you seldom say more than three words in a row."

"I do so."

Samuel arched his brows. "That was three words."

"You're being silly."

"Three more." Samuel wiggled three fingers in front of Levi's face.

Levi decided he would be wise to quit before the others wanted to know what was so amusing. He had delayed leaving long enough. He turned to go, but Ruth and her *daed* stood between him and the door. For now, he thought the smartest thing would be to stay where he was. He leaned back against the sink again.

By the door, Ruth untied her bonnet as she finished her story, and everyone else began to talk at the same time. Aunt Sadie looked even rounder than the last time Ruth had seen her. Esther had changed from a girl into a young woman. Ruth was astonished to realize that her cousin might already have embarked on her *rumspringa*.

Mark Lambright squinted up at his tall cousin. "If the car was so fast, then why are you here so late?"

"We had to wait," Ruth explained, "until after our driver was finished with some other trips he'd promised to make." She looked at the younger *kinder*. "He drove all the way to

Philadelphia and back today before he came to pick us up. Imagine that!"

They giggled, and she wondered which ones were old enough to go to school. For the first time, she realized she would be teaching some of her own cousins. She couldn't wait to begin, but first . . .

"Sadie," she said, "it's so kind of you to open your house to me. I'm looking forward to getting to know all of you better. Oh, I see the quilt *Mamm* made for you when the twins were born." Again she was babbling, but she couldn't stop herself. "She wanted two of everything on the quilt, so we had a lot of fun stitching it together. She will be so pleased to hear that you have it displayed. I—"

"Daughter." *Daed*'s voice wasn't raised, but she heard the warning in it.

Silence clamped down on the kitchen. Ruth shifted uneasily from one foot to the other, and her hands seemed uncomfortable whether they were by her sides or clasped in front of her. Heat swarmed up her face.

Please don't let me blush, she prayed as she looked away from her cousins who were gathered around her.

For the first time she noticed the man standing by the sink. She was surprised she hadn't taken note of him before, but she'd been so busy talking with her cousins. Now she wondered who he was.

His tanned skin was a sign of long hours of work in the fields. He was tall and lean, as many Amish farmers were. Taller even than she was. When he put one hand on the edge of the sink, she was astonished by his long fingers. Most farmers had short, stubby hands with heavy knuckles scarred from injuries over the years with farm equipment. His hands were work-worn but not gnarled.

His indecipherable gaze swept over her and away. Without a word, he took a step toward the back door.

He halted when Sadie said, "This is our *gut* friend Levi Yoder. Levi, this is my sister's husband, Zeb Schrock, and his eldest daughter, Ruth."

Daed and Levi nodded at each other.

Ruth didn't look at him as she said, "Hello, Levi."

"*Komm* and sit, Zeb, Ruth." Sadie gestured at the table.

Ruth edged past Levi, careful not to let her arm brush his. She had assumed he was leaving, but Esther grabbed his arm and drew him toward the table.

Levi shook his head. "There isn't room."

"*Mamm* says we've always got room for one more." Esther giggled as she waited for him to sit next to her eldest brother and across from Ruth. She hurried to where Sadie was slicing a pie, and she picked up the *kaffi* pot to begin serving.

Ruth offered to help, too. She hoped nobody would guess that she wanted to avoid having to make small talk with Levi until she discovered why the Lambrights acted as if he were a member of the family.

"Stay where you are," Sadie told her. "It will take longer to tell you where everything is than to do it ourselves." She came back to the table, making sure each of her *kinder* was seated and had a piece of pie. "We're very excited to have you with us, Ruth."

"I'm so excited to be here," she replied after taking a bite of the warm pie. "Oh, your apple pie is delicious!"

"It should be. It's your *mamm*'s recipe," Sadie said with a smile.

"How is your *mamm*?" Mervin asked.

"*Mamm* is doing well. The hot weather has been wearying, and Ella and I try to convince her that she needs to sit and finish the quilt she started when she was expecting Mattie." Ruth grinned. "Mattie turned four last week. We told *Mamm* if she didn't finish it for this one, Mattie would soon be helping her."

Laughter rushed around the table again, but *Daed* put down his cup and said, "Mervin, I am grateful that Ruth can stay with you during the upcoming school year."

"We're glad she's willing to teach at our district's school."

"*She's* our new schoolteacher?" asked Levi.

Ruth bit back her retort as her cousin Samuel held up four fingers and chuckled. It must be a joke between the two men, but that held no interest for her. She wanted to know why this admittedly fine-looking stranger sounded so disbelieving when he heard she was the new schoolteacher. Did he not think her capable? Was he judging her when he didn't know anything about her? Even *Daed* didn't make up his mind about someone until he knew them well. Levi didn't know that she had experience teaching. He didn't know that she hoped the position would show everyone that she could do a *gut* job. That it would show her *daed*, so he would relent from his stern inflexibility and be the *daed* he had once been.

"Didn't you hear that Paul and Joseph asked Ruth to come here to be our teacher, Levi?" asked Mervin. "I was sure you'd know by now."

Levi shook his head, but said nothing.

"We are very grateful that Zeb was willing to allow Ruth to come to our aid," Mervin said with a warm smile.

Daed put his cup on the table. "I had my concerns about Ruth coming here to teach, but your district's need outweighed my personal concerns. I pray you feel it was the right decision, after Ruth has been teaching here a while."

Every eye turned toward Ruth. She lowered her gaze to the table. *Daed!* Why did he have to express his opinion like that? What concerns? It sounded as if he doubted the people in the district would think they'd made the right decision in hiring her. Did he really think so little of her, or was he saying that he would regret that she wasn't home to help *Mamm*? Either way, she felt a moment of fear and uncertainty, as if she had missed a step and felt herself falling.

The uneasy silence was broken when young Mark brought the box containing Ruth's things into the kitchen, carrying it past the table and into the front room. As before, everyone began to talk at once.

Everyone but Levi, Ruth noticed. He chased the apples on his plate around with a piece of crust and stared at the table so intently she wondered if he was trying to see through the thick oak. She should be grateful he wasn't looking at her. Each time he had, she had either blushed or been annoyed.

She tried to pay him no mind as she listened to her *daed* talking with her *onkel* about farming.

"You can use a front-end loader?" asked *Daed*, his eyes widening. "Our bishop would never allow that."

"It's only for moving heavy items like bales of hay and

27

other feed," Mervin replied. "Would you like to see it in action?"

Daed shook his head. "Not tonight, but I'll stop by some other time and see how it helps with your chores." His glance at Ruth held a silent warning that he expected to hear only *gut* things about her when he came back.

She realized nobody else had noticed *Daed*'s expression when her *onkel* pushed back his chair and said, "Speaking of chores, I need to get out and finish up in the barn. With two boys sick, we're barely getting the milking done."

"I'd be glad to help with the milking until Lewis and Ray are feeling better," Ruth said.

When she heard a quickly hushed gasp from across the table, she looked at Levi. Astonishment widened his eyes. They were an odd shade that wasn't quite green and not quite brown, as if he had spent so much time checking his crops that his eyes had taken on their colors.

What had surprised him so? Surely nothing she'd said. She glanced from him to her cousin Samuel, who wore the mischievous expression she remembered from when they were young. Maybe her cousin had said something to him?

"Any decision about you helping here must be your *on-kel*'s," *Daed* said.

Ruth nodded. "I only wanted him to know that I'd be glad to help."

"Such a decision must be your *onkel*'s," he repeated in a tone that brooked no debate.

She lowered her eyes. *"Ja, Daed."*

"Your offer is appreciated, Ruth," Mervin said, "but

you'll be busy with teaching. Having a school of your own won't be like assisting in the one you attended."

From the other side of the table, Levi asked, "You haven't taught before?" He grimaced when Samuel held up four fingers and chuckled again.

This time, she was tempted to ask what game they were playing, but decided she should focus on Levi's question. "I helped our teacher," she replied, "and when she was unable to teach for a few months, I took her place. That's not a lot of experience, but it was enough for me to know I like to teach."

She waited for him to ask another question, but he said nothing more. His eyes narrowed, and she couldn't help wondering what he was thinking.

Daed pushed back from the table and stood. "I told the driver I would be only a few minutes."

Ruth rose as Sadie and Mervin did and walked to the back door with her *daed*. "*Danki* for coming with me, *Daed*." She took a step forward to embrace him, but stopped when he spoke.

"Do as you should, Ruth." Then he turned and walked toward the door with Mervin.

Tears filled her eyes. Not only were *Daed*'s parting words a reminder that he wasn't sure she could do as she agreed to, but she realized that when he left she would be without her immediate family for the first time in her life. She barely knew the Lambrights; she had seen them only at weddings and funerals. Now she would be living with them. In the excitement of being offered a teaching job, she hadn't really thought about everything she would be giving up.

Daed didn't look back as he closed the door behind him. She blinked rapidly to keep tears from falling. What was wrong with her? She had asked God for an adventure, and He had given it to her. Why was she about to cry like a *boppli* now in front of her cousins and Levi Yoder?

As she thought his name, she glanced across the kitchen. He had gotten up, too, and he looked at her as if struggling to solve a puzzle, which made her feel uncomfortable. She didn't need another man judging her.

Sadie must have noticed where Ruth was looking because she put her hand on Ruth's arm and guided her over to Levi and Samuel. Ruth didn't see Sadie look at her son, but Samuel announced he had some chores to do outside.

"You know how it is for a farmer," he said with a grin. "The work is never done."

"Much like for a farmer's *fraa*," Sadie replied. "If you'll move out of my way, Levi, I can finish up the dishes."

"Let me help," Ruth said. She didn't want to face Levi until she had regained her composure. It seemed to flee each time he looked in her direction.

"Nonsense. Esther always helps me. You've had a long journey here." Sadie turned away, giving Ruth no chance to argue. "Why don't you sit and talk with Levi? You two should get to know each other better. After all, you'll be seeing a lot of him."

Ruth stared in disbelief at her *aenti*. Others had tried to play matchmaker for her, but nobody as blatantly as Sadie.

"Time for me to go," Levi said, and frowned as Samuel

started to raised five fingers. "Enough of that counting non-sense."

"Levi, sit down and let Ruth get to know you," Sadie said, waving a soapy hand in his direction.

As Samuel went out the door, laughing, Ruth watched Levi perch on the very end of the bench across from where she sat.

By the sink, Sadie and Esther talked quietly. Sounds came from the living room as the *kinder* played or worked on projects. The rumble of the car's engine outside swallowed the peepers' songs. Even so, Ruth guessed every ear in the house was aimed at the table, where she and Levi sat.

"Do you live here, too?" Ruth asked. It wasn't unusual for a family to take in relatives, as the Lambrights were taking her in. She didn't remember anyone named Levi in her family, and he couldn't be someone's husband because his square jaw was clean-shaven. Plain men didn't grow beards until after they married.

He shook his head. "Couple of miles up the road."

"I don't understand why we'll be seeing each other of-ten."

Esther grinned over her shoulder. "Levi lives across from the school."

"And he donated the land for the school when we needed a new one last year," Sadie added.

"You did?" Ruth was astonished that a bachelor would do such a thing. Maybe he had siblings who attended the school.

"Ja," Levi said.

Wiping her hands on a towel, Sadie walked to the table.

"When we realized our new schoolteacher wouldn't be coming from this district, it was decided that if she needed to drive to school, she could put her buggy and horse in Levi's barn during the school day."

"If it's only a couple of miles, I can walk." Ruth regretted her words when Levi affixed her with a cool frown. Did he think she wanted to avoid him? That wasn't far from the truth, but she hadn't meant to insult him. "That is, I appreciate your offer, Levi, but the *kinder* must walk that far, so I can as well."

"Samuel takes the *kinder* to school on his way to work." Sadie returned to the sink. "As the teacher, you'll need to be there before them and may have to stay after the scholars go home. In a couple of months, it'll be dark, and it's not safe to walk along the roads then."

Ruth forced a smile. "That's true. I'll accept your offer, Levi."

"Gut." Rising, he took a straw hat from the pegs by the door. He put it on and went out without another word.

The second the door closed behind him, Ruth released the breath she'd been holding. How long had she been holding it? It felt as if she hadn't drawn a deep breath from the moment she entered the Lambrights' house and her gaze was captured by Levi Yoder.

"I'm glad that's settled," Sadie said as she helped Esther put away the last of the pots. "Esther, show Ruth where she'll be sleeping."

"In my room!" the excited girl said. *"Komm* with me."

Ruth followed Esther up the steep stairs. At the top, Esther turned left and into a room with two narrow beds, a stand between them, and a bureau. A window with a seat beneath it was set into a dormer. The ceiling sloped opposite the window.

"You'd better take this bed over here," Esther said, picking up the box Ruth had brought with her and putting it on the bed closer to the window. "As tall as you are, you'll bump your head on the low ceiling on this side."

"If this is your bed—"

"It isn't." She lowered her voice. "Don't tell anyone, but I don't like the shadows the moon makes on the wall at night."

"I won't tell anyone." Ruth grinned, her excitement rushing back through her. Yes, she was a bit homesick, but she had an adventure ahead of her. She intended to enjoy every minute of the blessing God had given her.

Esther dropped onto her stomach on her bed while Ruth opened the box and began to hang her extra dresses and *kapps* on the empty pegs next to Esther's clothes. "Levi couldn't take his eyes off you."

"What do you mean?" An apron fell from Ruth's suddenly numb fingers.

"I saw him watching you," Esther said, grinning. "And you were watching him, too."

"Everyone is always curious about newcomers." She picked up the apron and hung it in place.

"And he talked to you." Esther propped her elbows on the bed and leaned her chin on her palms.

"He didn't talk to me much."

"More than he talks to other people. He's awfully shy."

Ruth drew in a deep breath and released it slowly. Had

she mistaken his shyness for being aloof? In her mind, she'd accused him of being judgmental without taking the time to learn the truth about her. She had done the same with him; she must not make the same mistake the next time they spoke. She wasn't sure when that would be. He would likely be busy with chores when she stabled the horse and when she left at the end of each school day. She probably wouldn't see much of him.

And that would be fine with her. Then she wouldn't have to be bewildered by how a glance from him unsettled her.

Three

❧

Ruth drew in Jess, the horse the Lambrights had lent her, as the buggy topped the hill. Fields spread out between white farmhouses. A few barns were painted red or gray, but most were white. The fields had an abandoned appearance except for the soybeans, which hadn't yet been harvested. The corn was being chopped in many fields, and low stalks could be seen everywhere.

"Almost there," Esther said from beside her. She pointed down the hill. "Do you see it? It's the red building with the brown roof."

"By the big maple?"

"*Ja*. The scholars use that tree as a starting place for hide-and-seek."

"Do the scholars play baseball, too?"

"*Ja*. It's the favorite sport in this district, but I'm looking forward to playing volleyball on my *rumspringa*. It looks like so much fun when the youth groups get together."

Ruth let her cousin chatter on. Everything for Esther came back to her upcoming *rumspringa*. Most of her friends were already sixteen and had "running around" privileges.

Flicking the reins so Jess would continue down the road, Ruth thought about her own *rumspringa*. It had been fun to stay out late at singings and go on picnics and for rides through the countryside with members of the youth group she had joined. Once, they had gone by bus to an open-air concert, where they joined *Englisch* teens to listen to a singer.

She pulled to the side of the road as a car rushed around them. It pulled in too close to the horse, and Jess shied. Ruth kept the horse under control, but frowned at the careless driver.

"I wish we had buggy lanes as they do in Bird-in-Hand. That's what we get for living so far out of town." Esther shook her head. "Though a few of the *Englischers* drive too fast there, too. I know we're not supposed to judge others, but those *Englischers* who drive too fast are *ab im kopp*."

Ruth laughed. "I don't think they're crazy. Just in a big hurry." She winked at Esther. "Exactly as you are to get to your sixteenth birthday."

"And you to get to school."

"True." She was glad Esther had come with her today. Even though her cousin had finished eighth grade before the new school was built, Esther could help her get better acquainted with how the district's school was run.

Holding the reins loosely, Ruth gazed at everything. She couldn't imagine why anyone would want to live anywhere but Lancaster County. She was fascinated by each curve on the country road and the houses they passed. Those with electric wires and cars in the driveways belonged to *Englischers* or less conservative Mennonite families. She smiled at the miniature windmills in some yards, turning gently in the September breeze.

"That's Levi's farm over there," Esther said, pointing across the road.

The house and the barn were set back along a country lane. A *dawdi-haus* protruded from the white farmhouse at a right angle. Ruth could see chicken coops and a small building for goats or pigs behind the white barn. The fences around the pastures looked freshly painted, and she wondered who'd had the time to do that during the busy planting and harvesting seasons.

She stopped the buggy by the brick schoolhouse. A bell hung over the front porch. Behind the schoolhouse was a smaller building with two doors that must be the outhouse. A baseball backstop was set on the neatly mown grass to the right of the schoolhouse. Four swings hung from a thick wooden pole.

Climbing out, Ruth looped the reins over the split-rail fence. Eventually she would have to ride over to Levi's farm and see where he wanted her to put the horse and buggy.

Not now.

Now she wanted to visit the schoolhouse.

Her schoolhouse!

She fought her feet, which wanted to twirl about in a

happy dance. She had promised *Daed* to show the esteemed behavior he expected of her. If he heard that she was—what was the word he'd used?—*cavorting* again, he might insist she return home.

From the back of the buggy, she lifted out supplies and books. Ruth had kept the books she'd had as a *kind*, and she had brought a box for the scholars.

Esther grabbed two more bags and followed Ruth up the porch steps. Ruth fumbled with the key. She wasn't used to locked doors.

She opened the door and smiled. Three windows on either side of the room let in light and would keep the room pleasantly cool. Two more windows were set on either side of the front door. A side door would let the scholars reach the outhouse quickly. That would be very important when winter's cold settled in.

An aisle ran between the rows of desks beneath the ceiling's peak. The girls would sit on one side and the boys on the other. Each desk had a seat connected to its front. That allowed for a front row of seats, which Ruth could use when she worked with individual grades.

At the front of the room, a larger desk was set close to the blackboard, and a woodstove claimed one corner. Ruth had assumed a new schoolhouse would have a propane stove. She hoped she could figure out how to keep a fire going.

Everything from the pegs and empty bookshelves to the stack of readers on the teacher's desk was tidy. After Ruth put her box on the desk, she turned slowly to take in every inch of the room.

Esther set the bags by Ruth's desk. "The scholars' parents held a work frolic to get the school ready for the new year."

"I must be sure to thank them on Sunday after the service. Their kindness has saved us a lot of work."

"Do you want me to put the textbooks on the desks?"

Ruth pulled out the list that Joseph and Paul, the two school board members, had given her. They had told her that she would be introduced to the other school board members at their next meeting, the night before she started teaching.

As Ruth read the names and grades off the list, Esther placed the correct reader and workbook on each desk. The youngest ones sat up front, and the oldest in the back. With just over twenty scholars to prepare for, they were done quickly. Esther put the remaining books on a bookshelf near the side door.

"Now what?" asked Esther. "This is fun."

"Ja." Ruth grinned, her joy like a shower of soap bubbles within her.

"Do you think I might help you at school sometimes? I'd like to be a teacher someday."

"I'll have to ask the school board, but if they agree, I would love to have your help." She didn't add that she would also speak with Esther's parents first. Sadie and Mervin might not be in favor of their daughter being a teacher.

"Danki."

"There are a few other things we can do now to make everything simpler the first day of school." Ruth walked to the middle of the room and looked up, where kerosene lamps hung from hooks in the ceiling. "We shouldn't need lamps for a few weeks, but some are in the wrong places. This one and that one"—she pointed to two in the center—"they need to go over the desks by the windows. Otherwise, those scholars will be working in the shadows."

"How can I help?"

Stretching up as high as she could, Ruth grimaced. The lamps were far above her fingertips. "Is there a stepladder?"

Esther grinned. "Levi must have one."

Ruth's smile started to slip, but she forced it into place. "I'm sure he's out in the fields by now."

"He won't mind if we help ourselves."

Reluctant to have to ask Levi for anything, Ruth pointed at the side door. "Let's check if there's a storage room out back. If there is, there may be a stepladder in it."

"All right," the girl said. "I'll go look."

Ruth was glad. She wanted a moment alone in her schoolroom. The familiar odors of chalk dust and scholars' lunches would soon fill the space. But for this one point in time, everything was new and exciting.

Thank You, God, for heeding my prayer to learn more about other places and people. This is, indeed, what my heart yearned for.

When Esther returned without a stepladder, Ruth again waved aside the girl's suggestion that they check Levi's barn.

"I've got an idea that will save us a lot of time," Ruth said, pretending not to notice that Esther was curious about why Ruth was avoiding Levi's farm. She wasn't ready to explain how he perplexed her when, during their single conversation, he had been kind one moment and the next, acted as if she barely existed.

"You're looking fine," Levi said to the sparrow caged in a stall not far from where he milked his cows. Two other cages were in the stall, but both were empty. By week's end, he would be able to release the sparrow.

He had discovered it by the main road. One leg was missing, and he guessed it had been hit by a car or barely escaped from a cat. He had stanched the bleeding and kept it fed and away from the barn cats while it healed. The sparrow had learned to balance on one leg and now could land without falling. It was about ready to fly free again.

Folding a small packet of birdseed, Levi put it on a shelf by the stall. He walked to the next stall to check on the young doe he'd found in the barn several weeks ago. Something must have chased her inside. He couldn't guess how she had broken her left hind leg, but he had set and splinted it. She shied at every noise and watched Levi with fearful eyes.

He understood that. God's creatures didn't know he wanted to help them, so he always approached them slowly and with gentle murmurs. That he fed them helped, too, but they would bolt for the nearest door if they had the chance.

Something moving past the open door caught his eye. Across the road at the schoolhouse, Ruth and young Esther ran about like young scholars. Ruth jumped up and then kept running, turning quickly to leap into the air once more. Why would a grown woman act like that? He hoped the school board hadn't hired a flibbertigibbet.

His horse nuzzled his arm. He absently patted Strawberry's head. Unlike the wild animals, Strawberry had an uncanny ability to know when something was bothering Levi.

"What will parents think if they see her acting like that?" Levi asked, as if his horse could answer.

He needed to warn Ruth that, no matter how things were done in her district, such actions weren't acceptable in his. He thought about how even her *daed* hadn't seemed to be in favor of her teaching here. Could it be because her *daed* was concerned that she would act outrageously and shame her family? Grabbing his battered, straw hat, he put it on and strode down the lane.

Several cars sped by. A tractor-trailer blocked his view of Ruth and Esther. Once the vehicles passed, he didn't see them anywhere.

Suddenly he heard a shriek. Then another. Ruth ran around the schoolhouse. She held Esther's arm, almost dragging the younger girl. What were they doing *now*?

He lost sight of them as two more large trucks and a tractor hauling a load of hay rumbled along the road.

As soon as the wagon was past, Levi sprinted across the road. He heard weeping. Coming around the back of the Lambrights' buggy, he saw Ruth and Esther on the porch. Esther sobbed, her face hidden in her hands. Ruth was trying to comfort her.

What Ruth was saying was too low to reach beyond the sudden rushing sound filling his ears as he stared at her.

Ruth's *kapp* was missing, and her hair shimmered like spun gold around her shoulders. He couldn't force his eyes away. He couldn't release the breath burning in his lungs. He could only gaze at her beauty.

She looked up, and their gazes locked, as they had in the Lambrights' kitchen. Color rose up her face as she hastily tucked her hair behind her ears. No man, except the man she married, should ever see her hair loose like this.

"Levi . . ." Her face grew pale.

He could read her thoughts as if they were his own. If he mentioned this to anyone, she could be chastised by the deacon or even the bishop.

He scanned the ground. Where was her *kapp*? There. On the grass. Scooping it up, he handed it to her. She twisted her hair into its bun and set the *kapp* in place. He was startled by the regret that clamped around his chest when her lush, blond waves were restrained once more.

"I'm so glad you're here, Levi," she said. "Esther stepped on a yellow jackets' nest. She's been stung several times. Do you have any vinegar?"

"*Ja*. Wait here." He turned and ran toward his house.

Glancing back, he saw Ruth put her hand under Esther's arm and help her into the school. He rushed to his kitchen door and threw it open. His foot slipped as he stepped in a puddle by the door. The tiny puppy he had seen wandering alone around the farm last week was curled on a blanket by the sink. Levi had always believed that animals belonged in the barn, but the puppy was barely a month old, so he had made an exception.

He grabbed some paper towels and tossed them on the

puddle. Pulling open the cupboard, he took out the vinegar. The bottle was almost empty. He hoped it was enough.

He raced back to the schoolhouse, glad the road was clear of traffic. The school's door was open, and he saw Esther sitting at a desk, Ruth standing beside her.

"Levi will be here soon," came Ruth's soothing voice. "I'm sure he's coming as fast as he can."

Levi started to say he was back, but words vanished as he stared at the scholars' desks. They had been moved out of neat rows and into a circle. The teacher's desk was in the very center. Was *that* how she planned to teach?

"Levi, hurry!" Ruth called, wondering why he was hesitating.

Impatient, she strode up to him and plucked the vinegar bottle out of his hand. She tilted the bottle against a rag from a bag she'd left on the teacher's desk then pressed the vinegar-soaked rag against Esther's left leg.

"Wet another, Levi!" she ordered without looking in his direction.

He obeyed, taking the bottle from her. His fingers brushed hers, and she jerked back, startled by the warmth of his touch.

"Where do you want it?" His voice was easy, as if he hadn't even noticed her reaction.

"On her right shin," Ruth said, relieved her voice sounded normal.

She untied Esther's shoe with one hand while holding the pungent cloth to Esther's left leg with the other.

Levi knelt and loosened the ties on Esther's other shoe. Ruth pulled off her black socks then soaked more cloths with vinegar until it was gone. She wrapped the rags around the bright red welts on Esther's lower legs.

"Does that help?" she asked.

Esther nodded, biting her lower lip.

"Any we missed?"

"No," the girl whispered.

"*Gut.*" Ruth pushed herself to her feet with a sympathetic smile. She turned to Levi as he stood. "*Danki* for your help. The vinegar takes the fire out of stings. The yellow jackets' nest is close to the boys' side of the outhouse, about five feet away. Do you have something to kill them?"

"*Ja.*"

"*Gut,*" she said as she had to Esther. "I don't want the *kinder* getting stung, too."

"What were you doing?" He regarded her with a puzzled expression. "When I looked across the road, you and Esther were hopping about wildly near the swings."

Ruth smiled wearily. "I am sure we appeared to be acting oddly."

"*Ja.*"

In spite of herself, she laughed at his quick agreement. "We were trying to catch bugs for the scholars to study." She reached into a bag on the floor and pulled out a bugfilled jar. "I never guessed," she added with a sigh, "that Esther would step into a yellow jackets' nest."

"What about in here?" He spread out his hands toward the desks. "Are you really planning to teach with the room set up like this?"

"Of course not! Levi, I think you've got the wrong opinion of me. Is it because of what my father said when we were at the Lambrights'?" She looked from him to Esther and back. "*Daed* wanted me to remain at home with *Mamm* so I could help before and after the new *boppli* is born. My *daed* didn't mean that I'm not a *gut* teacher—"

"I didn't mean to suggest—" Color rose in Levi's face.

"*Ja*, you did. You thought *Daed* believed I was a bad choice to teach here. Why else are you questioning everything I'm doing?" She pointed to the ceiling. "The lamps weren't in the right places, so we pushed the scholars' desks out of the way and pulled mine over. Once I stood on it, I was able to unscrew the hooks and move them."

"I've got a ladder you could have used," he said quietly.

Esther looked up. "I told you that we should have asked him."

It was Ruth's turn to have her face burn hot as if she'd been the one stung by the yellow jackets. First, she had lost her *kapp* and half her hairpins. Now, Esther's innocent comment revealed that Ruth had tried to avoid Levi. He had been *gut* about coming to Esther's aid, and Ruth's earlier reluctance to ask for his help seemed rude.

"*Ach*, we managed, didn't we?" She tried to make a jest, but her question fell as flat as a deflating balloon. "But, now that you're here, I must ask you for a favor, Levi."

"*Ja?*"

"Could you show me how to work the stove? The school I attended had a propane heater, and so does my family's house. I don't know anything at all about woodstoves."

He looked at his feet, then at the ceiling, then at the blackboard, then at the door. Anywhere but at her. Could he make it any clearer that he didn't want to spend one minute longer in her company?

"Levi," she said when he didn't answer, "I would really appreciate you explaining how this stove works."

He motioned for her to follow him to the stove. With the barest minimum of words, he showed her how to start a fire and how to keep it going. She asked some questions, and his answers were terse. She fought the yearning to yank out his words, but she remembered Esther saying that Levi was shy. Maybe that was why he refused to meet her eyes and didn't say more than a dozen words in a row to her.

When he finished demonstrating how to bank the fire for the night, she turned to check on Esther, who was no longer crying.

Levi stepped in front of Ruth, saying, "*Komm* with me."

"Where?"

"I can show you where to put your horse in my barn."

Ruth nodded. "In a minute." She went to the younger girl, who was adjusting the vinegar-soaked cloths on her legs. "How are you doing?"

"Better." Esther gave her a wan smile. "Next time, I'll watch where I'm going. I just wanted to catch that butterfly."

"Will you be all right if I go see where Levi wants me to put the horse and buggy?"

"*Ja!*"

Ruth grinned at Esther's quick answer. If she had any doubts that her cousin was a matchmaker-in-training, they were gone. She wanted to say that Esther's plans were

47

doomed, but if thinking about Ruth and Levi courting helped her cousin now, she would let Esther have her fun.

Looking at where Levi was returning the scholars' desks to their usual spots, Ruth said, "Esther will be all right here for a few minutes."

His mouth tightened, and she realized her words sounded as if she didn't want to spend any more time with him than necessary. But, if that was the truth, then why had her heart leaped at the thought of spending more time with him?

Four

❧

The barn's upper floor was dusky. Aromas of hay and wood shavings welcomed Levi. The wide, double doors were left gaping open, as they were from spring until the first snow. Light slanted down from overhead, and dust motes danced in a silent song. He looked up through the open rafters to the loft window, where spiders spun gossamer webs in each corner.

This was his favorite place in the whole world. The place where he could be himself. The place where, in the quiet and the healing, he could feel God's presence.

"Where do you want me to leave the buggy and Jess?" asked Ruth.

Levi faced her. "Can you unhitch and hitch up the horse to the buggy by yourself, or will you need my help?"

"You are making a joke, right?" she shot back. "Of course, I can do that by myself." Her chin rose a fraction. "Let me know if you need help hitching your mules to the plow next spring, because I can do that, too."

"Bragging?"

"Stating a fact. I often work with my *daed* in the barn."

"Really?"

"Why are you questioning me, Levi?" she retorted in a voice that sounded every bit the stern schoolteacher.

"I didn't mean that," he said, amazed that she could be angry and pretty at the same time. Her eyes glowed like the heart of a flame. "Just surprised."

"Because the barn is the domain of men while women oversee the house?"

"*Ja.*"

"That's usually the case, but my *daed* has seven daughters and not a single son. As I'm the eldest, I did chores with him before school."

Levi felt a flush of shame. He had assumed when she offered to help with the milking at the Lambrights' that she refused to recognize a woman's place. Instead she had made a generous offer to help her *onkel*.

Exactly what he would have done.

"You won't have to help me," she went on. "If you'll show me where to leave the buggy during the school day, I'll try to stay out of your way."

"You can put the buggy over there," he said, pointing past the hay wagon he also used to carry his potatoes to market. "You should have plenty of room to turn it so you don't have to back out."

"Plenty."

He was surprised her answer was as curt as his usual ones.

"And Jess?" she asked. "Where can I leave the horse?"

"*Komm* with me." He walked out and down the bank to the barn's lower level, which was even with the bottom of the hill.

Ruth followed him into the barn, easily skirting animal droppings. Suddenly she stopped and asked, "Is that a doe in that stall?"

"*Ja.*"

"What's she doing here?" Without waiting for an answer, she walked to the stall where the deer watched her with cautious eyes. "She has a broken leg."

"*Ja.*" He grimaced. He needed to say something more. He leaned his arm on the stall door. "After I found her, I set her leg. She should be ready to return to the woods soon."

"And hide before hunting season begins."

He started to say "*Ja,*" but halted himself. "With a healed leg, she has as much chance of survival as any deer. Her life, like all of ours, is in God's hands."

Ruth heard sorrow in Levi's voice, but she didn't question him. For the first time, they seemed to be having an actual conversation, and she didn't want to ruin it by pressing him for explanations. She continued along the stalls. When she saw rabbits in one stall and a sparrow in a cage in the next stall, she looked at him. "How many wild animals do you have here?"

"About ten, now. There were a few more last month." His mouth tightened. "Several died. Some are too far gone for me to save them. When that happens, I try to make the animal's last hours as comfortable as possible. It's God's will which ones recover and which die. I'm only His hands tending to His creatures. I've learned to accept some are meant to go home to Him before I'm ready to let them go."

"That can't be easy," she said.

"No, but each time I can release a healed creature into the wild, it's a blessing." He smiled as he looked at his patients.

She did, too. Puzzlement creased her brow. "Didn't you say you had ten animals here? I only see nine."

"I've got a puppy in the kitchen. It's too young to be in the barn." His smile became wry. "But not too young to make a mess of the kitchen. The whole room smells of puppy piddle, no matter how often the linoleum is scrubbed."

Ruth laughed. "That's why *Daed* believes God intended animals to live outside."

"Like my *mammi*. When I wanted to bring my first patient, a woodchuck, into the house, she put her foot down. That wasn't something she did often." He chuckled. "When *Mammi* put her foot down, we listened."

As he went on, talking about his *gross-mammi* and the animals he had tended, his laughter rippled through her like spring warmth after a long winter. His face, which had been so austere, was now lit from within. Was this how he was with the Lambrights? Her cousin Samuel was a jovial man, and she had puzzled over why he was friends with Levi.

But the man standing beside her was so animated, so dedicated, so passionate . . . so handsome. He smiled when he talked about the wild creatures in the barn. She could imagine his long fingers cradling a wounded animal, offering it hope as he prayed for its recovery.

Her gaze settled on his lips. Now that they weren't straight and clamped closed, there was a fullness about them that she found tempting. How would they feel if she ran her finger along them? Or her lips?

Shocked by her own musings, Ruth said, "I've left Esther too long. I should go."

"*Ja.*"

Were they back to one-word answers?

"*Danki* for showing me where I can leave the buggy. Now I won't have to disturb you or your *mammi.*"

Pain flashed in his eyes. "My *mammi* died two years ago. Last March."

She winced at his reaction, which told her that his grief hadn't lessened. The way he had talked about his *grossmammi*, Ruth had assumed she was alive. Somehow, she mumbled her condolences, and hurried out of the barn. She glanced over her shoulder once as she went down the lane. He stood by the barn, watching her.

Ruth didn't say much on the way back to the Lambrights' farm later that morning. Her thoughts were filled with Levi, and how he was still grieving for his grandmother.

Lord, please comfort him in his grief as he comforts animals in their pain.

She added a quick prayer for her cousin, who was slouched on the buggy seat beside her. "Esther, how are you doing?"

"The stinging is coming back," Esther admitted.

"We'll get more vinegar on your legs once we get back. Maybe your *mamm* has something else to help."

"Ach!" Esther sat straighter. *"Mamm* asked if we could stop at the farm stand and see if they need more of her egg noodles."

"Which farm stand?"

"Stony Field, the one Miriam Brennemann runs."

That didn't tell Ruth anything, so she asked again. Esther explained how Miriam's *daed*, Jacob Lapp, had started the Stony Field Farm Stand, which allowed the whole community to sell vegetables, baked goods, and crafts. After his death, Miriam had taken on the task of keeping it running.

"Is it the stand that burned during the summer?" Ruth asked, remembering her *daed*'s conversation with the school board members.

"Ja. How did you know?"

As *Daed* had, she said simply, "I read about it in *The Budget.*"

Esther gave her a weak smile. "I should have guessed."

When Ruth realized the Stony Field Farm Stand was more than a mile past the Lambrights' farm, she said, "I don't think we should go now. Why don't we wait for tomorrow?"

"All right." The reluctance in Esther's voice puzzled Ruth.

She flicked the reins to urge the horse to go faster. She wanted to get Esther home, and she wanted to evade further thoughts of Levi. She was sure to be successful at only one.

* *

Esther was waiting for Ruth by the buggy the next morning after the breakfast dishes were done. When Ruth had offered to help, Sadie shooed them out saying, "The best help is to take my *maedel* to the farm stand so she's not under my feet."

Ruth strode through the heavy dew to the barn. It smelled so much like Levi's barn, except that here no wild animals watched her. Samuel was working on a piece of harness, and waved before she went to help Esther hook up the horse.

"Stay away from bees!" he called as they climbed into the buggy.

Esther stuck out her tongue. He laughed and tugged on Esther's *kapp* strings, then did the same to Ruth.

She playfully slapped his hand away. "I'm not your sister, Samuel Lambright. I don't have to put up with your antics."

"Sister, cousin . . . not much difference." He waved and went back to fixing the harness.

"Are you feeling better, Esther?" Ruth asked as she drove onto the main road.

"*Mamm*'s baking soda poultices helped, but she said she was glad Levi had that vinegar."

Ruth's hands tightened on the reins at the mention of his name. "I hope Levi makes sure the yellow jackets are gone before school starts."

"He said he would, and Levi's word is *gut*."

Ruth was glad to hear that, but she was also glad when

Esther began talking about the farm stand. Last night, sleep had eluded Ruth. It hadn't been because of the summer's lingering heat; a battery-operated fan oscillated between her bed and Esther's. It hadn't been because her cousin had trouble sleeping; Esther fell asleep quickly after drinking a cup of tea. Ruth suspected Sadie had added valerian to it, and that may have been why Esther snored more loudly than usual. But those snores hadn't prevented Ruth from sleeping either.

Her thoughts kept her awake. Thoughts of Levi Yoder. She couldn't stop thinking of how gentle he had been with the animals and the grief in his voice when he spoke of his *gross-mammi*.

Those thoughts chased her to the farm stand. Two buggies and three cars were parked in front. An *Englisch* woman examined the dried-herb wreaths hung on a lattice to one side. Two very young *Englisch kinder* stared with eager eyes at the whoopie pies. Signs listed the flavors as traditional chocolate, chocolate with peanut marshmallow, and red velvet with sour-cream filling.

Ruth tied the horses' reins to an iron rail as Esther ran to greet a girl her age. Was that girl the reason Esther had been disappointed that they hadn't come yesterday?

"Can I help you?" asked a woman from inside the farm stand's double doors. She was shorter than Ruth and slim, but every inch of her radiated happiness and contentment.

"I'm Ruth Schrock."

"The new schoolteacher?"

Ruth laughed. "I see it doesn't take long for news to travel."

"So true. By the way, I'm Miriam Brennemann."

"You own the farm stand, right?"

"It's really everyone's farm stand. So many people contribute time and items to sell. And so many helped rebuild it after the fire." She motioned for Ruth to follow her. "*Komm*, let me give you a tour."

"*Danki*. I can't wait to see it."

The farm stand, which consisted of two buildings, was surprisingly spacious. In the larger building, vegetables and baked goods were displayed at the front. Shelves along the sides were filled with canned goods and preserves. Electric lights hung from white rafters, and a modern cash register sat on the counter. The smaller building was devoted to Plain crafts with handmade clothing, furniture, and bright quilts sewn with autumn colors.

A young woman was waiting on the English customers with calm, friendly efficiency. "That's Leah," Miriam said. "She's my main helper, but we've been so busy that many from the district volunteer their time. Any time you'd like to help, you're welcome." Miriam smiled. "Though I'm sure you'll have your hands full with teaching the *kinder*." Her voice gentled on the last word, and she put her hand on her stomach.

Ruth guessed Miriam must be in a family way, but she did not ask. It was not the way of Plain people to talk about a pregnancy until it became obvious. Even with her own *mamm*, Ruth had not said anything at first. She had simply assumed more of *Mamm*'s chores when she noticed how her *mamm* was more fatigued than usual, a sure sign she was quickening. "Are any of your *kinder* going to be at school?"

"Not yet." She flushed and then smiled. "Tell Sadie I

could use more of her egg noodles. Our customers love them. Oh, excuse me. Someone is trying to get my attention."

As she looked around for Esther, Ruth's eye was caught by a bright-green poster hanging by the doors. It announced an upcoming fund-raiser for the volunteer fire department.

"It's always a fun event," said a friendly voice from behind her.

Ruth turned to face an older woman. Silver laced through her dark hair, and a few wrinkles feathered out from her twinkling brown eyes.

"I'm Rachel Miller," the older woman said.

Introducing herself, Ruth wondered why that name sounded familiar. Then she recalled Sadie talking last night about the bishop and his wife. John and Rachel Miller.

"We're having an apple-peeling frolic the Saturday after next," Rachel said with a smile. "If you aren't busy, why don't you join us?"

"Apple peeling?" Ruth laughed. "I've been to many frolics, but never to one to peel apples."

"We do it every year to coincide with the local fire department's fund-raiser. Some of our men volunteer with them. This is a way the women can say *danki* to all the firemen for their willingness to protect our houses and barns." She glanced around and smiled. "And farm stands."

"Are the apples used for pies?"

"Some are. The rest are pressed into cider." Rachel chuckled and winked. "Pride is a sin, but I can tell you lots of folks believe the cider from our apples is the best in Pennsylvania. Sadie and Esther usually come. Will you?"

58

Ruth quickly agreed. The frolic sounded like fun, and it would give her a chance to meet her scholars' families. She wanted to let the parents know they were welcome to visit anytime and that she would be happy to answer any questions they had about their *kinder*'s progress.

But now she needed to get ready for her meeting with the school board that evening, and for the first day of school, which would begin tomorrow. She shouldn't linger any longer at the farm stand, even though it was tempting to examine the many items for sale.

She looked around. Where was Esther?

As if she'd called her cousin's name, Esther rushed into the farm stand with the girl she'd met when they arrived. The girl was shorter, and reddish hair peeked from beneath her *kapp*. Oversize glasses perched on her nose, but couldn't hide her freckles.

"Ruth, this is my best friend, Hannah Wagler," Esther said. "We met on the first day of school, and we've been friends ever since."

"Hello, Hannah," was all Ruth had a chance to say before Esther grabbed her friend by the arm and hurried her away.

Ruth smiled. She would give Esther a little more time with her friend before they returned home . . . and give herself time to admire more of the items for sale.

Esther sat with Hannah beneath an oak tree. She unwrapped a whoopie pie and bit into it. "Yummy! Did your *mamm* make these?"

"No, I think it was Amy Beiler," replied Hannah as she smoothed her dark-purple dress over her legs. "She makes the best ones."

"You're probably right." This time, Esther took a smaller bite, so the treat would last longer. Leaning against the tree, she watched a car pull into the parking lot. "I hope she bakes plenty when the singing is at her house."

Hannah shook her head. "That won't be for a month or two. The next singing is at the Umbles'." She leaned forward and said in an anxious voice, "Esther, you've got to ask your parents to let you go. You've just got to."

"They want me to wait until I am sixteen." Esther shifted and winced. The stings still hurt.

"That's not until next month." Hannah groaned. "I know we vowed we'd go to our first singing together, but I've been sixteen for two months now. I don't want to wait any longer. What if I lose my chance with the boy I'm supposed to marry? I don't want to end up an old *maedel*."

"But you promised we'd go to our first one together."

With a sigh worthy of a martyr, Hannah nodded. "I know, but I didn't know how hard it would be to wait when everyone else is going to singings."

"Everyone but me. If you go, I'll be the only one from our class who isn't going."

Hannah gave Esther a quick hug. "You're right."

"So you won't go?"

"I didn't say that! But I'll help you persuade your parents."

Esther rolled her eyes. "You act like you've never met my parents. The only person more stubborn in this world than my *daed* is my *mamm*."

"Your parents aren't as strict as some. They've let us stay overnight at each other's houses since we were little." Looking to the right, then the left, she lowered her voice. "I heard *he* will be going to the next singing."

"Your *he* or mine?" Esther smiled as she imagined Caleb Stutzman offering her a ride home in his courting buggy. He was two years older, but she prayed he would wait until she was old enough so they could court. His family farmed the land next door to the Lambrights'.

Esther had set her heart on Caleb her very first day of school, even before she sat beside Hannah for the first time. He and his four sisters and two brothers had walked with her and Samuel to the old schoolhouse. His brother, Timmy, who was also six, had teased her about her English, a skill she hadn't mastered yet.

Caleb had told his brother to stop taunting her. Then Caleb had walked her to and from school for that first week, even though he must have wanted to spend time with his friends.

That week, he won her heart, and she'd never considered another boy for a husband. Caleb Stutzman was the one and only for her, even though she'd heard that he had escorted several different girls home from singings, and he never invited the same girl twice. She was sure he must be waiting for her to turn sixteen so he could turn all his attention on her while they were riding in his courting buggy.

"How," asked Hannah, "would I know if your 'he' is going to be there when I don't know who your 'he' is?"

Esther laughed. Hannah hadn't paid attention to boys until the past year, but she now had one particular boy in mind, just as Esther did. Even best friends didn't speak a sweetheart's name.

Maybe Caleb wouldn't be at the singing. No, Esther was certain he went to them. After church recently, she had listened when the older girls talked about which boys attended singings. Caleb's name was always mentioned.

"You've got to convince your parents to let you go to the next singing," Hannah pleaded. "You've got to!"

"I don't know if I can," Esther said truthfully. "But if I can't, I'll release you from our vow to go to our first one together."

Hannah's face turned a bright pink behind her glasses. "That's nice of you, but—"

"But what?"

"My *mamm* told me that I couldn't go until your parents agreed to let you go."

"Why?" Esther was astonished. After all of Hannah's complaining about Esther not yet being sixteen, Esther hadn't guessed that she was having trouble getting her parents' permission to go, too.

"For some reason, my *mamm* thinks you're the sensible one." Hannah smiled wryly. "She believes if I'm with you, I'll stay out of trouble."

"But you won't be with me if your *he* asks you to let him take you home or my *he* asks me."

Hannah's eyes brightened. "*Ach*, let's hope that's what happens!"

Five

❧

Ruth tried to still her wobbling knees as she stepped down from the buggy that evening. Her fingers were clumsy as she tied the reins to the split-rail fence and lifted a cloth bag out of the buggy. She could barely look at the other four buggies parked by the schoolhouse. She had been told there were five school board members. She hoped the last one wouldn't be too late. She wasn't sure how long she could keep her knees from knocking together.

All day, her stomach had clenched tighter and tighter as she thought of her meeting with the school board. She had packed and unpacked a bag of materials to bring with her. Should she bring it or would the board members think she wasn't willing to follow the curriculum they had established? She finally had decided to bring it. Just in case she needed it.

When she had taught at her old school, everything had been so simple. She knew the routine. She had spent eight years as a scholar there, becoming familiar with the various teachers' styles. She had been an assistant for most of the time, and when her local school board came to ask her to take over temporarily, she had known each of the board members well. They had been a part of her life from the moment she was born.

She hadn't thought about the differences she might face in this district until she heard *Daed* discussing with Mervin the different, acceptable tools for farming. And there were other things that took her by surprise. Esther had a dress that was made of a lighter pink fabric than was allowed in Ruth's home district. She would have to pay attention so she didn't do anything improper here.

How foolish she had been to let her pride lead her to assume that she could handle teaching in an unfamiliar district with the same ease she had in her own! She had to fight her own yearning to jump back in the buggy and drive all the way home.

Stop it!

She had wanted adventure and a chance to prove that she could do a *gut* job. God had provided this opportunity, and squandering God's gift was a sin.

Please put the right words in my mouth, Lord. I don't want to say the wrong thing to the school board members. I want to do Your will.

A sense of peace comforted her like a sun-warmed quilt

as she reminded herself that God was always with her. That thought steadied her steps, and her hand was no longer shaking when she opened the door.

Five men waited inside. Four were setting out chairs they must have brought with them, and the fifth sat in her desk chair.

She closed the door, and the men turned to look at her. One called a friendly greeting. Some part of her brain identified him as Paul Beiler, but she couldn't reply. All she could do was stare at the tall, handsome man at the far left of the group. The only one without a beard.

Levi!

Levi was on the school board? Why hadn't he said anything about being one of the members? He'd had the chance when he showed her where to park her buggy in his barn. She flushed when she thought of that first night at the Lambrights' house. Levi had acted surprised when he heard she was the new schoolteacher. He could have explained he was surprised because he was a member of the school board and hadn't been told.

Now he stared at her as if nothing were amiss. Something very pleasant fluttered deep inside her when a faint smile tipped his lips. His simple, blue cotton shirt and broad-fall trousers were no different from what the other men wore, but the clothing seemed to suit him best, showing off his muscular arms. That made no sense. Her thoughts whirled in every direction until she felt dizzy.

Stop it! Focus!

Paul Beiler motioned toward the scholars' desks. Jerking her gaze away from Levi, Ruth walked stiffly to the first row. She perched on a seat. Her knees stuck up in front of her, and Levi offered his chair.

"Danki," she murmured. She took the seat but couldn't stop herself from asking in a sharp whisper, "Why didn't you tell me that you're on the school board? Did you think it would be funny to spring the truth on me *now*?"

He shrugged. "I assumed you knew."

Ruth didn't reply. Was that all there was to it? Embarrassment flooded her. She had let her anxiety about this meeting twist her even more tightly. It was too late to take back her whetted words because Levi walked to the front of the room.

While he leaned one shoulder against the clean blackboard, she sat and faced the school board.

Paul smiled. "You've met several of us, Ruth." He motioned to Joseph Hooley, who had come with Paul to ask her to teach. "And, of course, you know Levi, who donated the land for our new schoolhouse." He then glanced at the man who had been frowning since she entered. "You haven't met Micah Stutzman. And that's Simon Wagler." He nodded toward the fifth man. "We take our positions on the school board seriously. We hope you'll take your position as our schoolteacher just as seriously."

He paused, and she realized he expected an answer. Hoping her voice didn't squeak, she said, "I'm happy to be able to teach here, and I hope you'll be satisfied with my work."

"That's yet to be seen." Micah's frown never wavered.

Paul glanced at him, then back at Ruth. "Now we'd like to ask you some questions."

Ruth nodded, and the questions began. The men asked how she intended to teach the *kinder*. She explained each day would begin with the traditional prayer and singing. She outlined how she would pick better students to help struggling ones and how she would help the first graders learn to speak English. She went over handling recesses. She even talked about keeping discipline.

"No spankings?" Micah's frown deepened the lines in his forehead.

Ruth didn't hesitate. "I believe punishments should help the scholars learn. Don't think I'll be lenient. The first mistake will be dealt with by me here. If the scholar continues to make the same mistake over and over, the parents will be informed."

The school board members exchanged glances. She couldn't read what they were thinking. Instead, she looked at Levi. He was the only one who hadn't asked her a question. When his eye closed in a slow wink, she almost gasped in surprise.

Did he think this was amusing? Or was he trying to put her at ease? She was so muddled she wasn't sure what to think.

"Have we forgotten anything?" Paul asked.

"Missed days." Levi folded his arms in front of him.

"*Ach*, of course," Paul said. "As you know, we're starting school almost three weeks late. That's sure to cause a problem in the spring, when the scholars are needed to help in the fields."

"May I make a suggestion?" she asked.

He nodded.

"If the scholars attend school every other Saturday for the rest of September and October and then attend school every other Saturday after the wedding season and the holidays, the time will be made up before the usual date for school to be out."

The men, except for Micah, smiled. They told her to work out a calendar, and they would review and approve it. Then they asked about her plans for the first weeks of school.

Ruth was prepared, because she had been thinking about it since the night she'd been asked to teach. She went over which days she would concentrate on which subjects, telling the school board members that if she found the scholars having trouble with one subject, she might switch the days, so the hardest subject wasn't taught on the last day of the week.

"While the weather remains nice," she said, excited to share her ideas, "I also want to hold some classes outdoors. The scholars—"

"Outdoors?" Micah half-rose off his chair but sat when Paul gave him a sharp look.

"Ja," she replied, smiling. "One thing I've observed, both for myself and the scholars I've worked with, is that sometimes four walls are too confining. We Plain folks love being outdoors, and the best time to teach about God's beautiful creation is while we're walking through it. For example, I want them to discover which bugs are helpful and which can ruin crops." She opened her bag and pulled out one of the jars of now-dead insects. "I've started collecting some already for them to study. Whether they eventually plant a garden or a whole farm, they need to know

that. Reading about it in a book won't leave as strong an impression as seeing the bugs themselves."

Simon nodded, smiling more broadly. "I can see the *gut* sense in that."

"I agree," Paul said. "Any other questions?" When no one spoke, he added, "*Danki*. We're grateful you've agreed to teach in our school, Teacher Ruth."

Ruth felt a small glow of delight. He had called her *Teacher Ruth*. It was official now. She was the teacher for this district. She thanked him then remembered her promise to Esther. When she asked if the girl could be her assistant in order to learn more about teaching, the men quickly agreed.

After a short prayer to end the meeting, the school board members rose and carried their chairs out of the schoolhouse to their buggies so each man could take his chair back home.

Ruth stared at the desk. *Her* desk. Tomorrow morning, she would return to the schoolhouse as Teacher Ruth. She should be jumping with joy. Instead, she was too drained to move.

She stood up and made it as far as the front steps before her knees started shaking so hard she couldn't walk any farther.

"You'd better sit down before you fall down." Levi's voice was close to her ear.

She sat on the porch, her feet propped on a step.

"I'm sorry," he went on. "I saw how surprised you were when you saw me with the other members of the school board. As I said, I assumed you'd been told."

"You shouldn't assume," she said, her voice raspy from all her talking. "But you're not the only one. It seems that everyone thought someone else had told me that you're on the school board."

"Then I'm doubly sorry I didn't tell you myself." He shrugged as he had before. "But . . . you know now."

"Levi," she said as he turned toward the school's door.

"Ja?"

"I'm sorry, too. I shouldn't have suggested that you intentionally kept the truth from me."

"What else were you supposed to think?" He gave her a lopsided grin then went back inside.

He doused all the kerosene lanterns but one. When he came back out, he carried it and the chair he had lent her. He set the lantern beside her on the steps. He slung the chair over his shoulder, holding it with a couple of fingers, and she tried not to stare at how his muscles flexed as he passed her and went down the steps.

"I'm going to take this back to the house. Let me get you something to drink while I'm there. You sound like your throat's pretty dry after answering everyone's questions."

"Danki." Words flooded her head, but none reached her lips as she watched Levi cross the road and blend into the darkness.

In her mind, she replayed the conversation with the school board. Everyone had gone from serious expressions to smiles as she spoke of her plans—except Micah. She wondered what she could have said to satisfy him.

Levi had listened, but only once—other than when he brought her the chair—had he spoken. Even then, he'd said just two words. Was he always so reticent with the school board?

Ruth raised her eyes to the stars poking through the clouds. *Did I say too much, Lord? Did I not say enough?*

She chuckled wryly. She had never been accused of not saying enough.

Hearing a yip, she looked across the road. Levi was returning with a tiny brown-and-white puppy on a leash. In his other hand, he carried an insulated flask and two glasses.

She drank in the sight of the tall man being pulled along by a little puppy. When he bent to say something to the animal, its tail wagged so hard Ruth was surprised that the puppy's feet didn't lift off the ground.

They waited for several cars to pass, then Levi gently tugged the puppy away from whatever it was sniffing. With another yip, the puppy raced across the road, stretching the leash taut. It must have caught sight of Ruth because it ran to her. It tried to climb the steps and tumbled down. Before she could help, it clambered up the steps and onto her lap.

"Well, hello," she said with a laugh. Its spaniel ears flopped as it burrowed down into her lap and rolled over to offer its stomach to be rubbed. "Aren't you a precious little girl!"

"You wouldn't think so, if you were the one cleaning up after her five or six times a day." Levi set the insulated container beside Ruth. "Puddles on the floor, kibble on the floor, tipped-over water dishes, and I just discovered she's chewed the brim of my best hat."

Ruth laughed. His martyred expression and droll recitation of the puppy's mischief tickled her. "How old is she?" she asked as Levi sat beside her, his long legs stretching to the ground.

He turned the lantern down until only a dim light came from it. He waved away the bugs that had gathered around it. "About five weeks old."

"But that's too young to be away from her *mamm*."

His smile tightened into a frown. "*Ja*, but that didn't matter to whoever abandoned her. I don't know how they live with themselves."

"Maybe because they know you'll watch over her."

A blush crawled out of Levi's collar and shadowed his neck, then his face. The puppy must have sensed something was amiss because she leaped toward him, tangling her rear right leg in the leash, and tumbling headlong down the stairs.

Ruth caught the puppy at the same time as Levi did. Their fingers met, and she yanked hers back as heat arced between them. Then their gazes caught—just for a pair of heartbeats, but that was long enough. Something shifted within her. She couldn't explain what it was, and that disconcerted her even more.

She should say something, but she had no idea what. She couldn't tell him how thoughts of him kept her from sleeping. That would sound silly, because they barely knew each other. Yet, it was the truth. He intrigued her and baffled her. One minute, he seemed cool and critical. Other times, like now, he was warm and tender as he nestled the puppy close and calmed it. Could he soothe her uncertainty if he took her in his arms, too?

Ruth looked quickly away, hoping her thoughts hadn't

been visible on her face. She desperately searched for something to say as the silence stretched and grew taut between them. She had no idea how long they would have sat in silence if the puppy hadn't crawled off Levi's lap and back onto hers. The puppy cuddled into her arms, putting her head over Ruth's heart.

"So precious," she whispered.

"Every creature is precious in God's eyes."

She discovered Levi watching her. She averted her eyes, not wanting to chance his gaze holding hers again. Surely, he could read her emotions if he did.

"What do you call her?" she asked, glad for the excuse to talk about something else.

"Graceless."

"What a horrible name for a cute puppy!"

"It was either that or Piddle Pup." He grinned, and she felt the tension across her shoulders ease. "This way, if she ever outgrows her awkward ways, her name can be changed to Graceful. How about some root beer?"

For a moment, she considered saying she needed to get back to the Lambrights' farm. She should put an end to this conversation before she did something stupid. Something *else* stupid.

But he didn't give her a chance. He opened the container, filled two glasses, and handed her one.

"This is delicious," she said after she took a sip of the fragrant drink. "Did you make it yourself?"

He nodded. "My *dawdi* taught me. He said a woman is known for her cooking, but a man needs to be able to make *gut* root beer and blueberry wine."

"Does your *dawdi* live on the farm with you?"

"No. Both my grandparents are dead."

She set the puppy between them on the porch. "*Ach*, Levi, I'm sorry."

"He died quite a few years ago."

"You must miss him."

"*Ja.*"

"So who else lives on the farm with you?"

"Just me."

"The rest of your family—"

He patted the puppy's head and didn't look at Ruth as he said, "My grandparents were all I had after my parents died."

Ruth looked directly at him again. Lines she hadn't noticed before cut into his stern face. Lines gouged by grief. "No wonder you've got a zoo in the barn to keep you company," she said softly. When Graceless crawled over her, she added, "And a puppy in the house."

He raised his glass to his lips, and his hand trembled. He stared out into the night as he said, "*Danki.*"

"For what?"

"You understand. Not many do."

His simple words touched her deep inside her heart. They revealed the deep wounds he hid. Had he always been shy, or was he using that reputation to keep a wall between him and the world? She longed to put her hand on his arm, to offer him solace.

Before Ruth could give in to that temptation, a motion caught her eye. "Levi, watch out!" she cried. "Graceless is going to tip over the root beer."

He picked up the puppy and set her on his other side so she couldn't reach the container. Again Ruth imagined herself being held by his strong hands. She had to stop thinking of such things, but she didn't know how.

Casting about for something to say that wouldn't give him a clue to her thoughts, she said, "I hope the school board members saw how much I want to be a *gut* teacher."

"It doesn't matter what we think."

Would he ever say something she expected? "What do you mean? You hired me, and you can dismiss me if your faith in me is misplaced."

"God has given you a gift of teaching, so you must trust that He has brought you to this place to use His gift."

"I know, and I try to submerge my will to His. It isn't always easy, and I'm not always successful, but I try. I pray it's His will that I do a *gut* job. I love helping scholars learn."

He nodded.

"Thank you, Levi. You've been a *gut* friend to me tonight."

He patted her arm and smiled. "You looked as if you needed one."

Or at least that's what she thought he said. The moment he touched her, her ears filled with the thunder of her heartbeat, and the warmth from his fingertips seemed to flow through her.

Overwhelmed, she stood and handed him her empty glass. She thanked him. She patted the puppy on the head. She walked down the steps and to her buggy. Each motion was wooden and difficult, but she didn't stop.

As she untied the horse and climbed into the buggy, she told herself she should be grateful that he hadn't heard her pounding heartbeat. She drove away in the dusk, forcing herself not to look back. She could flee from Levi, but it was impossible to flee the memory of his warm, rough skin on her arm.

Six

❧

Esther picked up the honey jar from the table and wiped a damp cloth under it. From the sink, the clatter of the breakfast dishes told her that *Mamm* was washing the bowls they'd used for oatmeal.

"*Mamm?*" she asked, trying to keep her voice casual.

"*Ja?*"

"I heard there's going to be a singing at Umbles' farm on the next church Sunday."

"The Umbles are generous to host both the Sunday services and a singing." *Mamm* bent over the sink to scrub harder on a bowl. "It always wonders me how oatmeal can turn to concrete in such a short time."

Esther didn't want to talk about oatmeal. "Hannah was talking to me about the singing."

"That's right. Hannah is already sixteen." *Mamm* rinsed the bowl and put it on the drying rack. "Does she enjoy singings?"

"She hasn't gone to one yet."

"Why not?" She looked over her shoulder, and for once, her hands were idle in the sink.

Now that she had *Mamm*'s attention, Esther knew she had to choose her words with care. "She said her parents want her to wait and attend the first time with me. It's been so difficult for her to wait when she wants to go so bad." *And I know how she feels, because I can't wait to go!*

"What a *gut* friend she is! I hope you have thanked God for putting such a true friend in your life." *Mamm* began washing another bowl.

No, no! This wasn't the way the conversation should go.

"*Mamm*, Hannah really wants to go to the singing at Umbles'."

"I understand, and you should thank her for making such a sacrifice so you could attend together. She can always go to the singing at the Hooleys' in a couple of weeks." Without pausing, she added, "You had best get going. You're going to be late for the first day of school. Go ahead. I'll clean up the rest of the kitchen. Ruth is depending on you to be there." She made shooing motions with her hands.

Esther put the cloth on the table, recognizing defeat. But she didn't have to accept it. There had to be some way to make her parents see how important it was for Esther to go to *this* singing. She just wasn't sure how to sway them.

Not yet.

* *

Ruth couldn't have asked for better weather for the first day of school. The air had a hint of crispness. She was up and driving the buggy toward the schoolhouse an hour earlier than she'd planned. She loved the early morning when birds called from the trees, the fences, and the electric wires. Cows emerged from barns after the morning milking.

Turning onto the road to Levi's farm, she hoped she would see him. Even a few days ago, she would have scoffed if anyone suggested she and Levi might become friends. Were they friends now? She wasn't sure *what* they were, but she was glad they weren't hissing at each other like two cats.

Levi was nowhere to be seen when Ruth pulled into the barn. She turned out the horse in the field then hummed her favorite hymn as she walked to the schoolhouse. She wasn't going to take a chance of singing secular music, not even the country music Samuel played in the barn.

The first thing she did in the schoolhouse was to raise the green shades and open the windows. She smiled as sunshine flooded into the room. She was grateful Esther would be arriving after she helped Sadie clean up after breakfast.

Ruth went to the board and wrote the assignments for the day. She took slips of paper with the scholars' names and taped each one to the appropriate desk. Every year, her teacher had done that on the first day, and it was a tradition she wanted to continue in her own school. Ten boys and eleven girls would be depending on her. She couldn't wait to begin.

Sooner than she expected, she heard excited voices outside. She smiled at the *kinder* playing in the schoolyard. She reached to ring the bell just as Esther arrived. Once her cousin had put her bonnet on a peg near where the scholars would hang theirs, Ruth pulled the bell rope to call the scholars inside.

"Gude mariye," Ruth said to each *kind*, and each responded with a "good morning" of his or her own. "Look for your name, and that will be your desk."

The scholars chattered and giggled as they looked for their seats. Several winced in new shoes after having gone barefoot all summer. One little girl, whom Ruth discovered was the youngest Wagler *kind*, sat where the first graders should. She flushed as Ruth gently guided her to a second-grade seat. The newest scholars milled around, clearly not sure what to do.

Ruth gestured for the littlest ones. Kneeling, she said in English, "Welcome to school. This year, you will sit in the front row. That is a special place for our newest scholars. Do you want to come with me?"

Two of the girls nodded and said, *"Ja."* They understood at least some English. The shortest girl and the boy looked confused, but followed when Ruth led the way to the front. The girls took the three empty desks on the girls' side, and the little boy sat in the only vacant desk on the boys' side. Tears filled his eyes as he looked toward an older sibling. Ruth gave him a hug and told him in *Deitsch* that he'd soon love school. He gave her a watery smile.

Once the scholars were seated, she called roll as she planned to every morning. Each name was answered with a "here" in either English or *Deitsch*, depending on how old the *kind* was. As the scholars answered, she smiled, making sure she matched the face and the name.

"David Zook," she called.

Nobody answered.

She repeated the name. The scholars looked at a third grader with the lightest blond hair Ruth had ever seen. He wore a neatly pressed light blue shirt beneath his suspenders. His hands were pressed against the top of his desk as if he wanted to jump up and run away.

An eighth-grade girl—Mary Beth Umble, if Ruth remembered correctly—raised her hand. "Teacher Ruth, David doesn't talk. Not ever."

"Hush," scolded her brother Seth, who was in sixth grade. "*Mamm* said not to say anything about David being *dumm*."

Ruth frowned as David shrank into his seat. "That's enough. We don't speak of others unkindly. David, please raise your hand, so I can mark you as present."

He obeyed, and she thanked him before continuing with her morning schedule as if everything were normal. But it wasn't. Why didn't David talk? Could he? Those questions echoed in her head while the scholars began with a prayer and then sang three simple songs. She began lessons, working with the first graders on the alphabet and then letting Esther oversee an art project that taught shapes. Ruth had the older scholars open their readers and start with the first story. She watched to see which scholars finished quickly, which ones had trouble staying focused, and which mouthed each word they read. During the afternoon, she would test every class to determine how well each *kind* had absorbed what he or she read.

Ruth was as eager as the scholars for the mid-morning break. When the *kinder* rushed out for the fifteen-minute recess, she asked Esther about David Zook.

"He hears what I say," Ruth said as she wrote spelling words for each class on the blackboard.

Esther pinned some of the first-graders' art on a bulletin board. "*Ja.* He can hear. He just doesn't talk."

"Surely at home—"

"Not even at home. I've asked both his cousins"—she pointed toward the second-grade desks and then the fifth-grade ones—"and they told me that they can't remember ever hearing him talk."

Throughout the day, Ruth considered what Esther had said. Each time she looked at David Zook, he had his head bent over his work. He did his spelling and picked up his reader. The third-grade reader was the first to introduce the scholars to poetry. She had planned to have the third graders write their own poems and read them aloud. But if David didn't speak . . .

Lord, I need Your guidance on this problem. Help me help David.

Instantly, as if a lamp had been lit, the image of Levi's face appeared in her mind. She was so startled she dropped a book. The scholars looked up in surprise.

"Oops," she said, giving a quick laugh as she picked it up.

The scholars giggled then returned to their work.

Ruth answered a boy's question and tried to regain her

composure. Was the thought of Levi a message from God? Or was it simply that he invaded her thoughts so often?

Someone knocked on the door, and Ruth was grateful for the interruption, a distraction from the troublesome questions flitting through her head.

Or she was until she opened the door and saw two *Englischers* on the porch. The man wore a bright-green, short-sleeved shirt and jeans while the woman next to him was dressed in a more conservative burgundy blouse and a black skirt that was almost as long as Ruth's. She had a camera around her neck and dark glasses propped on her short hair.

"Are you lost?" Ruth couldn't think of another reason why they would knock on the schoolhouse door.

The woman looked past her and gushed, "Stan, doesn't it look like something on *Little House*?"

Ruth eased onto the porch, closing the door behind her. "How can I help you? If you're lost—"

"No, no, we're not lost." The woman smiled broadly. "Yesterday, we took a buggy ride in Intercourse and passed your cute schoolhouse. We thought we'd come back and take a peek. You don't mind, do you?"

Ruth bit her tongue before she blurted out that, of course, she minded. But she couldn't. *Daed* had instructed that turning the other cheek wasn't a choice. It was the Plain way of life. The man and woman probably felt their tour of Lancaster County wouldn't be complete until they visited a school.

"C'mon. Give us a peek," Stan said, shifting from one foot to the other. "We won't get in the way."

Again Ruth hesitated. No tourists had ever intruded in her district's school, so she wasn't sure what she should do. *Mamm* always taught that being generous and gracious to tourists was the easiest way to deal with them. They were asking nicely, and the idea of being rude left a sour taste in her mouth.

"You can't take any pictures," Ruth said, glancing at the fancy camera. "It isn't our way."

"Not even through the window? I know you Amish don't like your faces photographed, but surely it won't hurt if I take pictures from the back." The woman sounded so disappointed. "I thought it was okay for kids to have their pictures taken because they haven't been baptized yet."

"That's a parent's decision," Ruth explained, "and their parents aren't here, so please leave your camera outside. Later, if you wish, you can take pictures of the school, but not of the *kinder* or of me."

For a moment, she thought they would argue, but the woman lifted the camera over her head and set it by the door.

Ruth prayed she wasn't making a huge mistake. She opened the door. The scholars turned to look at the *Englischers.* When the *kinder* began to whisper, Ruth told them to return to their work.

It was impossible to ignore the *Englischers* who wandered around the room, looking at the posters and the blackboard. Esther bit her lip, but said nothing. Ruth allowed the *Englischers* five minutes, then moved to steer them out of the schoolroom.

The man noticed. "Leslie, we've disrupted the classroom long enough." He took her arm and drew her toward the door. "I think we should go. Thank you," he said to Ruth. "You've been very kind."

"*Danki*—I mean, thank you for understanding. Now, I need to return to my students."

"One more question," Leslie said. "Won't the children go home soon? It would be *wunderbaar gut* if we could talk with them."

"Not quite yet," Ruth said, trying not to laugh at the phrase that tourists believed Plain people used all the time.

"Okay, we'll wait."

Ruth's stomach tightened. Until the *Englischers* left, she wasn't going to allow the *kinder* outside. *Lord, I need help to keep these tourists from bothering the scholars. Show me what I should do.*

As she prayed, she looked across the road. She smiled and said, "You might be interested in that barn, where Levi Yoder has several injured, wild animals he's tending while they heal."

Leslie looped her arm through her husband's. "C'mon, Stan. We'll see the animals while we wait." As they walked down the steps, she said, "You've still got the lollipops in the car, don't you? You know how Amish children love them."

Ruth closed the door and frowned. She'd heard of tourists who thought they were being kind when they gave *kinder* candy in exchange for posing for pictures. She hadn't expected them at her school.

"They're gone," Seth Umble said from where he watched out a window.

Ruth, too, looked out the window. As soon as the tourists vanished into the barn, she would send the *kinder* home. Then she wouldn't have to worry about them being tempted by sweets.

Clapping her hands, Ruth ordered the scholars to put away their books and collect their head coverings and lunch boxes. She told the scholars to hurry home and not to talk to strangers. When the younger *kinder* looked alarmed, she hurried to reassure them. The older scholars understood, and she was glad to see them watch over the little ones as the *kinder* went out the side door and across the fields toward home.

Ruth closed the door and raised her brows at Esther, who burst out laughing. She joined in, overwhelmed by the silliness.

When she stopped, wiping tears from her eyes, Ruth said, "I never expected something like that today."

"I'm glad you knew what to do." Esther bent to pick up a paper dropped by the first graders who'd been cutting shapes. "I didn't."

"I hope I did the right thing. I never thought to ask the school board what I should do under such circumstances." She began to erase the day's lessons off the board and write the next day's.

"Do you want me to help you with that?" Esther asked. Ruth heard a restlessness in her tone.

"Let me guess," she said, "you want to go visit your friend Hannah?"

Esther nodded. "If you don't need me for anything else."

"Go ahead, Esther. Once I get tomorrow's lessons on the board, I'm leaving."

"Okay. Let *Mamm* know I went to the Waglers'. Hannah will give me a ride home."

Ruth gave her cousin a quick hug. "I'm so happy you were here today."

"Me, too." With a wave, Esther went out the door.

Ruth finished listing the lessons then cleaned the rest of the board. She went outside and clapped the erasers. Through the chalk dust, she saw the *Englischers* walking from Levi's farm. She ducked back inside before they discovered her trickery.

Going to her desk, she got her book bag and lunch box. She glanced at the blackboard and frowned. She had forgotten the lessons for the fourth graders. She started to add them as the front door opened.

Ruth whirled, wishing the *Englischers* had left. Her eyes widened when Levi stomped through the doorway. He closed the door. It didn't slam, but it was loud.

"What were you thinking?" He walked between the desks, his work boots punishing the floor with each step. "Sending *Englisch* tourists to my barn to ask dozens of questions and upset the animals?"

Ruth put the chalk in its trough. Brushing her hands together to knock off the white dust, she said, "I was thinking of the scholars. I overheard those tourists talking about giving lollipops to the children if they'd agree to pose for pictures. I couldn't let that happen, so I suggested the tourists visit your barn to give the *kinder* time to go home."

"When did you hear that they intended to give candy to the scholars?"

"When they were leaving."

"You let them in the school?"

"Levi, what choice did I have? They would have disrupted the school day by taking pictures through the windows."

"Did you ever consider asking them to leave immediately?"

"Of course I did," she retorted, stung by his attitude. "But what would I have done if they refused?"

"You could have sent one of the boys to find me, and I would have handled it as a member of the school board."

She deflated. "Oh. I didn't think of that."

"You need to, Ruth. The scholars' parents trust you to watch out for them."

"Which is what I was trying to do."

He put a thumb under the rim of his straw hat and tipped it back. "I know, but you've got to consider every aspect of a decision as you make it. Not afterward."

"I suppose you'll have to tell the rest of the school board," she said stiffly, stung by his tone.

Levi sighed. "*Ja.* The other members of the school board need to know."

"I understand. The *kinder* will tell their parents about what happened." She picked up her bag and lunch box. "But I'm glad that they'll get home without being bothered by cameras and promises of sweets."

Levi ran one thumb along his suspenders, then took off his hat and placed it on her desk. "Forgive me, Ruth. I see now that your decision was a very *gut* one."

"*Danki.*" She was astonished by his abrupt change of

heart. If he could relent, so could she—at least a little bit. "I know you believe I didn't think about the consequences, and you're right. My only thought was to protect the scholars."

Squaring his broad shoulders, he said, "No damage has been done other than some school time was lost and some animals were frightened. If you would like, I'll explain to the other school board members what happened."

"You would do that for me?"

He nodded.

"Why?" She knew she should leave well enough alone, but she had to find out why Levi was once again her ally.

"Why do you think?"

She wished she were brave enough to say that it was because he cared for her. "Perhaps because you're fair-minded?"

A flash of emotions sped through his eyes, too quickly for her to recognize even one. He picked up his hat and motioned toward the door. She flung the strap of her book bag over her shoulder. Together they walked out onto the porch.

He bid her a *gut* afternoon and walked toward one of his fields farther along the road. He never answered her question.

Seven

Levi yawned and stretched, trying to stay awake a little bit longer. It had been a long day with harvesting the last of the potatoes. Last night, he hadn't slept as he tried to save a cat that had been hit by a car. It had been futile right from the start, so he had sat with the cat, talking to it and praying for it to be released from its pain. Just before dawn, the cat released a deep breath and never drew in another. He had buried it by the small copse where he buried all the other animals that hadn't survived, and he had said a prayer before walking back to the barn. Then he began milking and spent the day with his chores, catching a quick bite at lunch and for supper, and cleaning up Graceless's messes in the kitchen.

He rested his shoulder against the stall door while he

watched the doe eat the hay he'd brought in for her. Maybe he should send the puppy out to live in the barn, too, but he couldn't bring himself to do that. He was tired of the puddles on the floor and the chewed-up newspapers. Yet he liked having someone there at the door to greet him when he came in. The puppy made the house feel a bit more alive, and he hadn't realized how dead it had felt since *Mammi* passed.

But he wouldn't keep the puppy once it was big enough and housebroken. He would find a *gut* home for Graceless with *kinder* who would love her seemingly endless energy. That had been his plan from the beginning.

Maybe he should reconsider . . . It was nice having the pup rush to the door to welcome him home so enthusiastically. No, he couldn't change his mind. The puppy needed a loving family, and that was the one thing he would never be able to give Graceless.

Suddenly he heard, "Wake up!"

Blinking, Levi looked over the stall door to see Samuel Lambright grinning at him. "I'm not asleep."

"No? When did you start snoring while awake?"

Levi grinned. "I must have drifted off. With barn chores, taking care of my animals, taking care of my house, and staying up with a dying cat all last night, I didn't get much sleep."

"The solution is simple." Samuel folded his arms on the stall door as Levi went to check the bandage on the doe's leg. *"Ja?"*

"You need to find a *fraa*, Levi. You can't keep putting it

off, or you'll be so old that no *maedel* will give you a second look."

Levi snorted. "Look who's talking! How many times has your *mamm* said it's time for you to find a farm of your own? You and I both know that means she's hoping you'll settle down with a nice *fraa* who can give you lots of *bopplin* for her to spoil."

"She's just looking out for her eldest son."

Focusing on the doe's leg, Levi unrolled the stretch bandage on it. The deer must have sensed he was about to free her because she didn't fight him as she had before. Still, he made sure each movement was slow. Her eyes were white-edged as she looked past him at Samuel.

"Talk quieter," Levi said in a whisper. "If she panics, she may hurl herself against the stall and hurt herself again."

"*Ja,*" Samuel said softly.

Levi continued to remove the bandage. The doe's leg looked straight. Once she regained muscle strength, he could release her. It shouldn't take more than a few days.

He tossed the bandage to Samuel. His friend knew the routine, because he had assisted Levi, since they were *kinder*, with the animals. "You don't think she'll try to jump out?" Samuel asked as Levi opened the stall door and eased out.

"Her leg muscles won't allow that yet. I'll check her in the morning. If she's doing better, I'll let her out into the pasture. That way, she can graze on her own and leave when she's ready."

Samuel grinned. "If I didn't know better, Levi, I'd think you could talk to these animals."

"I understand they're in pain. And I understand that all they want is to be free."

"Sort of like you."

Checking that the stall doors were secure, Levi didn't answer. Samuel wasn't wrong. Levi had days when he wished he could abandon the heartache hanging over the farm where he had lived his whole life, but he had promised *Dawdi* and *Mammi* that he would take care of their land.

"So what do you think of my cousin?" Samuel asked.

"Edna Lambright?"

Samuel grimaced. "You know I'm not talking about Edna. What do you think of Ruth?"

"She's . . . unpredictable," Levi said with a grin. He picked up the lantern he'd brought to the barn. "She also cares a lot about the *kinder* and being a good teacher."

"I think she could care a lot about you, too. Just don't tug on her *kapp* strings. I made that mistake, and she got all riled up."

Levi chuckled as they walked along the aisle between the two rows of stalls. "Why don't you leave matchmaking to the women? You're not very *gut* at it."

"No? I saw how Ruth looked at you the night she arrived."

"With annoyance, more likely than not."

Samuel clapped Levi on the shoulder. "I know you didn't have much of a *rumspringa*, but even you must know enough about women to realize that annoyance is often the first step to her wanting you to court her."

"Is that so?"

"*Ja.*"

94

"You seem to think you've got great knowledge about women."

"More than you, Levi." He laughed again. "Watch Ruth the next time you're around her. She may be irritated, but she has a special twinkle in her eyes when she looks at you. All you need to do is look back, and you'll see."

Levi let his friend go on talking. He didn't have any intention of looking for a special twinkle in Ruth's eye. He might be lonely with only a rambunctious pup for company, but he'd been taught too well what the costs of love and loss were.

"It's a good thing that there's no school today, *ja*, Ruth?" Esther asked as they rode in the back of the Lambrights' buggy.

"*Ja*," Ruth agreed. "I'm glad that this isn't one of the Saturdays when we make up classes. I wouldn't want to miss the apple-peeling frolic."

Ruth relaxed back against the seat, letting her thoughts wander. She enjoyed every minute of teaching and spending time with the *kinder*. Even so, she struggled to keep up with preparation work and grading papers and reading back copies of the *Blackboard Bulletin*, the teachers' guide. In addition, she helped her cousins with their chores.

Every day for the past three weeks, she had left her buggy in Levi's barn. She had seen him only once or twice. Each time, he offered a pleasant greeting but nothing more. He acted as shy and distant as he had that first night at the Lambrights' house. She wasn't sure why. Was it because, in spite of his words to the contrary after the incident with the *Englischers*, he was disappointed with her? Nobody else had mentioned the *Englischers*' visit. Maybe the parents were accustomed to such intrusions. Perhaps they believed, if their *kinder* mentioned the intrusion that she had handled it the best possible way. No other school board members had asked her about it. So why was Levi acting disappointed in her? That thought upset her so much she didn't dare to ask. She was afraid he would confirm her suspicions that she wasn't living up to the school board's hopes, even though none of them had spoken to her about her teaching.

She wasn't meeting her own hopes with David Zook. When she called roll, he raised his hand but never spoke. She watched him during recess. On occasion, he would play with the other *kinder* as long as the game didn't require him to talk. She chose teaching plans so he could participate silently. Whenever she could, without making him the center of attention, she spent time with him, going over his lessons. He was a bright *kind* who mastered each lesson quickly. He shared well and was *gut*-hearted. A fine boy in every way.

Except he never spoke.

And why hadn't she heard anything from home? She had written three letters to *Mamm* and two more to the whole family. No return letters had arrived in the Lambrights' mailbox. She'd considered calling, but *Daed* seldom checked the answering machine in the phone shanty they shared with neighbors.

If she didn't receive a letter next week, she would call. No matter if *Daed* considered worry a frightful sin, because she should be trusting in God's will. She had realized long ago that was one trespass she would commit over and over, especially when ones dear to her were involved. *Daed didn't understand.*

Her thoughts went in endless circles until Esther said her name impatiently. Ruth wondered how long her cousin had been trying to get her attention.

"I'm sorry, Esther," she said. "I was daydreaming."

"I know." Esther laughed. "*Mamm* and I were discussing how much I'm enjoying being at school with you. I said that Hannah would like to help, too."

Sadie turned the buggy down a long farm lane edged on both sides by dried cornstalks. "I suggested she ask you before she and Hannah made any plans." Smiling at Ruth, she added, "Young girls get excited about any chance to get out of household chores."

"*Mamm!*" Esther rolled her eyes. "I'm not trying to avoid my chores. Don't I always get them done?"

"With Ruth's help."

Ruth patted Esther's shoulder. "She helps me, and I help her. It's only fair. Esther, next time you speak with Hannah, ask her to stop by the school and see me."

"You can see her today. She's coming to the frolic."

"Very convenient," her *mamm* said drolly.

When they arrived at the Umble farm, Sadie halted the buggy by the rambling white farmhouse. The Umbles owned one of the larger orchards in the district, so Barbara had offered to host the frolic.

Seth Umble popped out of the barn and waved. He offered to take the buggy to a spot where others waited under

97

the large maple trees. He grinned and called, "*Gude mariye*, Teacher Ruth!"

"*Gude mariye.*" She wasn't surprised Seth was helping with the frolic. The sixth grader always had his hand up to volunteer to wipe the board or slap the erasers or lower the window shades. "*Danki* for your help."

His grin broadened, and she remembered how praise from her own teachers had left her with a warm glow.

Ruth followed the Lambrights to the house between two large trees that wore the first tints of autumnal glory. All three of them carried baskets with food to share. Sadie's basket held stuffed green peppers and sweet pickles. Esther brought a peach pie, and Ruth had baked her *mamm*'s favorite cinnamon rolls.

The large kitchen looked almost identical to Sadie's, except the linoleum was dark green and the large table was an oval instead of a rectangle. Eager greetings invited them to join a dozen women already at work. The women made room to give Ruth and Sadie seats. Piles of apple peelings looked like strangely colored shavings in a woodworker's shop.

As soon as Ruth sat across from Sadie, an empty basket was set on her left and a bushel of apples on her right. Soon she was creating her own pile of peelings while Esther went to help Hannah watch the *bopplin* and younger *kinder*.

Ruth found it simple to match each of her scholars with his or her *mamm*, because the resemblance was strong. Figuring out the complex web of how families were related to each other, however, would take longer.

Esther came back into the kitchen and whispered in

Ruth's ear, "Can you come and see Hannah now? She's so anxious."

"Of course," Ruth said.

She followed Hannah into the other room, where she found nearly twenty *kinder* in addition to Esther and Hannah. Both girls' faces were alight as they read to the *kinder*. That sight, more than answers to any questions she might ask, told Ruth how well Hannah would do at school.

Bopplin were lying on quilts spread on the floor. Two older *kinder* also sat on quilts, playing with blocks, dolls, and toy animals. They looked up curiously as Ruth approached them.

She knelt by two *kinder* who must have been seven or eight years old. The little girl waited for the boy to pile blocks up then she knocked them down. They laughed and started over again.

Footsteps came from behind her. Barbara Umble and Sela Miller, who had been introduced to her as Barbara's sister, paused in the doorway. When they saw Ruth by the two Down syndrome *kinder*, they paused.

She knew the women were watching but kept her attention on the *kinder*. "*Wie geht's?* I'm Ruth. What are your names?"

"Abby," the little girl said with a grin. "Abby Miller."

The boy hesitated then said in a near whisper, "Gabe."

"He's Gabe Umble," Abby said.

"Nice to meet you, Abby Miller and Gabe Umble."

They grinned.

"I like your blocks." Ruth sat back on her heels. "Did someone special make them?"

"*Daedi.*" Abby seemed the more talkative, and Gabe seemed used to letting her take the lead. "*Daedi* made them for Abby."

"What a lucky girl you are!"

Abby beamed and picked up a block. She handed it to Ruth. "Pretty."

"*Ja*, it is a pretty block."

"Not block pretty. You pretty." Abby gave a peal of laughter, and Gabe joined in.

Ruth did, too. Giving the block to Abby, she stood. The *kinder* returned to their game, their laughter unrestrained.

She went to Barbara and Sela and lowered her voice so their *kinder* wouldn't overhear. "Such sweet *kinder*. God gives His special *kinder* an extra share of the joy He must have felt on that first day when He created light to shine on the heavens and the earth."

Sela's eyes filled with tears. "Abby is a blessing. She's never met anyone she doesn't love."

"And Gabe is the same, isn't he?" Ruth asked, turning to Barbara.

"He's quieter." Barbara's laugh was as warm as her son's. "But he's never happier than when he makes someone else smile or laugh."

"Do they attend a special school?"

Both women shook their heads, and Sela said, "There isn't one close enough."

Ruth didn't hesitate. "You're welcome to send them to school with your other *kinder*. When I was a scholar, a Down syndrome *kind* attended my school, and it was my

100

job to make sure he learned all he could." She smiled as she thought of the loving *kind* who had taught her as much—or more—than she had him.

"But you've got so many scholars already." In spite of her words, Barbara couldn't hide her hope.

Ruth took one of Barbara's hands and one of Sela's. "I wouldn't have asked if I didn't think we could handle it." Looking at where the youngest *kinder* crawled over Esther and Hannah, she raised her voice. "Esther Lambright helps me, and I'm about to ask Hannah Wagler, as well."

The two girls squealed and hugged each other. Esther jumped up and ran over to give Ruth a big hug. Hannah followed, and thanked Ruth over and over.

Shooing them back to the *kinder*, Ruth said, "As you can see, they are loving girls, and I know they'll help Gabe and Abby."

Both women had tears in their eyes as they looked at Ruth.

"*Danki,* Ruth," Barbara said.

"Abby wants to go to school with her brothers and sisters," Sela added. "This is so *gut. Danki.*"

Their gratitude made Ruth uncomfortable, so she shifted the conversation to practical matters. "Why don't you bring them to school next week, so you and the *kinder* can spend time with us? You're welcome to stay until they're comfortable with us, and, of course, you can visit whenever you wish."

A hand settled on Ruth's shoulder as Sadie said, "I heard what you've offered, Ruth. That's very kind of you."

"Every *kind* deserves to learn as much as they can." She grinned. "I know Esther and Hannah will feel the same . . . as soon as I tell them what I've volunteered them to do."

They laughed. For the first time, Ruth felt at home in this new district. No, it was more than that. She felt accepted. It was *wunderbaar*.

Barbara poured more *kaffi*. With the last apples peeled, the women began to slice the least brown ones for pies. The rest would be put, along with the peels, into the Umbles' cider press that afternoon.

"Anyone else?" Barbara asked.

Ruth shook her head. Their break for lunch had offered so many varieties of delicious food, she couldn't swallow another bite.

Setting the pot on the stove, Barbara put her hands on her ample hips. "It's time to talk about what's on everyone's mind today."

Ruth smiled, sure she knew the topic. Wedding season would be arriving in November, and soon Sunday services would include the publishing of wedding announcements. She listened as the women discussed who they thought would get married.

Some clues were easy to read. Extra celery planted in a neighbor's garden was the sign of an upcoming wedding, because celery was such an important part of the wedding feast. If a man gave a woman a clock the previous Christmas, that guaranteed a wedding before the next one. Young women hosting a quilting frolic for a friend often foreshadowed a wedding.

"What about Ruth?" asked someone from the far end of the table.

Laughter enveloped her. She was glad that the women liked her enough to tease her, but a husband would have to wait. If Levi was right, her becoming a teacher was God's will. The thought warmed her. Because she was accepting God's will or because she thought of Levi?

"Don't look for a husband for her too quickly," Barbara said with a wink. "Once she's married, she'll probably stop teaching."

"Then she needs a husband who'll let her teach until they start having *bopplin*." Sadie laughed.

"There's Cyrus Beiler. He needs a *fraa*." Sela gathered up apples and put them in a bucket. "And I don't think he has any plans for *bopplin*."

Ruth joined in with the laughter when Sadie explained that Cyrus Beiler was a confirmed bachelor who was almost sixty years old.

"Don't forget," Sadie's sister-in-law, Mavis, said with a wink, "there's Samuel Lambright."

"It may be too late," Esther said from the other room.

That set everyone to chattering about who had caught Samuel's eye. Ruth suspected the younger women already knew because they suddenly seemed intent on sorting apples. That they knew wasn't a surprise. Newly married couples often chaperoned at singings. They would see which boy asked which girl to go home in his buggy after the singing.

Ruth was relieved the conversation had turned from finding her a match. Her parents had agreed to let her teach for a year. They might not want her to continue, especially when *Mamm* had a new *boppli* and a daughter on her *rumspringa*.

Hannah reached past Ruth to grab apple slices. She handed them to Esther to take to the *kinder*. Turning, Hannah called over her shoulder, "How about Levi Yoder? He's eligible, and he's right across the road from the school."

"Now that's a thought," Sadie said. "Levi was always a *gut* boy. He never gave his grandparents a second of trouble."

"Except when he brought home hurt animals," Sela said with a shake of her head. "His *gross-mammi* worried that he would get rabies. Do you like animals, Ruth?"

That brought a new round of laughter. Even though Ruth laughed along—and despite the spark that jumped between her and Levi whenever they touched—she could not imagine letting him court her. Levi was far too serious. Had he ever done anything spontaneous in his whole life, or had he restricted himself to being a *gut* grandson?

She glanced at Abby and Gabe, who now rolled a ball back and forth as they giggled. *Kinder* were supposed to have fun, even if it meant being naughty. How many times had *Mamm* told her and her sisters that making mistakes was part of learning?

For the first time, she wondered what Levi would have been like if his parents had lived. She couldn't imagine anything sadder than him giving up his youthful joy to be the *gut* grandson every day of his life.

* *

"I can't believe we're going to be back in school together!" Esther gave Hannah a hug.

"Isn't it strange? I could hardly wait to graduate and be done with school."

"Me, too." She giggled. "But now we're going back as assistants to the teacher."

"I'm so excited." Hannah picked up a fussy *boppli* and checked its diaper. Her nose wrinkled as she reached for a clean one. "What do you think we'll be doing?"

"Ruth has asked me to work with the little ones on art projects, and I help the older ones with their numbers."

Hannah shook her head as she changed the diaper. "I won't be any help with that. Numbers and I don't get along."

"You're going to need to know how to do accounts when you are a *fraa* and have a house of your own."

"I'll marry a man who's so *gut* with numbers that he won't want me to bother."

"And who would that be?"

"I'm not telling." Hannah wadded up the dirty diaper and dropped it in the diaper pail, that was kept close to the *kinder* during frolics. "But I will win his heart all on my own. I'm not going to take a chance on being an old *maedel*."

"Me, either. I don't want to be like poor Ruth. I'd *die* if the women were trying to match me up like that."

"They're only funning her." She put the *boppli* back on its quilt. "Why are you upset, Esther? You know how women talk when they get together. It's always the same."

Esther sighed. Her friend was right. The topics were always new recipes or new *bopplin* or which *maedel* might be the best match for which unmarried man.

"I don't want them to talk about me like that."

"Then get married right after you are baptized."

Esther stopped a toddler from taking a book from another *kind*. "I'd gladly do that."

"If your *he* was willing." Hannah dropped her voice to a whisper. "Is he?"

"I hope so."

"Maybe you'll know more after tomorrow night's singing at the Hooleys'. Have your parents told you that you can go?"

Esther's happiness vanished. While playing with the *kinder* and planning how she and Hannah would work together at the school, she had let the singing slip from her mind.

"Not yet," she admitted.

Hannah's face fell. "But I want to go so badly!"

"Me, too."

"So find a way to get your parents to give you permission to go."

"I'm trying." After *Mamm* hadn't taken the hint from all the times Esther had mentioned the singing this week, she had to come up with another way to persuade *Mamm*. But how?

She heard laughter from the kitchen. When she looked out there, Ruth was standing up to carry more sliced apples to the other end of the table. *Mamm* admired Ruth and how well she was doing with the teaching. Maybe Ruth could help get *Mamm* to listen—really listen—to Esther.

"Try harder." Tears sparkled in Hannah's eyes. "I can't miss *another* singing."

Esther squeezed her friend's hand. She almost blurted out her plan to ask Ruth, but she didn't want to get Hannah's hopes up. "I'll do my best. I promise you that."

Hannah threw her arms around her and hugged her. "I know you will, and I know we'll have a great time together at the singing."

The rest of the afternoon passed quickly. After the sliced apples were divided up so each woman could take enough to make a half-dozen pies, *Mamm* said she wanted to help Barbara with the cleaning up.

"Then Ruth and I will go home and make supper," Esther said, delighted she'd have a chance to speak to her cousin alone. "Samuel will bring the buggy back and pick you up."

In short order, Seth brought the Lambrights' buggy. He handed the reins to Ruth and grinned shyly. Esther held back her laughter. Seth had a big crush on his teacher, and Ruth had no idea.

Ruth turned the buggy onto the main road, holding the reins loosely and letting Jess find the way home. Esther kept glancing at her cousin. How should she bring up the topic so close to her heart? She considered and discarded idea after idea, wondering why it was so hard to talk to Ruth about this.

"Go ahead," Ruth said. "Say what you've got to say before you explode. I don't know how I would explain to your parents if that happened."

Esther smiled. Ruth's teasing was what she needed to

loosen her tongue. "I need your advice," she said. "How can I persuade my *mamm* and *daed* that I'm mature enough to go to the singing tomorrow? I'll be sixteen in a few days. It's not like I'm going to get a lot more mature before then."

Ruth shook her head. "I can tell you from experience that an argument like that will get you nowhere."

"Then what can I do?"

"Ask Samuel if you can ride with him. Your parents might let you attend if they know he's watching out for you."

"But I don't want to ride home with my brother! I want to ride home with Caleb. He . . ." She pressed her hands over her mouth. "I shouldn't have spoken his name."

Ruth put an arm around her. "Don't worry. I'd never share what's in your heart with anyone else."

"Really? Not even with *Mamm*?"

"No, not with her or anyone else."

"Not even with Levi?"

A car approached from behind, so Ruth grasped the reins with both hands. Once it was past, Ruth said, "Levi and I don't talk about such things."

"What do you talk about?"

Ruth hesitated for a split second. "Usually about the school and the scholars. Why are you asking?"

"I was curious what I should talk about when a boy asks me to ride in his courting buggy."

"That's simple, Esther."

"No, it's not!" she moaned. "What if I can't think of anything to talk about?"

Ruth's smile returned. "That's only a problem if you go with the wrong boy. If he's the right one, you won't have to worry about what to talk about because you'll both want to share your opinions and dreams and wishes with each other."

"Do you feel that way about Levi?"

"We're talking about you, not me," Ruth said with a laugh.

Esther grinned. "After the suggestions you got for a husband at the frolic, I'm not surprised you don't want to think about it right now."

"That's right. Now, let's cook up some ideas to convince Samuel to be your ally while we're cooking supper."

Now that her cousin was willing to help, Esther felt a surge of hope. Tomorrow's singing was going to be the best night ever!

Eight

As Levi sat on a bench next to the Lambright men, he wasn't thinking about the Sunday service that would be starting soon. He was thinking about Ruth, hoping she wouldn't ask him why he'd been avoiding her when she brought her buggy to his barn each day. He had laughed at Samuel's clumsy attempts at matchmaking, but he hadn't been able to shake the conversation from his thoughts.

Samuel was wrong; Levi didn't need a *fraa*. He needed a housekeeper, a cook, a laundress, a gardener, and a seamstress. Yes, a *fraa* did those things, but a *fraa* took on all that work because of the love she shared with her husband. He didn't have love to give. He would never expect Ruth to marry him with no love. Even if he were foolish enough to make such a proposal, she would turn him down flat.

When the women entered the Hooleys' house for the worship service, Ruth walked in with her Lambright cousins. Her gaze was lowered. She sat and picked up her *Ausbund*, so she'd be ready for the hymns.

Three hours later, when the service came to an end, Levi had no idea which hymns they'd sung or what the sermons or district announcements had been. He had attempted to keep his eyes from cutting to where Ruth sat, seemingly absorbed by the service. Her attention never wavered. Not once had he noticed her looking in his direction. He should be relieved, but having the inevitable conversation delayed was an exquisite torment.

Levi's hope that he would find a chance to speak with her after the service withered when parent after parent asked her about their *kinder* in school. Ruth appeared to welcome questions, and as far as he could tell, she answered each one with genuine concern for her scholars.

He hid his irritation when he heard Mose Christner and his friends, who were close to his age, talking about humorous things Ruth had said after service. When had she spoken to them? Their comments made it sound as if Ruth had flirted with them.

His gut tightened. He didn't want to think she was one of those women who chatted up every man she met. He asked himself why he was upset. He should be glad that she might meet the man God wanted her to spend her life with. She was a *gut* person, and she deserved a man who could love her.

So why was he bothered by his friends' comments about Ruth?

Levi strode to the barn, where the singing would be held

tonight. He always thought most clearly when he was doing something physical. He found Samuel, Mose, and Peter Hooley, who was almost eighteen, setting up tables and chairs. He offered to help. The space beside the baled hay had been swept, but wisps of dried grass and dust clung to the rough boards. A single row of tables ran the length of the space, and four other tables would hold cookies and cider for everyone attending the singing.

"Where do you want these?" asked Samuel as he held up kerosene lanterns.

Mose pointed toward a rafter above the table. "There are hooks up there."

"Guess I'll fill them first then." Samuel motioned to Levi. "Want to help?"

"Sure." He didn't. The only thing he wanted to do was talk to Ruth.

Levi and Samuel hadn't gone more than a few steps from the barn before Samuel asked, "Are you going to mope all day?"

Levi regarded him with a single, raised eyebrow.

Samuel shook his head. "It wonders me how a man who can tell what animals are thinking doesn't even know his own mind."

"I know my own mind."

"And?"

"It's my own business."

"So that's how it's going to be, is it?" Samuel began filling the lanterns. The pungent smell of kerosene surrounded them. "Just like always. If you ignore something long enough, you can pretend it doesn't matter to you."

Levi didn't reply as he shifted the lanterns to make it easier for Samuel to fill them.

"Are you going to ignore me, too?" asked Samuel as he put the top back on the kerosene container. He picked up two lanterns. "Maybe that's what you want. For everyone to leave you alone. Just you and your critters. Even those you kick out of your life the moment they can get by on their own."

"I do not kick them out of my life. They want to return to the wild," Levi said. He grasped two other lanterns by their wire handles. "You are making things sound worse than they are."

"I'm not the one wandering around with a scowl on my face and a chip on my shoulder."

Levi tried to find words to deny what Samuel was saying but couldn't. He reached for the other two lanterns as Samuel strode away. Now he had angered his best friend. Could this day get any worse?

God, You know my mind and my heart. You know, too, why I guard them with such care. I'm struggling to understand what You have planned for me. Guide me, please. Let me know Your will for my life.

He raised his head and hoped he would find his way with God's help.

Soon.

Ruth tried to keep Esther calm as evening approached. Even after Ruth had promised to keep a close eye on Esther, Sadie had been reluctant to let Esther attend the singing tonight. She had acquiesced when Esther reminded her mother that she would be sixteen soon and would be able to attend . . . without Ruth to watch over her. Once Sadie agreed, Esther had been able to talk of nothing else. Her cousin was floating on air, and Ruth imagined her as a balloon being held to Earth by a slender string. She finally sent Esther to sit with Hannah, where they could whisper and eye the boys who intrigued them.

She slipped her hand into her pocket under her apron and touched the letters she had received in the mail. No one had checked the mailbox out by the road until after the family had divided into the big wagon and Samuel's buggy for the drive to the Hooleys' farm. When she had discovered three letters, one from *Mamm* and two from her sisters, she'd read each one slowly, savoring every tidbit of news from home. Her *mamm* assured her nothing was wrong; only the extra-long hours of work to get the farm ready for winter had kept her from writing. Ruth prayed her *mamm* wasn't hiding the truth. Her sisters hadn't said anything about *Mamm*'s condition, writing instead about school and their friends.

Going into the Hooleys' barn, she saw everything was ready. Benches ran along both sides of the tables, and food was already being set out by the other women.

"Do you need something?" asked the deep voice she'd been hoping to hear.

She faced Levi, and her breath caught over her heart that seemed to have forgotten how to beat. "I thought," she said, pleased her voice sounded casual, "I'd see if I could help with anything."

"The songbooks need to be put on the tables."

"I believe I can do that," she said, her voice teasing. "As a teacher, I've had experience passing out books."

He didn't smile, and she wished she hadn't mentioned anything about school. She snatched up the songbooks and placed them along the table, then left to return to the kitchen. She thought she heard Levi call her name, but she didn't stop. Her yearnings to be with him and learn more about the man behind the cool wall were tricking her. She had to keep them from betraying her.

Esther paused in the doorway beside Hannah. She still couldn't believe they were attending their first singing. Others in their age group were standing around talking, and the long tables waited for the singers to take their seats. More tables pushed to the side of the barn held food and lemonade for the breaks.

"Where do we sit?" Esther whispered, not daring to talk louder.

"I asked, and I was told we can sit anywhere."

"I'm not sitting down first. We'll look desperate for any boy to sit across from us. I'm waiting for someone else to sit down first."

"Me, too."

They stood in the doorway until some of the other teens drifted to the table and took seats: girls on one side, and the boys facing them, for some well-chaperoned flirting between songs. Couples who had been courting long enough that it was no secret sat across from each other at the far ends of the tables.

"C'mon," Esther said as the seats began to fill. She had to tug on Hannah's arm to get her friend to move.

Hannah didn't answer but followed Esther. Two places were still open in the middle of the long tables. Esther swung one leg over the bench, then the other. She patted the bench, urging Hannah to do the same. The places across from them were empty.

"What if nobody sits there?" Hannah whispered. "I can't end up an old *maedel*."

"Someone will, and stop worrying about being an old *maedel*. It's just our first singing, and there's a big crowd here tonight." She scanned the barn until she saw Caleb Stutzman standing with a group of young men, who were clearly watching the young women.

Her heart soared. Caleb wasn't here with a girl. Maybe . . . just maybe . . .

"Let's all sit down," Ruth called out in what Esther considered her "Teacher Ruth" voice, calm but authoritative enough so everyone listened.

Esther couldn't help watching as Caleb walked toward the table with the easy confidence he'd shown for as long as she had known him. He paused and spoke to one girl, and her heart plummeted. But he kept going and came toward the middle of the table.

Sit right there! Sit right there!

"Are these seats promised to someone else?" he asked, his smile as bright as the light reflecting in his black hair.

117

Esther managed to mumble, "No."

"*Gut.*" He motioned to another young man, who had sandy hair and freckles. "This is Amos Esch. He's from my *mamm*'s home district, and he's here to see how we do a singing."

They sat across from Esther and Hannah. Esther fingered the thin songbook they would be using tonight. She looked up at Caleb and saw him smiling at her. She wondered if she'd ever been so happy.

Even so, she was glad when a *vorsinger* for the first song was selected. It was Peter Hooley, and he had the honor of leading them. While she sang, Esther listened to Caleb's slightly off-pitch baritone. He seemed to be having a great time, and she hoped it was because she was there. When he joked with Amos between songs, she grasped Hannah's hand and held it tightly. Wouldn't it be perfection if Amos could become Hannah's special *he*? The four of them could have so much fun together.

A break was called, and Ruth came over to put her hand on Esther's and Hannah's shoulders and guide them to the table where the treats were. Esther looked back but the barn was so crowded, and didn't see Caleb or Amos anywhere. She wished she was tall like Ruth and could look over the others and see Caleb.

Hannah tugged on her arm, and Esther followed her to a corner. Hannah whispered, "I can't believe they sat across from us. Two handsome boys chose us."

"What about your *he*?" Esther hadn't guessed Hannah was so fickle.

With a laugh, Hannah waved a hand holding two oatmeal-raisin cookies. "It's all perfect!"

Esther had to agree when the end of the break was called, and they went back to the tables to find Caleb and Amos sitting right where they had before. It was all absolutely perfect.

"Ruth?"

At the sound of her name, Ruth whirled. The singing was over, and she was stacking dirty plates. She hoped the deep voice belonged to Levi, who hadn't come into the barn for the singing. It didn't. She recognized the man as one of Samuel's friends whom she had met earlier. His name eluded her.

"Ja?" she asked.

"If you don't have a ride home tonight, I would be honored to drive you." His face slowly turned red, making her wonder if his collar was too tight.

"That's kind of you, but I already have a ride home," she said as she had to the two other young men who had approached her earlier. She couldn't help wondering if the matchmaking at the apple-peeling frolic had stirred more than one woman to encourage her son to ask Ruth tonight.

"Gut." He beat a hasty retreat, and she guessed that he hadn't wanted to ask her any more than she had wanted to accept.

Maybe she should have Sadie speak with the other women so they didn't engage in matchmaking for her. As much as she wanted someday to have someone court her, she didn't want it to be because his feet had been held to the fire. She wanted love.

Ruth shook her head. She didn't need to be thinking about her heart's yearnings now. She needed to figure out what to do about what she had witnessed tonight.

Esther and her friend Hannah had sat across from two young men whose names, Ruth had learned, were Caleb and Amos. The young men had flirted with her cousin and Hannah throughout the singing, but the moment a break was called, they had disappeared only to return just before the singing began again. At the second break, Ruth had watched closely and had seen two girls waiting for them near the farthest reaches of the light from the barn. She had started to follow, not wanting Esther and her friend to risk their reputations at their very first singing.

But the girls hadn't been Esther and Hannah. Ruth's relief was short-lived; Esther would be devastated if she knew where Caleb had gone. Still, Ruth couldn't let the other two girls risk their reputations, either. She started to go outside to bring them back but before she reached the door, Mose Christner led the two girls and two boys back into the barn. Ruth was glad both Esther's and Hannah's backs were turned. From the flushed faces of the girls who'd been outside with Caleb and Amos, she guessed that they had been kissed, but neither Esther nor Hannah seemed to notice. They were too wrapped up in their own excitement.

During the rest of the singing, Caleb sat across from Esther and soon had her giggling. Ruth vowed to talk to her cousin. She wouldn't say what she'd seen, only urge Esther to be careful when starting her *rumspringa*. Ruth prayed that God would give her the right words. The last thing she wanted was for her cousin to be hurt the first time she risked her heart.

Mose Christner came over to where she was working. "Ruth, can I ask you something?"

She was ready to tell him that no, she didn't need a ride when she saw Amy Beiler beside him. The two had stayed close to each other all night, and she suspected they were courting.

"Of course," she said.

He glanced at Amy then asked, "Did you notice some of the girls and boys going outside tonight?"

"*Ja*, but you were already bringing them back into the barn by the time I got to the door."

"No others?"

She shook her head. "Is sneaking out common?" She couldn't remember any incidents when she attended singings during her brief *rumspringa*.

"Not until recently." Amy rubbed her hands together anxiously. "It seems to be only a few of the younger people." She looked at Mose.

He took a deep breath then said, "The truth is, the troublemakers seem to be my cousin Caleb and his friend, who's from another district. I gave them a *gut* talking-to tonight, but I don't know if it'll make any difference. They like to flirt with the girls too much."

"And the girls like it, too," Ruth said as she stacked more plates. "I'll be glad to help you two the next time I chaperone. If we can get a couple more adults, we could simply stand in the doorway so they can't slip out."

Mose grinned broadly. "That's a *gut* idea. We'll be prepared next time. I thought we'd be fine tonight, but Levi never showed up."

"That's not like him," Amy added. "He's always dependable. I hope nothing's wrong."

Ruth didn't answer; she guessed Levi had stayed away because she was in the barn. He had avoided her since their conversation on the schoolhouse porch. Once when she came into the barn to get the buggy, she'd heard his footsteps hurrying down to the lower level. She had thought they could be friends. She'd dreamed they might be more, but it was clear he liked his solitary life too much to have more than a few friends like Samuel.

Amy looked past Ruth to the table. "I'll be back to help. Right now, we need to make sure everyone has a ride home."

"I can take care of the rest of this by myself." In all honesty, she wanted to be alone now. She was tired of pretending that it didn't hurt that Levi was eager to avoid being in her company. *"Danki."*

As Mose and Amy headed for the door, Ruth collected paper napkins and tossed them into a pail that had been left under the table. Her fingers froze when she heard Mose say, "Levi! It's about time you showed up."

She refused to look over her shoulder. She kept working, putting the dirty dishes into stacks that would be easy to carry back into the house. Putting leftover food on the other end of the table, she drew back when a long arm reached past her and picked up a snickerdoodle.

"Ruth," Levi said from behind her, "it seems like I'm always apologizing to you for something or other."

Was he going to tell her that he was sorry for treating her so shabbily?

She glanced over her shoulder when he didn't go on. "Mose Christner and Amy Beiler were here."

"So I saw." A cloud seemed to pass before his face before he said, "I'm sorry, Ruth, for not being here. Joseph and Paul stopped me on the porch. We got to talking and I lost all track of time."

"That's all right. Did you discuss anything about the school that I should know about?" She turned back to gathering up the dirty dishes. That let her avoid looking at him again. What a change from him being the one to dodge her! But it didn't make her feel any better.

"No. We were talking about how Wayne Fisher was taken to the hospital this afternoon. It's the third time in the past month that Old Wayne has gone by ambulance to Lancaster Regional."

She turned to face him as she heard the genuine anxiety in his voice. "Is he going to be all right?"

"I don't know. Each time he's gone, it's because he forgot his medications or took too much. Joseph said a cousin is coming from Delaware to take Old Wayne back there with him, so they can keep an eye on him." He took a bite of the cookie then said, "Everyone's going to be talking about it soon, because Joseph said Old Wayne's cousin plans to sell his farm."

"Is it a *gut* one?"

"*Ja.* One hundred arable acres along with the farmhouse and barns. They're all in fine condition."

"Some young man who wants to get married is going to be very interested."

"If *Englischers* don't buy it first."

She turned back to pick up the closest stack of dishes. "That's always a possibility, which is a shame because they usually don't plant anything in the fields."

He put out his arm to halt her from walking away. "Ruth, the dishes should remain out here until all the young people have left for home." He quickly lowered his arm before she could bump into it. "Just in case."

She set the dishes back on the table and glanced around the room. Levi must have seen, as she now did, that no other adults remained in the barn.

Levi sat on a hay bale. He wasn't sure if Ruth would join him. The last time they'd sat side by side, their conversation had become very personal. He wasn't sure he wanted to open up that much again, especially with Ruth, who saw parts of him that he had long believed were hidden.

When she perched beside him, however, the scent of lavender washed over him. He didn't know if it was her soap or her shampoo, but the fragrance suited her perfectly. Gentle yet not willing to be ignored.

He wasn't sure what to say, so he fell back on the trite. "Did you enjoy the singing?" he asked as laughter came from the teens on the other side of the barn.

"Ja." She folded her hands on her lap. "Are your fields ready for winter?"

"Other than a few acres where I planted soybeans. The potatoes are all out of the ground. Soon it'll be time for winter work—repairing equipment and taking more time to read God's word."

"That's one of the blessings of winter." She grinned. "I could do without the cold mornings, though. I've been meaning to ask you how your patients are doing."

He realized that, even though he hadn't asked, she had forgiven him for avoiding her. Grateful, he said, "The doe and two of the rabbits are back in the wild. I can't let the birds go until spring, because they missed flying south with their flocks. And Graceless has decided she needs to stay in my house."

"She'll be *gut* company for you."

Levi looked across the barn as the teens started leaving. Several picked up the plates Ruth had stacked to take them back to the house. As she called, *"Danki!"* he hoped she would stay just a little longer. He had been a fool to miss speaking with her each morning. That was something he intended to change.

"Do you have any new patients?" Ruth asked.

"No, thank God! I understand, however, that you'll be having two new students soon."

She smiled, and he noticed a dimple on her left cheek that he never had before. "Word spreads quickly."

"*Gut* news is always happily shared."

"So you think it is *gut* that Abby and Gabe are coming to the school?"

"Most certainly." He searched her face. Today, several of the scholars' parents had told him and the other school board members how glad they were that Ruth had been hired. Yet, she seemed to doubt herself. "Why would you think that I'd consider it anything but *gut*?"

She looked down and picked a thread off her apron. "You haven't made it a secret how you feel about other decisions I've made."

"And I'm not making my opinion about this one a secret, either."

The corners of her mouth twitched, and suddenly she was smiling. He smiled back, glad that for once they seemed to be enjoying each other's company.

Ruth wondered if she'd ever seen Levi look so free of worry. *He should smile more often*, she thought. His whole posture seemed lighter, as if he had set aside a burden too heavy for one man to shoulder.

She wished she didn't have to be serious, but she wanted his advice as a member of the school board and as someone who knew everyone in the district. "To tell you the truth, Levi, I worry less about how Abby and Gabe will do than I do about David Zook. He never talks. He does well at his lessons, and I can see he understands more quickly than some of the other scholars his age. I wish I could find a way to persuade him to speak."

Levi's expression became sympathetic. "Don't expect too much, Ruth. Even his *mamm* and *daed* haven't gotten him to talk."

She got to her feet and he did, too. They crossed the empty space toward the door.

"I believe in God's miracles," Ruth said, "and who knows when we might be blessed with one? I've been praying for guidance on how to reach David."

"I'll add my prayers, as I'm sure his parents have every day since they realized he could hear but refused to talk."

"What did the teacher last year try?"

Levi didn't hold back his frustrated sigh as they stepped out beneath the star-dusted sky. "Last year's teacher gave up on David after a few months."

"That is very sad. I won't give up on him."

"*Ja*, I know." He put his hand on her arm.

It was just a friendly gesture. But it wasn't, because a pulse of heat spread outward from his fingertips, surging right into her heart. When he took a half step closer, she held her breath, waiting to see what he would do next. Would he ask her to let him drive her to the Lambrights' house? On such a cool night, they could wrap a blanket around their shoulders, which would mean sitting close in the buggy.

"Ruth, I don't know if you've made plans to . . ." He cleared his throat.

Was he going to ask her if she would let him take her home? *Oh, please, let him ask me!*

He began again. "That is, Ruth, if you're willing, I—"

"Ruth!" Esther's heartbroken voice rang through the night. She ran over to them, almost knocking Levi out of the way. She threw her arms around Ruth and began babbling through her sobs.

Ruth couldn't understand anything Esther said, but she had a *gut* idea of what had happened. Singings were meant to be fun. When there were tears at their conclusion, it always meant one thing: A *maedel* hadn't been offered a ride home by a young man who interested her.

Still, Esther hadn't had her sixteenth birthday yet, so shouldn't expect a young man would ask to take her home.

Until a *maedel* began her running-around time, she was off-limits to boys.

"Let's go home, Esther. We can talk there," Ruth said, turning her cousin back toward where Samuel stood beside his buggy.

She looked back at Levi. His face was bare of any emotion, so she couldn't guess what he was thinking. He probably had no idea what to do with a weepy teenager.

"I'll see you tomorrow morning, Levi," she said, wishing she could have told him that if he really was asking her to ride home with him, she would have agreed.

"Yes, you will."

She smiled back at him as she heard the lighter tone of his voice. For the first time, she dared to believe their friendship could last longer than a single conversation.

Ruth walked Esther to Samuel's buggy, her arm around the younger girl's shoulders. "Listen to me, Esther," she said in a quiet voice. "I saw how Caleb sat across from you tonight, and I understand how happy that made you. But during the breaks, I also saw him talking with others."

Esther began to sob again.

"Hush," Ruth soothed her. "It may not mean anything. After all, you are not yet sixteen, so he couldn't ask you to ride home with him. But you are just entering the time when you can meet many boys and see who is best for you."

"He's the only boy I've ever wanted," Esther said through her tears.

"I know," Ruth said. "All I mean is that you should try not to give your heart away so quickly. That way, you can find the one whom you are truly meant to be with, the man God intends for you."

Esther nodded as they reached Samuel's buggy, and he helped her up into it. Ruth made sure the girl had blankets over both her lap and her shoulders. Esther turned her face to the side of the buggy, still upset.

"Are you sure you want to go with us?" asked Samuel as Ruth started to climb into the buggy.

"I don't want to walk back after dark."

"That's not what I meant." He gestured with his head back in Levi's direction. "I thought when I saw you two talking so close together . . ." He hesitated and cleared his throat like Levi had. "That is . . ." He stubbed his toe against the ground, unable to meet her eyes.

Ruth rushed into the buggy and sat beside Esther. She drew the girl's head down on her shoulder, so she didn't have to meet Samuel's eyes. She prayed he wouldn't say anything to Levi, even in teasing, about what he'd just said to her. Levi was such a private person that he might be upset enough and start avoiding her again.

And that would break her heart as surely as Esther's had been broken tonight.

Nine

◈

Ruth lifted the last of the littlest *kinder* off the wagon. She motioned for them to stand back beside the boxes of apples as Joseph Hooley drove the hay wagon onto the road. He had been kind enough to give the scholars a ride to Stony Field Farm Stand. Esther and Hannah stood like bookends on either side of the scholars. Abby and Gabe had stayed beside them all day, but now they joined the other *kinder.*

Tilting her bonnet away from the cloud of dust that rose behind the wagon, Ruth grimaced. As sticky as the air was today, she didn't want the dust glued to her face and clothes.

"*Ach*, what do we have here?" asked Leah Gingerich, the young woman who worked at the stand, as she came over to where the *kinder* were waving away the dust. "Lots of customers?"

"Actually," Ruth said, "we're bringing you something to sell. These scholars spent the morning picking apples at Old Wayne's orchard. Now they'd like to see where the apples will be sold."

Leah smiled, and told the scholars to follow her. With Esther and Hannah herding them, the *kinder* followed like an odd collection of ducklings.

Miriam came out from behind the counter, wiping her hands on her apron. "What a *gut* thing you're doing! Not only for Old Wayne, but for the *kinder*."

"My *daed* is a deacon," Ruth said, "so I learned early how important it is for the district to work together to help those who can't help themselves. I hope they've learned about helping others. Now they can find out how you run a business here."

"Leah has been looking forward to showing off the new cash register since she heard you were bringing the scholars here." Miriam chuckled. "She's as excited as a *kind* herself." Her smile wavered, and she put her hand up to her mouth.

Esther had told Ruth that Miriam was expecting after many years of wishing for a *boppli*. Surely the pregnancy was a gift from God, but nausea was never welcome.

"Maybe you should sit," Ruth said, putting her hand on Miriam's elbow.

"It passes quickly, but you're right." Miriam sat near a rack holding baked goods.

"Would you like a cool cloth?" Ruth asked. "It's so hot and humid today."

"I'm fine." Miriam looked at the apple baskets. "They must have stripped every tree."

"The little ones gathered windfall apples, and the biggest boys went up ladders to pick the highest ones." Ruth lowered her voice. "If I tell you a secret, will you not repeat it to anyone? I got queasy today, too. Just from watching the boys climbing up and down like carpenters at a barn raising."

Miriam laughed. "I won't tell a soul, but I can tell *you* that it's clear teaching brings you great joy."

"I love being with the *kinder*, even though there are some challenges." From her first day in the schoolhouse, Ruth had known that this was what God meant her to do. Still, she couldn't keep from glancing at David Zook, who stood off to one side as the *kinder* peppered Leah with questions.

How she wished she could help him escape his silence. While they were picking apples, she'd seen the longing in his eyes to be like the others, who chattered like a flock of sparrows. If he would say a single word, the other *kinder* would certainly welcome him as they had Abby and Gabe. There must be some way to reach him, but nothing she had tried worked. She wasn't ready to admit defeat. She had considered checking with Bishop John to see if she could ask the librarians at Pequea Valley Public Library to obtain materials to help her. She wasn't sure if the district's *Ordnung* would allow her to ask them without his permission.

Ask Levi.

The words came from the place in her heart where God whispered to her. Such simple advice, and she hoped to follow it. Though she had seen Levi each morning this week, they hadn't had time to say more than a polite *"Gude mariye."* He

133

was so busy with chores, and she was so busy with school. She tried to tell herself that she must accept the situation, but she longed for a chance to have a real conversation with him. "Challenges," Miriam said, her quiet voice bringing Ruth out of her thoughts, "are a part of life. I have mine here at the farm stand on mornings when nobody can come to help and on mornings when everyone wants to help. But your challenges are more important because you work with our scholars."

"I hope we're all learning from each other," Ruth replied.

Ruth joined her scholars while Leah gave them a tour. Almost all of the *kinder* had visited the stand at least once during the summer, but they were eager to see what went on "behind the scenes." Ruth put her hand on David's back and guided him toward the others. He looked up and smiled. Her heart tugged oddly.

Clapping her hands, she said, "All right. Time for the rest of our frolic. First graders and second graders, Hannah will show you how to sort apples by size. Esther will teach the rest of you how to weigh the baskets and price them."

Ruth watched as the *kinder* eagerly began. Walking between the groups, she answered questions. She doubted any scholars guessed their fun tasks were part of the arithmetic lessons for the week.

When the *kinder* finished with the apples, Miriam and Leah brought out treats they had prepared. The scholars were excited about the selection of whoopie pies and cookies. Cups were filled with fresh lemonade again and again until even the eighth-grade boys were full.

Ruth gathered the scholars and led them to the field behind the farm stand while Hannah and Esther remained inside, talking with the women and glad for an excuse to stay in the cool shadows. She pointed at the trees along the fence line.

"See how the leaves are showing their bottom side?" she asked. "What do you think that means?"

"They're going to do somersaults when they fall," suggested Mary Beth.

The *kinder* laughed along with Ruth.

"Some people believe," she said when everyone was listening again, "that when the leaves show their underside, rain is on the way."

"The clouds show that, too." Seth pointed toward the west. "They're getting really dark."

Ruth glanced at them and felt a stab of alarm. Seth was right. The clouds were building up fast. She needed to get the scholars back to the schoolhouse before it began raining.

"Let's go," she said, not surprised when two first-grade girls grabbed her hands.

A distant rumble of thunder floated over the farm stand. Miriam and Leah were bringing in crafts and produce. Esther and Hannah hurried over to help Ruth.

Where is Joseph? Ruth wondered. She came to a sudden halt as she realized: She meant to ask him to return for them and give them a ride back to school. But in all the excitement of arriving at the farm stand, she hadn't told him to come back.

Ruth fought back a wave of panic. Joseph wasn't coming for them. They were all going to be caught in the storm.

A wagon pulled into the farm stand in a cloud of dust. One of the boys called, "It's Levi!"

Ruth motioned for him to be quiet even as her insides were jumping up and down at the idea of seeing Levi. She made sure all the *kinder* were out of the way when he drew his wagon with bags of potatoes close to the farm stand.

Rushing out to greet him as he jumped from the driver's seat, Leah called, "We'll get you unloaded quickly."

"Danki," he said, and then glanced to where Ruth stood surrounded by the scholars.

His gaze locked with hers, and she could only stare back. Once again, those sweet sensations swept between them in an endless loop, weaving them together.

"We didn't expect this delivery until tomorrow, Levi. Did you decide to combine two trips into one so you could take the scholars back to school?" asked Leah as she picked up a bag of potatoes. "It is *gut* of you to do that."

Before Ruth could explain that had never been the plan, Levi spoke up. "Of course, I'm taking the scholars back to school," he said. "When I heard Ruth was bringing them here today, I knew there wasn't any use going home with an empty wagon."

It was a lie, but she was so grateful for it. She and Levi hadn't made any plans for today. If she had mentioned she was taking the *kinder* to Old Wayne's farm, it would have been only in passing. Maybe Joseph had told him about his part in transporting the *kinder*. Even so, Levi couldn't have known about her forgetfulness ahead of time. He was covering for her.

It took every ounce of her self-restraint not to throw her

arms around him and thank him. He smiled in her direction, and warmth filled her as she smiled back.

She wasn't sure how long they would have stood there if the *kinder* hadn't rushed to help unload the wagon.

More thunder sounded. Closer now.

Ruth called, "*Komm*, everyone. Climb into the wagon. We can still beat the storm back to school."

As Levi pulled out some empty potato bags and spread them across the dirty wagon, she picked up a few more and did the same. He glanced at her. "I guess you and the scholars really need a ride."

"*Ja*, and *danki*, Levi," she said as quietly. "I'm sorry I put you in this position. I planned to ask Joseph to take us back, and then I forgot."

"It's fine," he said, and turned to hoist the smaller *kinder* onto the wagon.

Ruth hurried to thank Miriam and Leah for patiently answering the scholars' questions, as well as for their help in selling Old Wayne's apples. Then she turned back toward the wagon, where Levi was picking up a first grader. He swung her high in the air and made her giggle before setting her on the wagon. The other *kinder* clamored to be the next.

Levi's smile was as enthusiastic as the *kinder*'s. His deep laugh resounded beneath theirs. It was puzzling why a man who had such a generous laugh released it so seldom.

"Teacher Ruth is next!" called Mary Beth. The *kinder* repeated her name in a joyous chant.

Ruth started to quiet them because she didn't want to put Levi in an uncomfortable situation. Then Levi's hands set-

tled on her waist. As if she weighed no more than milk-
weed fluff, he lifted her onto the wagon's seat. His hands
lingered a moment longer than necessary as he gazed into
her eyes. His gaze warmed her; it made her feel as if everything inside her was somehow more alive.

Then he released her, and she hurried to sit. What must
he think of her when she looked at him that way? He'd
never offered her anything more than friendship, and even
that had been hard won. She should be satisfied.

But she wasn't. When she admired his strong hands, she
thought of them holding her. The sight of his broad shoulders led her to imagine leaning her head against him. His
laugh reached into her heart and lodged there like a memory.

Levi climbed up onto the wagon's seat. She couldn't help
noticing he left enough room between them for another person. As the wagon bounced out onto the road, her shoulder
bumped into Levi's. She gripped the seat when he stiffened
and slanted away from her.

It was such a small gesture and yet, it hurt her. She
wanted to ask him what she had done to make him want to
avoid her. She couldn't imagine. He hadn't regarded her
with his disapproving frown. Instead he acted as if everything were normal . . . except that he wanted to keep her at
arm's length.

She shook off the thought. She was being silly. Instead
of dwelling on a puzzle she couldn't solve, she should be
thinking about the *kinder* and the storm darkening above
the western horizon.

Beneath the clatter of the iron wheels on the asphalt road

and the scholars' excited voices, she said, "*Danki* again, Levi, for coming to our rescue."

"Glad to help."

"I appreciate that you made it sound as if we'd planned this in advance, but I'm sorry you had to lie."

"It wasn't exactly a lie. If I'd known ahead of time that you and the *kinder* needed a ride, I would have offered it."

"*Danki.*"

He didn't reply, and she released a silent sigh. When he'd offered to drive the *kinder* back to school, she had hoped that he might actually talk with her. But, if he truly wanted to keep her away, why hadn't he released her quickly when he lifted her into the wagon?

She was more confused than ever.

Ten

❦

Levi pressed one foot against the wagon's dash and tried to ignore how his hands shook as he guided the horses along the road. He hoped Ruth didn't notice. At least his legs weren't jelly, the way they'd been when he had climbed onto the seat beside her. *That* had been unexpected. She wasn't the first woman he'd assisted into a buggy, but never before had it made him go weak in the knees. He gritted his teeth, knowing he had to forget that moment when he put his hands around her waist and lifted her. She'd gazed down at him as if she trusted that he would never drop her. His life was fine just as it was, and he didn't need anyone else in it. He had learned that the price of that happiness could be too high. Better not to risk it and just focus on his farming and tending to his animals.

He gathered his composure around him like a shield and focused on the road. Cars and trucks sped by in both lanes, their occupants probably as eager to avoid the thunderstorm as he was.

Thunder clapped, and Ruth glanced over the trees across the road. The wind wafted some of her lavender fragrance toward him.

"Do you think we'll get to school before the storm hits?" she asked.

"Ja." It would be close. The storm was moving quickly now, but he didn't dare urge the horses to go any faster, because the *kinder* might bounce off the back of the wagon.

"I hope you're right. The sky is turning a peculiar shade."

Levi looked to the west and scowled. He recognized that brownish-green tint to the clouds, though he had never seen it so late in the year. Spring was the season for tornadoes in Lancaster County, and even then they were rare. But the sky had that unmistakable color.

He slapped the reins on the horses' backs. "We can always stop at the Keims' corner store."

"It's closed. Sadie told me now that the tourist season is over, the Keims have headed south to Pinecrest for the winter."

Levi put his hand up to keep his straw hat from flying away with a gust of wind. "But there are other places we can stop." Lowering his voice, he asked, "How are you managing with your newest scholars?"

"Very well." She smiled gently as she looked over her shoulder, then back at him. He was amazed how openly she wore her emotions. He was also a bit envious. He wished he could be so candid. Or did he? As flustered as he was today, he should be glad that nobody knew what he was thinking.

"Thank God for Esther and Hannah. I couldn't help Abby and Gabe and also teach the other *kinder*. Both girls will be *wunderbaar* teachers."

"And your other special scholar?"

The wind grew stronger and whipped loose strands of hair from beneath her *kapp*. Thunder almost drowned out her words as she asked, "You mean David?"

"*Ja.*"

"He's still not speaking, but he's joining in with the *kinder*'s games. If he doesn't, I give him a gentle push."

"David is fortunate that you haven't given up on him."

"I'm running out of ideas," she admitted. "I've drawn him out of his shell, but he's still not talking." She started to say something else but hesitated.

"What is it, Ruth?"

"Can I ask your opinion about something?"

"*Ja.*"

"I've been thinking about asking Bishop John if the librarians at the local library can find information on the Internet that might help me to help David. Do you think the bishop will agree?"

"I don't know," Levi said honestly.

"*Ach*, I'd hoped you'd tell me that he would agree." She tensed as lightning flashed in the distance.

"Bishop John is a *gut* man and a godly one. Go to him with your request. Don't expect an answer right away, because he'll want to pray on it." He grinned at her. "The worst he can say is no. Then you're in no different position than you are now."

"*Danki*, Levi," she said. "You're right. I'll ask Bishop John, and I'll keep praying myself, too. Maybe God will give me some new way to help David. If you think of any ideas that might work, please let me know."

"I will. I want to help him, too." He slipped his hand onto her sleeve, and she felt her heartbeat quicken. Did he feel the same thing?

Lightning flashed, sending a three-pronged strike on the far side of the hill. Several of the *kinder* let out frightened cries.

"Will you stop the buggy for a moment?" she asked. "They need me back there with them."

Rain began to fall as Levi drove onto the shoulder of the road and stopped the buggy. He helped Ruth into the back, where she pulled the smallest *kinder* close to her. "Go, Levi! Get us out of here!"

Levi climbed back up onto the buggy's seat. He shouted to the horses and slapped the reins. The horses sped forward along the road, the wagon jouncing and jostling.

"Teacher Ruth, I'm scared!" a third grader cried as sharp needles of rain pierced their clothing. "What if we fall out of the wagon?"

"Just hold on!" Ruth told him. "Everyone hold tight to each other."

Levi was trying to find the smoothest route, but passing cars kept pushing the wagon toward the shoulder. Horns blared. At first, she thought the *Englisch* drivers were annoyed at their slower pace. Then she noticed them pointing toward the storm with anxious expressions. The storm was coming fast.

It was not much farther to the school, but it might be too far. The wagon shuddered as wind struck it.

Ruth looked over her shoulder. Levi was bent forward as if he could make the wagon go faster with just his will. The dark edge of the roiling clouds was almost overhead.

"Are we going to make it?" Ruth struggled to be heard over the wind and the thunder.

"I hope so." Levi turned the team up his lane.

"Where are you going?" she cried. "The school is right there."

"Before you can get all the *kinder* inside, the storm will be upon us. There's no time to get into the house either."

Ruth twisted to look forward. He was heading for the barn. The hayloft doors were open and banging against the walls. He steered the horses and the wagon into the hayloft. She shouted for the scholars to hold on as the wheels bounced on the stone ramp.

As soon as the wagon was inside the barn, Levi drew in the horses. He tossed the reins to Ruth. Jumping down, he called to the older boys to help him close the double doors. The wind fought them and tried to pull the heavy doors away.

Ruth didn't hesitate. She ran to the door and pressed her hands beside Levi's. More of the *kinder* rushed forward to help.

Inch by inch, struggling not to slip as rain soaked the wood floor, they forced the doors closed.

"The bar!" Levi shouted as the doors threatened to explode inward with the wind.

Ruth released the door's bar, and it fell into place. The doors still moved in and out as if on a giant's breath. She leaned back, panting. Her *kapp* was askew, but at least it hadn't vanished like Levi's straw hat. The *kinder* stood watching the heaving door, their eyes wide.

"Is everyone all right?" she asked.

They shouted back excited answers, but froze when thunder slammed the barn, shaking the structure on its stone foundation. One of the youngest girls started crying, and several others joined in. Levi hurried to lash the horses' reins to one of the posts holding up the roof.

"Let's take them down to see your animals," she said when he was finished. "That will take their minds off the storm."

"The animals will be nervous, too."

"Oh, I didn't think of that." She turned to go to comfort the *kinder*.

He hurried after her. "Ruth?"

She looked at him, tattered, bruised, and covered with dirt from the door. She wondered why she had been so worried when this strong, quiet man had been there to get them out of the storm.

"Let's take the *kinder* downstairs," he said.

"But if your animals—"

"It's safer with the stone and earth between us and the storm."

Ruth gasped as she understood what Levi wasn't saying.

146

He suspected there was a tornado somewhere in the fierce storm. She motioned for him to lead the way, and she told the scholars to follow him.

The steps were so steep that they resembled a ladder. The youngest *kinder* needed help, but the rest scampered down and waited by the bottom. Straightening her *kapp*, she did a quick head count. Everyone was there.

Suddenly, Levi pushed past her and raced along the concrete floor. Hay and silage swirled around his ankles.

Wind blew through the barn. The lower door must be open.

"Boys, come with me." She had a feeling that Levi might need help.

By the time they reached the milking parlor, the cows were milling about, confused. The boys didn't hesitate as they guided each cow into a stanchion.

On the far side of the milking parlor, Levi struggled with a door. Ruth pushed alongside him. Again, working together, they were able to shut it. He twisted a deadbolt, and she jumped back when hail struck a window. With the windswept rain, she couldn't see anything outside.

He put his arm around her shoulders, shocking her until she realized his other hand pressed against his ribs. Had the door struck him? She raised her eyes to discover his face had gone pale.

"What happened?" she asked.

"I'll . . . be . . . all . . . right." Each word came out with a gasp.

She led him to a three-legged stool and sat him on it. He nodded his thanks, but motioned toward the boys.

She told them they'd done a *gut* job getting the cows secured and then led them back to where the other *kinder* were trying not to look scared. The wind banged hard against the barn, and they crouched down. Overhead, the horses' hoofs resounded against the wooden floor.

"I can quiet the horses, Teacher Ruth," Seth said.

"I would rather have you stay down here."

"If they panic, they could hurt themselves."

Ruth couldn't argue with his logic. "All right, but if I call, you've got to come immediately. No matter what."

Seth nodded and climbed the stairs at top speed.

Ruth soothed the other *kinder*, but kept thinking about Levi. Was he really all right? Maybe she shouldn't have left him sitting there. She glanced toward the milking parlor, but saw no sign of him.

Squatting by the *kinder*, she noticed big brothers and sisters sat on the concrete floor with their younger siblings and cousins. Esther and Hannah held on to Abby and Gabe as well as their own younger sisters and brothers.

"Why don't we sing?" Ruth didn't wait for an answer as she began one of the scholars' favorite morning songs.

As she sang "Jesus loves me, this I know . . ." the *kinder* joined in. She urged them to sing louder and louder until their voices rang through the barn. The thunder cracked hard and loud, but now the *kinder* giggled, believing they were safe.

She kept them singing, but something was missing. Someone! Where was David?

Gesturing to Esther and Hannah to keep the *kinder* singing, Ruth walked toward the pens where Levi kept his injured animals. David couldn't be in the other direction; she would have seen him. Near the stalls, rain battered the windows so hard the noise hurt her ears. She paused when she heard a deep voice beneath the pounding.

Levi!

She hurried forward. He stood beside David at the stall that held two cages, each with a small songbird inside it. He had his hand on the little boy's shoulder as he pointed toward the birds.

David must have heard her footsteps, because he looked toward her. She had never seen such happiness on his face. She wanted to ask Levi what they had been discussing but couldn't. Not in front of the *kind*.

"I think," she said, keeping her voice light as the barn strained against the wind, "all the *kinder* would enjoy seeing your animals, Levi."

"*Ja.*"

"David, would you like to come with me to get them?"

He nodded and held out his hand. When she held out her own hand, he put his fingers trustingly in hers.

Her heart filled with joy. It was the first time he had willingly reached out to her. *Thank You, Lord, for sending a ray of sunshine along with the storm.* As she led him to where the scholars sang, she saw a broad smile on Levi's face. He understood what an important moment this was.

Levi warned the scholars to be quiet and not make any quick motions. "These are wild animals, and they don't know that we want them to get well and return to their homes in the woods or fields."

"Can we hold them?" asked Irma Rose.

"Not unless you want to be bit, pecked, or clawed."

Ruth knew that she and Levi would have to keep a close eye on the *kinder*. She walked between the stalls as Levi spoke about each animal, how it had been injured, and what he was doing to help it recover.

David hung on every word. Several times, Ruth saw the little boy open his mouth as if he wanted to ask a question, but he never said anything. Maybe because he didn't need to. Levi would glance at him then ask the scholars if they wanted to know more about that animal or bird. Each time, David would brighten and nod happily. Somehow, the shy man and the mute boy had found a way to communicate that needed no words.

As the other *kinder* drifted away to watch the storm through the windows, David remained by the animal pens. Levi knelt beside him and began describing how he had bandaged a hawk's wing. He pointed out the signs of healing. Each time he looked from the bird to the boy, he waited for David to nod. If the boy didn't or gave him a puzzled expression, Levi would explain until David smiled his understanding.

Ruth's heart was so filled with gratitude that she wondered how it could hold all her joy.

"You like animals, don't you?" Levi asked as he stood.

David nodded.

"You and the other *kinder* are welcome to come back to see the animals. Maybe then we can take some out of their cages. Today, they're too anxious because of the storm."

Again David nodded, but this time with a wide smile.

Levi patted his head and walked to where Ruth watched the other *kinder*. Twice already, she had warned them to stand away from the windows. She didn't blame them for being curious, but she didn't want them struck by broken glass if a window shattered.

"How are you feeling?" she asked Levi.

"Better. I'll probably have a few bruises from where the doorknob jammed into my side, but at least the cows are safe. That David is a smart little boy."

"I know." She sighed as she watched David stand to the side as the other *kinder* jostled to look out the biggest window, which gave them a view of the field between the barn and the schoolhouse. She realized that, no matter how many times she warned them away, the scholars would give in to their curiosity and rush back to look out the windows. Even so, she ordered them away from the window again before saying to Levi, "You've done more today to reach past his wall of silence than I've managed in almost a month."

"If he didn't trust you, he wouldn't have trusted me."

"I don't know about that."

"No?" He faced her, leaning back against the rails where the mules shifted uneasily as the wind blew even harder. "I saw how he took your hand. It wonders me, Ruth, how you can't see what a difference you're already making in his life."

"I haven't done much."

"No?" he repeated then grinned. The expression transformed his austere face. "You're making more of a difference than you realize. Once the storm has passed, you must tell Samuel that I gave your scholars a tour of my barn to-day. He'll be shocked."

"Why?" Ruth asked.

"Because I am not the type to give tours." He kept his eyes on the *kinder* as he asked, "Did you notice how often Samuel holds up fingers in front of my face?"

"*Ja.* A different number of fingers every time."

"It's an old joke between us. He says I seldom say more than three words in a row if I'm not talking about animals. When I say only a few words, he holds up one finger for each word."

"But you say more than a few words to me."

"Now."

She grinned at his terse answer. Her smile widened when she realized the wind was dying down. Rain slid down the windows instead of slamming into the glass.

"I think the storm's going past," she said.

As if to refute her words, lightning crackled, raising the hair on the back of her neck. The animals' warning cries were silenced by the instantaneous clap of thunder. The barn shook so hard that the wagon rocked overhead.

Ruth grasped Levi's arm, praying the barn hadn't been hit. The younger *kinder* rushed to Ruth and Levi and clung to them. The odor of burned air hung around them, tasting bitter.

"Was the barn hit?" she cried.

Levi shook his head. "No, but it was close."

"Teacher Ruth!" called Nelson. The eighth grader ran up to her and seized her hand. "*Komm!* See what's happened to the schoolhouse!"

Her heart sank. Had lightning hit the school? She ran to the window and stared out. The schoolhouse hadn't been hit, but the large maple shading it had. The tree had split and fallen through the schoolhouse's roof.

Eleven

Water dripped in a slow, steady rhythm through the schoolhouse's roof. It plinked in metal buckets under the holes. Weak sunshine flowed in, an apology for the destruction left by yesterday's storm.

Ruth leaned on the rag mop she was using to push water out. The wood floors had already started to swell, but the winter's cool, dry air should flatten them again. The glass in all but one window had shattered or cracked. The desks could be dried out. If the wooden tops split, they could be replaced. Those that had been knocked over by the massive branches might still be salvageable. Ruth's own desk was beyond repair, broken by the tree's impact. Her chair was covered with leaves and bark, but only needed cleaning. The woodstove was a complete loss. The heaviest branch had smashed right through the metal firebox, and the door hung by a single hinge.

Even with the damage, pencils, chalk, and erasers already were lined up to dry on windowsills. The plastic-coated maps and lessons had been taken down, wiped dry, and spread out in the corners.

But the books had been soaked. The paperbacks on the low shelves were ruined. Soaked workbooks were piled up to be thrown away. Even before the water was pushed out the door, Ruth had collected the hardcover textbooks. Now they were in the kitchen of Levi's *dawdi-haus*, on the table, on the benches, on the counters, and on the floor. She hoped they could be saved.

She heard footsteps on the porch and looked out the open door. School had been canceled after yesterday's storm, but several scholars and their parents had stopped by to help. She had gratefully let them tote stacks of books to the *dawdi-haus* and told them that the school board would be meeting immediately to decide what to do. The *kinder* already had so many days to make up.

Levi stuck his head past the door, and Graceless raced in to greet Ruth. She bent to pet the puppy then drank in the sight of Levi as he entered the classroom. His wet and dirty clothes showed that, like her, he had been working on the school since dawn, checking the stability of the roof, both inside and out. His shirt clung to his muscular frame, and she imagined what it would be like to be held to his chest. She turned away so he couldn't see her blush.

"The school board is meeting at my house now," he said. "We'd like you to be there."

"*Ja*, of course." She leaned the mop against a desk and went to the door. She pushed her hair back toward her *kapp* and wished she had a mirror to make sure she was present-able for the school board.

"You look fine." Levi hurried down the steps. "Better than fine."

"*Danki*, but I never expected I would sit down with the school board while my feet are swimming in soaked socks."

He laughed and scooped up the puppy before Graceless could run into the road. They started across the schoolyard toward his house. When Ruth asked about the roof, he said, "Once we replace some sheets of plywood and reshingle it, the roof will be fine. If the tree had to fall on the school, it picked a *gut* spot. It missed the main rafters."

"The inside needs lots of work."

"I saw that." He edged around a puddle on his lane. "That's what the school board needs to talk about."

Ruth hurried with him into the kitchen. The school board members and Bishop John sat at the table in the im-maculate room. She was amazed that Levi was such an excellent housekeeper, and then she wondered why she was surprised. He was *gut* at everything he did.

The men welcomed Ruth and invited her to sit with them. When Levi offered them some of his homemade root beer, everyone accepted with an eager smile except Micah, whose only expression seemed to be a frown. How different he was from his son Caleb, who had such charming smiles for all the girls.

"How is the clean-up going, Teacher Ruth?" Paul asked.

"*Gut*." She listed the progress they had made. "But the

scholars can't return to the schoolhouse until the roof is repaired. When I talked to you about having classes outdoors, I didn't mean all the time."

The men chuckled. Micah joined in reluctantly when Bishop John glanced in his direction.

"It shouldn't take more than a couple of weeks," Joseph said, "to get the materials to repair the roof and put in a new stove. I've already spoken to the hardware store, and they'll put a rush on our order."

"But that doesn't solve the problem of what to do in the meantime," Micah said. "The scholars can't sit outside for their lessons." He glowered at Ruth when he said the word "outside."

She looked away from him. The men ignored his negative comments, so she would, too. Sitting straighter, she said, "There must be some other place where we can have school until the building is repaired."

"There is," Levi said as he poured another glass of root beer and set it in front of Paul. "You can hold school in my *dawdi-haus.*"

Micah's hands fisted on the table. "That's silly. A *dawdi-haus* isn't set up to be a school."

"No, but a school is more than desks, four walls, and"— he gave them a wry smile—"a roof. Jesus wasn't in a schoolhouse when he taught his parables. Like his disciples, our scholars can learn their lessons anywhere."

"Excellent point," Bishop John said.

"First she takes them on a work frolic on a school day," argued Micah. "Now you're suggesting that she teach in your *dawdi-haus.* Where else will she drag our scholars this year, wasting time when they could be learning their lessons? I've heard that some parents aren't happy with her odd ways of teaching."

Ruth wanted to ask which parents were upset so she could speak with them at school or on a church Sunday. She didn't have a chance because Levi put down the jug of root beer so hard, she was surprised it didn't shatter.

Anger flashed through Levi's eyes, but he didn't even raise his voice as he said, "Micah, look past your personal opinions of Teacher Ruth and think what could have happened here yesterday if she hadn't taken the *kinder* to Old Wayne's orchard and the farm stand. All we lost yesterday were the roof, some windows and books, and the teacher's desk. We should be thanking God that He led Ruth to choose yesterday to take the scholars out of the building."

No one spoke, and Ruth guessed the other school board members and the bishop were as shocked as she was by Levi's lengthy reply.

Bishop John rose and clasped Levi's shoulder. "Your offer is generous, and your words are wise. Too often when we see God's will, it is when we look about in sorrow. Today, as we did yesterday, we've seen God working in our lives and through us, and we need to rejoice at His benevolence and love for all His *kinder*, both young and old."

Levi nodded then looked toward Ruth. She smiled, wishing she could tell him how much she appreciated him coming to her and the scholars' rescue. Again. She couldn't imagine what would have happened if he hadn't been there yesterday, or if he hadn't spoken up today.

The men pushed back their chairs, and Ruth realized the

meeting was over. When she saw Bishop John heading out the door, she rushed after him and caught up with him by his gray buggy. He had the reins in his hands and one foot on the step.

"Did we forget something?" he asked, facing her.

"May I speak to you about one of my scholars?" she asked, feeling suddenly shy.

He gave her a warm smile. "*Ja*, but the school board usually handles anything with the *kinder*."

"This isn't a school board issue. It's an *Ordnung* issue."

"Go ahead."

She explained how she wanted to ask the librarians to help gather materials to help David. "I'm not familiar enough with the *Ordnung* in this district to know if that's permissible or not." She hesitated, but knowing she must be honest with the bishop, added, "In my own district, I doubt I would be allowed to seek their assistance. I hoped it was different here."

"It isn't only a matter of the *Ordnung*. You're questioning God's will for this *kind*, Ruth," he said. "David is as God made him, just as Abby Miller is how God intends her to be."

"And I am as God meant me to be. He brought me here to teach these *kinder*, and I want to do His will." She gasped as she realized that she was lecturing the bishop on holy matters. "Forgive me, Bishop John. I shouldn't have spoken so."

He put a hand on her shoulder. "I'd forgive you, Ruth, if there was any need for forgiveness. Your longing to help young David is nothing to be ashamed of."

"But speaking to you like that is."

He smiled. "If I had a penny for every person who wished that they had spoken to me from the heart rather than talking around what they needed to say, I'd be a wealthy man. What you're asking for isn't so extraordinary in this district. Some of our *kinder* use computers during their *rumspringa*, and in some Plain shops, the shopkeepers sign for deliveries on a handheld computer. You wouldn't be using the computer yourself?"

"Definitely not. It would take me so long to learn how to use one that David will have *kinder* of his own before I find any information that might help him."

Bishop John smiled. "I can't see any harm in what you're asking. You're a deacon's daughter, so you'll know if you wander into an area where you shouldn't. And if you're uncertain, come and ask me. We'll pray together about it and seek God's advice."

"*Danki*, Bishop John. I don't know if I can help David speak, but I know that I must try."

"If anyone can, I believe it is you, Teacher Ruth." He turned to his buggy as he added, "Before you put any of those *Englisch* ideas to work, make sure David's parents agree. The Zooks are *gut* people who love their son deeply, but he's their son, so the choice must be theirs."

"I planned to speak to them after I spoke to you."

"*Gut.*" He climbed into his buggy and drove toward the main road.

Ruth twirled about in excitement. She faltered when she saw Levi on his porch. *Daed* had previously scolded her for acting so childishly. She had promised not to act so again. Now she was.

But Levi laughed as he walked toward her, Graceless running around his feet.

"Don't stop on my account," he said. "Sometimes being happy is just too much to keep inside."

"Were you listening?"

"To you and Bishop John?" He shook his head. "I saw you talking to him, so I kept my distance and made sure the others did, too, until they left." He stopped only inches from her, so close that a single step would bring her up against him. "Ruth, your joy glows from you as bright as a firefly on a summer evening."

She was conscious of her breathing as she never had been before as she gazed up into his eyes that hid so much from her. Not as much as when they first met, however, because now she could tell that he was happy for her.

"Bishop John gave me his permission to get information to help David," she said.

"That is *wunderbaar*." His eyes matched his broad smile. "He's a *gut* man, so I'm sure he's eager for you to do what you can."

"All I need to do is get David's parents' permission. How can they refuse an offer to help their son?"

"I can't imagine they will." He motioned toward the *dawdi-haus*. "Would you like to see your temporary school?"

"Ja!" Her answer was so enthusiastic that Levi laughed. *Ach*, she wished he would laugh and laugh. It was such a jubilant sound.

When Levi unlocked the door, she walked into the kitchen, which was a smaller copy of the one in the main house. The books they had rescued from the schoolhouse were on every surface, open and drying. Graceless pushed past her, but Levi picked up the puppy and set her back on the porch. He hooked a leash on her collar before lashing the leash around a post.

The puppy yipped in frustration as she tried to go into the *dawdi-haus* with him.

"No," he said firmly. "Making puddles in one kitchen is enough. The *kinder* shouldn't have to watch where they're walking."

"Maybe if you leave the door open so she can see you," Ruth suggested.

"*Gut* idea." He closed the screen door but not the wooden one.

With another yap of protest, Graceless settled down on the porch, her snout on her paws and her eyes focused on Levi.

"You have a shadow," Ruth said as she went to the table and began turning the books over to help them dry evenly.

"She hasn't let me out of her sight since yesterday's storm."

Ruth smiled at the puppy. "Poor thing."

"It'll be better when she lives with a family with *kinder*. Then there should always be someone around."

"You're giving her away?" Ruth couldn't keep the shock out of her voice. "But she loves you."

"She'll love having *kinder* to play with more."

"But, Levi—"

"Ruth, don't try to convince me to keep her. She'll be happier with a family." Without a pause, he asked, "Have

163

you heard of any other damage from the storm? Several other trees went down around here, taking the wires with them, so some of our *Englisch* neighbors don't have electricity."

"I know," she said, though she wanted to ask him how he could give Graceless away. She'd seen him with the puppy. He loved her as much as the puppy adored him. Yet she couldn't argue with his logic. Graceless would be happy having *kinder* to run and play with her.

She picked up some more books and turned them over. "A couple of *Englisch* families who live near the Lambrights' farm came over last night to get some kerosene for their lamps, and Sadie insisted that they stay and have supper with us. She's happiest when the table is surrounded by more people than there are seats for."

Levi held up a paper workbook that was disintegrating. "I don't think this one is worth saving."

She examined it and was pleased to see it didn't have a scholar's name on the inside. "Fortunately it's one of the extras. And, Levi, I don't think I said it, but *danki* for opening your home to the scholars and me."

He shrugged as he sorted through more soaked books. "It makes sense. The *dawdi-haus* is right across the road, so the *kinder* won't have to walk much farther."

"I know how you like your privacy."

"Not as much as I thought I did." He continued shifting the books and wiping up water. "When I showed the *kinder* the animals yesterday, I began to understand why you like teaching. Seeing those eager faces was fun. I would be glad to share more with them about the animals, if you'd like."

Ruth flipped a few pages in a drenched first-grade primer then raised her eyes to look across the table at him. "The scholars would like that, Levi."

"And you? Would you like that?"

She started to answer that of course she would, but she hesitated as her gaze was captured by his. Strong emotions burned within his eyes. Were they still talking about lessons for the scholars or something else entirely? Or maybe she wanted him to be talking about something else—about the two of them.

She was falling in love with him. When had that happened? Maybe when he'd helped with Esther's yellow jacket stings. Maybe when he'd named his puppy Graceless. Maybe just now, when she thought of how often he had been there when she needed him.

He was a *gut*-hearted man. He liked *kinder*. He was respected within the district. Even though he seldom offered his opinion, when he did, others listened closely to what he had to say.

At that thought, Ruth tore her gaze from his and stared down at the wet spots on her dark-blue dress. She didn't want to fall in love now. She had come to this district to give herself a chance to learn more about what she hoped to find in her life. She wanted to see new things . . . and prove to her *daed* that she could be a *gut* teacher and a *gut* daughter. And she couldn't imagine giving up teaching to become a *fraa*. With every passing day, she felt more and more certain that teaching was what she was meant to do at this time in her life.

So what was she going to do with her heart, which ached to belong to Levi? For once, she didn't have a quick answer.

Twelve

Esther finished sweeping the floor in Levi's *dawdi-haus*. She opened the cupboard and put the broom and dust-pan away. She had promised Ruth that she and Hannah would clean the kitchen and lock up when they were done. Ruth had taken the buggy on an errand right after school. Esther was curious about where she was going; Ruth had seemed both excited and nervous.

"This is such a cute kitchen," Hannah said as she finished wiping down the whiteboard that had been donated to the school by Levi's *Englisch* neighbor. "I'd like one just like it when I'm married."

"You'll want something bigger if you have a lot of *bopplin*." Esther flung out her hands. "It's so crowded when all the scholars are here."

"I don't plan to have twenty *bopplin*. Ten will be enough." Hannah giggled then dropped heavily onto the bench. Leaning back against the table, she said, "But I like that clock." She pointed to one, which had the name of a local seed distributor on it.

Esther sat next to her friend. "I like the rack on the wall. It looks like it could hold a whole load of towels, so you wouldn't have to hang them outside in the winter. My *he* is so thoughtful, I'm sure he'll make something just like that for me."

"Thoughtful? My *he* is the best-looking boy in the district."

"If you don't count my *he*, your *he* *may* be the best-looking boy." Esther sighed and stared at the clock. "I know nobody's perfect, but my *he* is as close as any person can get. He's handsome, and all the other boys look up to him. The girls, too. I've seen how they look at him and heard how they talk about him."

"Well, my *he* is the smartest boy in the district."

"Really?"

"Of course, because *he* is going to court me. That proves he's the smartest."

Esther laughed. "Maybe it's a tie. Maybe they're both the smartest and handsomest boy in the district."

"That isn't possible. One of them has to be the best."

"I think that my *he* is the best, and you think that your *he* is the best, so that makes two bests."

Hannah draped her arm around Esther's shoulders. "You know, you can be pretty smart yourself."

"True. Look who's my best friend."

They looked at each other and smiled.

Hannah asked, "Are you coming to the next singing?"

"*Ja!*"

"I was worried your *mamm* might not want you to go when you got so upset last time."

Esther grinned wryly. "Neither Ruth nor Samuel said anything to her or *Daed*. I was just being *dumm*."

"You were." Hannah grinned when Esther made a face at her. "I asked Dorcas about it."

"You told your big sister about me blubbering like a *boppli*?"

"No!" She rolled her eyes. "Esther, I wouldn't tell Dorcas anything like that. She's such a *blabbermaul*. She can't keep a secret ever. Not even the secret that Matthew Stutzman has been coming over to the house late at night to sit with her on the porch."

"Really?"

Grimacing, Hannah said, "Oh, I shouldn't have said that. I'm as big a *blabbermaul* as my sister."

"No, you're not." Esther hugged her friend. "And I can keep a secret."

"Good. I just mentioned to Dorcas that some of us younger girls were wondering when a boy might ask us to go with him in his buggy. She told me that no boy who's really serious about a girl will ask her to ride home from the first singing they both go to. He wouldn't want to draw attention to them."

Esther nodded. It made perfect sense. Courting should be done in secret.

"I wish I had an older sister, even one who's a *blabbermaul*, to help me understand these things."

"You have Ruth."

"But she's not married, and she must be almost twenty-five."

"That makes her an old *maedel*, doesn't it?" Hannah shuddered. "I pray every night that God has a boy in mind for me. I couldn't bear to be an old *maedel*."

"Do you know what Ruth told me?"

"What?" Hannah leaned toward her.

"That I shouldn't set my heart on one boy now. I should enjoy getting to know all of them." Esther's nose wrinkled. "I already know all of them, and there's only one for me."

"Ruth is a *gut* teacher of numbers and ABCs, but I don't know what she could teach you about courting." Hannah sighed. "Did you see how the unmarried men were looking at her after the service on Sunday? And she wasn't even aware of it. She thinks more about talking with the scholars' parents than spending time with one of the bachelors."

Again Esther considered her friend's words before saying, "I know Samuel wishes she and Levi would marry."

"Ruth and Levi?" Hannah's laugh echoed through the small room. "What a pair! The old *maedel* and the man who doesn't say two words in a row!" Her eyes widened. "But think about it. If she marries Levi, do you think she'll keep teaching? Or do you think she'll quit, and you and I can be teachers together before we get married? Wouldn't that be *wunderbaar*?"

"*Ja.*"

"Maybe you should give your cousin a nudge toward Levi, so we can be the real teachers."

Esther grinned. "Until I marry my *him*."

"And I marry my *him*!"

"Now that we've got all that planned out, I need to get home and help *Mamm* with supper."

"Me, too!"

Laughing, they hurried out of the kitchen and locked the door behind them. As they headed off in opposite directions at the end of the lane, Esther thanked God for such a *gut* friend. It was a blessing to have one person she could always depend on to share her dreams with. Soon she hoped she could tell Hannah that her *he* was Caleb Stutzman. Hannah would be so happy for her. She couldn't wait for that special day.

Patting her *kapp* to make sure it was straight and her hair was neat, Ruth stepped out of her buggy near the Zooks' house. She had sent a message with David that she would like to speak with his parents after this evening. She hoped he had delivered it, so her arrival wouldn't be a complete surprise.

She walked to the simple, white house that was smaller than most houses she had seen in this district. When she saw an unlit electric light by the door, she was astonished. Did she have the right house?

As she hesitated, the door opened. A short woman with a *boppli* snuggled against her shoulder and a toddler clinging to her plain dress stood in silhouette. Light from inside the house glowed through her heart-shaped *kapp*.

"Teacher Ruth?" the woman asked, her voice light and airy.

"Ja." She hid her bafflement about the electric light. "David must have given you the note I sent home with him."

"He did. *Komm* in." She stepped back into an immaculate kitchen filled with the aroma of freshly baked cookies. "I am Susan Zook, David's *mamm.*" Pale-blond tendrils peeked out from beneath her *kapp* and glistened in the light from the propane floor lamp as she put her youngest in a playpen in the living room. "This is Timothy, my husband and our David's *daed.*"

When Timothy came to his feet, he wasn't much taller than his wife. He shook Ruth's hand and welcomed her, but she could tell he was anxious about why she was there.

"Kaffi?" asked Susan while she sat the toddler next to the playpen and handed him some blocks.

"That would be nice. *Danki.*" Ruth looked around the comfortable room. "Is David here?"

"We sent him to his *aenti*'s house," Timothy said, "because we thought you might not want him here when you came to discuss what's going on at school."

"Danki."

He motioned for her to go into the living room while Susan poured *kaffi* and placed a tray with a generous serving of fresh oatmeal-raisin cookies on the low table between the light-brown sofa and the two overstuffed chairs.

"Pardon the appearance of the house," Susan said. "We bought it a couple of months ago. There's still a lot to do to make it a proper Plain house." She smiled. "The electricity has been disconnected, and I'll be glad when all the outlets and switches are gone. We were blessed, though, that the house already had propane connected to it."

"You were fortunate," Ruth said, taking an oatmeal cookie. "There are so few houses left with any land in the county."

"Ja," Timothy replied. "We have only ten acres, but so many of the *Englischers* from Philadelphia are eager to buy weekend homes. If the previous owners hadn't known we were looking for a home, I doubt we could have gotten this place. We were living in the *dawdi-haus* at my parents' farm, but my youngest brother will marry soon, so *Daed* and *Mamm* will need the *dawdi-haus* to move into."

"It's *gut* that David didn't have to change schools. That can be difficult for any *kind*."

"And particularly for a *kind* like our David," Susan said in almost a whisper.

Timothy stroked his beard then asked, "Has our David been a problem for you, Teacher Ruth? Is that why you're here?"

Ruth smiled. "I'm sorry. I should have made it clear in the note that I wasn't asking for this meeting because David is any trouble. He's a dear boy. He's attentive, and he never fails to complete his deskwork. His papers and workbook are always neat. Any teacher who has your son in her school would count herself lucky."

Timothy reached for his *kaffi.* "I'm glad to hear it."

"Ja," Susan said. "But if he isn't a problem, then, if I may be blunt, why are you here?"

"I want to work with your son to convince him that it's all right for him to talk."

Timothy stiffened, and Susan hurried to say, "You should know, Teacher Ruth, that we've tried everything we know to do just that."

"I'm sure you have, and I've done all I could think of, too. Then I thought of another way that might help." She quickly explained that Bishop John had given his permission for her to go to the public library and enlist one of the librarians to search for articles about mute *kinder*. "I don't know why David doesn't talk, and that presents some problems. Once I have a chance to read whatever the librarians can get for me, I may find the best way to work with David. It would be better if the other *kinder* aren't around, because that would just single him out as different again. Will you allow him to remain after school?"

Susan and Timothy exchanged a glance that she couldn't read. Couldn't they see how much she wanted to help their son? They must want him to talk like other boys.

"You're new here, Teacher Ruth," Timothy said slowly. "We know that each teacher brings something new and *different* to the scholars, but sometimes new and *different* aren't the best thing."

Was it only her imagination, or had he really put a bit more emphasis on "different?"

"I agree," Ruth said, trying to smile. "That's why I've taught the scholars the lessons approved by the school board."

He glanced at his wife then asked, "If that is so, why has Ida Stutzman complained to the school board about your odd ways of teaching?"

"A complaint?" Ruth was almost knocked off the sofa in astonishment. "I haven't heard of a complaint." She wanted to ask *why* she hadn't heard about it, but the Zooks weren't the ones she should ask. Why hadn't Levi told her that someone had expressed displeasure with her teaching?

She guessed Ida was Micah's wife and mother to Caleb as well as the two Stutzman *kinder* at school. Why hadn't Ida come to her if she had a problem with how Ruth taught? Just because her husband was on the school board was no reason not to try to resolve the problem with Ruth first.

She didn't even know what Ida was upset about, but immediately Ruth felt that lump in her throat and a sick sensation in her stomach she knew all too well. It was the awful feeling that came over her when she knew she had disappointed her father.

She pushed thoughts of her *daed* out of her head and spoke up. "Bishop John approves of my ways of teaching."

"While I am glad to hear that," Timothy said, "I'm still reluctant to agree to this *different* plan."

There was no mistaking his stress on the word that time.

"I'm sorry you feel that way. I've been looking forward to working with David and hoped I could convince him to speak. Levi has offered to help as well."

Timothy leaned forward. "Levi? Levi Yoder?"

"*Ja*. David's very interested in Levi's animals, so we— Levi and I—hoped David might be more willing to talk while working with the animals after school."

Susan turned to her husband. "Levi is a *gut* man and a sensible one."

"He is." Timothy again exchanged a glance with his wife.

Ruth wished she could decipher it. Would she ever be so close to a man that they could "speak" without saying a single word? She had seen *Mamm* and *Daed* do the same. For the first time, she longed to have that with someone else.

No, not just someone. She wanted to have that with Levi.

"All right, Teacher Ruth," Timothy said. "Since Levi is helping you, we'll give it a try. For one month. If there's no change in our son during that time, then we must accept it is God's will that our David remains silent."

Ruth wanted to protest she couldn't accept that God wished for the little boy to go through life without a voice, but she didn't want to risk this small victory. It hurt that they didn't trust her enough to accept her help alone.

But why should they trust her? They didn't know her, and they had already heard of complaints about her teaching. She needed to be grateful with the outcome of the conversation.

"Danki," she said to the Zooks. "Levi and I will do our best to help David. We're eager for the chance to work with him."

"Do what you can." Susan's eyes filled with tears.

Ruth took Susan's hand and squeezed it. "We will. I promise."

When the conversation moved to the repairs at the school and how the *kinder* liked being in the *dawdi-haus*, Ruth tried not to show her impatience to leave. She couldn't get past her shock that Ida Stutzman had complained about her. She needed to know why. At this late hour, when most families would be getting ready for Bible readings, baths, and bed, she was going to get an answer from the one person who should have told her about the complaint.

Levi.

Thirteen

☙

Ruth went straight from the Zooks' house to Levi's, but
when she knocked on his kitchen door, he didn't answer. He couldn't have gone to bed because a lamp was lit
in the kitchen. If he wasn't in the house . . . She looked at
the barn and saw a light moving past one of the windows.

She went into the hayloft and directly to the stairs to the
lower level. She should have guessed that Levi would check
his animals each night before bed.

As she came down the steep stairs, Levi was kneeling
by an open stall. Inside, the floor was covered with shavings, and a blanket was thrown over a wooden box. He
placed a bowl with what looked like dog food by the box,
then stood.

"Ruth!" He quickly closed the stall door. "What are you doing here at this time of night?"

Instead of answering him, she pointed at the stall. "Have you given up on housebreaking Graceless?"

"Not yet." He smiled and wiped shavings off his black trousers. "I'm nursing a fox back to life. If he eats the food and doesn't gnaw his way out of the stall, he has a chance."

"What's wrong with him?"

"He was caught in a double-jaw trap, and his right front leg is badly mangled." Levi rubbed his chin as he glanced into the stall. "It may be too late to save him."

"I'll pray for him."

"As I will, but God may be ready to take him from this earth. If that's God's will, then I know his final hours will be the best ones I can give him." His mouth tightened. "There are other ways of trapping. Cable restraints work, and they don't torture an animal by slicing into a limb. And trapping season for foxes isn't even open yet. I don't know if someone started early or if the trap was never retrieved after last season."

Ruth wanted to console him but reminded herself why she had come to his barn at such a late hour. "I just heard that Ida Stutzman made a complaint to the school board about me. Why didn't you tell me?"

Levi shrugged, not looking at her. "The school board hasn't acted on it, so there's nothing to tell you. We aren't supposed to talk about unresolved issues."

"You didn't think that I would want to know if someone has a problem with the way I teach?"

"It's not the way you teach, Ruth. It's where."

Instantly she understood. Ida's husband, Micah, had been vehemently against her teaching anywhere but in the traditional classroom. That she had taken the *kinder* on a frolic and saved them from the storm hadn't changed his mind one bit.

"Tell me exactly why Ida lodged a complaint against me," she said. "Please, Levi."

"I shouldn't—"

"Please, Levi! I need to know."

He raised his eyes and met hers. She saw his regret that he had to tell her about the complaint, and she realized he didn't want to hurt her. That thought set her heart to thudding harder.

"Ida came to the school one day," he said, "and you and the scholars weren't inside. She was upset that she had to go and find her *kinder* farther along the road."

"I remember that day. I took the scholars out to collect leaves so we could examine which trees turned when." She frowned as she paced back and forth along the narrow, concrete floor between the stalls. "I told you about that when I dropped my buggy off that morning."

"I know."

"If you thought there would be a problem, why didn't you tell me?"

"I didn't think there would be any problem, Ruth. You had explained to the school board how you were going to teach."

She stopped pacing and faced him. "And everyone agreed, except Micah, who hasn't liked anything I've suggested. If I told him the sky was blue and the grass was green, he would argue the sky was green and the grass blue. Why does he dislike me?"

"I doubt he dislikes you personally. Micah had hoped that his niece would be chosen to teach but, after speaking with her, Joseph and Paul didn't think she would be suitable." He raised his hands to prevent her questions. "Don't ask me why. I didn't ask, because I trust them to make a *gut* decision."

"Why haven't you told me this before?"

"I prayed Micah would come to his senses." He gave her a lopsided grin. "It wonders me how a smart man like Micah Stutzman can be so foolish at times."

"If the *Leit* believes the rumors that I'm not a *gut* teacher—"

His smile vanished, and he pushed himself away from the stall door. "Rumors?"

"The Zooks knew about the complaint, and that made them wary of accepting my offer to help David. School board members aren't supposed to talk about matters that haven't been resolved. Didn't you just say that?"

He shook his head and sighed. "Micah is restrained from speaking of specific complaints, but Ida isn't."

Ruth tightened her hands by her sides then opened her fingers as she sent up a quick prayer for God's help in dealing with this unforeseen complication.

"So the Zooks didn't accept your offer to help their son?" he asked.

"Actually they agreed, but only after I mentioned that you would be involved, too."

"They know me well."

"And they think I'm *different*." She wanted to take back the words as soon as she blurted them out, but it was too late. "I'm sorry, Levi. All of this has upset me. I think that I'd hoped they would be as excited about my offer to help as I was. Only blind pride made me believe that they would welcome my help without asking questions."

Perhaps pride was the source of many of her problems. For how long had she believed that because she could do something, she must prove to the whole world that she could? The only one she needed to please was God, and He knew what she was capable of before even she did.

Levi put a hand on her shoulder as if to comfort her, and without thinking she leaned against him. He pulled back but only slightly. Then he put his finger under her chin and tipped her face back so she looked up at him. "Pride is a common sin."

"But I seem to have given in to it far too often." She slid her gaze away from his and stepped back. "It's difficult when I want to help someone as much as I want to help David. As much as I want *us* to help him. You will help, won't you?"

"*Ja.*" He took her hands and held them between his much larger ones. "You must realize that nothing may come of our efforts."

"I told you, I believe in miracles. Don't you?"

"I believe that God works through us and with us, and His gifts can be miraculous. But I also know how hard it is for a shy person to speak."

"Something more than shyness keeps David from talking." She moved her hands so she could lace her fingers through his. "Something hurts inside him. I've seen you heal these animals with gentleness and patience. Maybe you can help me do the same for him."

"You're giving me more credit than I deserve, but I'll do what I can. I promise you that, Ruth."

He released her hands and, at a small sound, looked back at the stall where the fox remained out of sight in its makeshift den.

"Go," she told him. "God brought the fox to you because He knew you would take care of it as you do all His creatures."

"I try to do what I can."

Could she ever be as humble as Levi who did so much for so many and never wanted or expected any acknowledgment in return?

"*Danki* for helping me, Levi." Without thinking, she reached up and kissed him on the cheek. For the briefest moment she savored the sensation of her lips pressed against his warm, smooth skin. Then she stepped back, startled by her own gesture. What had she just done?

Levi, too, stepped back, his expression shocked. She stared at him, horrified at how bold she had been. She spun on her heel and ran to the ladder, her *kapp* strings flapping on her shoulders, before she did something even more foolish.

As the sun set over the western hills, the Stony Field Farm Stand was quiet after a busy Saturday. Autumn's changing leaves brought a whole new crop of tourists to Lancaster County, but only a few customers remained as the early darkness began to claim the hills. Miriam had asked Esther and Hannah to help that afternoon, because Leah was visiting with relatives, and she had an appointment in town.

Eli King, whom Leah would soon marry, was a cabinetmaker, and Miriam was going to his workshop to choose pieces to sell at the farm stand.

Hannah rushed over to where Esther was stacking more apples on the pile that had been depleted by customers. In the two weeks since the scholars had picked apples in Old Wayne's orchard, almost all had been sold. Many customers, both those of their district and *Englischers*, had paid more than the posted price after learning that the money was going to help pay the elderly man's medical bills.

"Did you hear that?" Hannah demanded.

"Hear what? Not more stories about Ruth being in trouble with the school board, I hope."

Hannah shook her head. "Why are you letting those rumors bother you? You know Ruth is a *gut* teacher, and that the scholars are learning a lot from her."

Esther continued stacking apples. How could she tell her friend that normally she would have ignored the rumors, but the one who had complained was Caleb's *mamm*. The woman who'd given birth to such an amazing son couldn't be a liar, and she had heard more than one person say how much Caleb was like his *mamm*. But if Esther explained all that to Hannah, her friend would know Caleb was the boy she wanted to give her heart to.

When she didn't answer, Hannah grew impatient. "Don't you want to know what I heard?"

"What?"

"There's going to be a mud sale next Saturday."

"A mud sale in October? What fun!" Esther's face fell. "But we have to be at school next week."

Hannah laughed. "Don't be silly! Ruth won't hold school when there's a mud sale. Everyone will want to go." She helped Esther arrange the apples as she went on. "Besides, the mud sale is for Old Wayne's benefit. His relatives have decided to sell the farm and the equipment and the animals so he has money for his medications down in Delaware."

"Then it will be very busy. Everyone wants to help Old Wayne."

"*Ja!* I think I'll wear my new purple dress and my new apron. That way, *he* will definitely notice me."

Esther smiled. "The mud sale is supposed to help Old Wayne, not you."

"It can do both. Maybe your *he* will be there, too."

"I hope so." Esther thought for a moment. "I've got an idea. Why don't we take some things to the mud sale to sell?"

Hannah shook her head. "I don't want to be tied to a table. I want to be able to wander around, especially if *he*'s there, and I can walk around with *him*."

"But everyone stops at the tables to see what's for sale. What if we make lemonade to sell? You saw how much lemonade the boys drank at the singing. They'll all stop by, and when your *he* and mine come by, we'll have a chance to talk to them."

"That's not a bad idea," Hannah said. "And we can ask Miriam about bringing some of the smaller quilted pot holders and hangings she sells here. That way, if the boys are there with their sisters or their *mamms*, they'll stop, too, because the women will want to look at the quilted items."

"Perfect!" The two girls walked over to the smaller building, where the crafts were displayed. As they discussed which ones they'd like to take to the mud sale, Esther paused.

"What's wrong?" Hannah asked.

"I can help you take everything to the mud sale, but I may not be able to bring back anything that doesn't sell."

"Why not?"

"I may have a ride home from the mud sale."

Hannah's eyes grew round. "With *him*?"

"*Ja.* He asked me last week." Esther wrapped her arms around herself, holding tightly to her treasured memory of Caleb. He had come over to ask Samuel to check a piece of harness that was wearing thin. While Samuel had looked it over, Caleb asked her if he could drive her home from the next singing. That was before the mud sale was announced. Maybe he would take the opportunity to ask her to go even sooner with him in his courting buggy.

Hannah frowned. "How could you wait so long to tell me? I'm your best friend!"

"You know I shouldn't talk of it. He asked me to keep his invitation a secret."

"All the boys say that. They think if all the girls know, everyone in the district will know."

"That's probably true."

Hannah shook her head. "I'm so envious of you."

"It will happen for you, too. I just know that your *he* will ask you to ride home with him from the next singing."

"I've waited what seems like my whole life for him to notice me." Hannah seemed to deflate as she leaned against one of the display tables. "Do you really think he's going to ask me?"

"*Ja!* Just as sure as I am that I'm riding home with Caleb—" Esther pressed her hand over her mouth, but it was too late. Her precious secret was out.

"Caleb?" Hannah choked on the name. "Caleb Stutzman?"

Esther put a finger over her lips. "Hush! You know we aren't supposed to talk about such things."

"Caleb can't be your special *he*. He can't!"

"Why not?"

"Because he's *my* special *he*!"

"Yours?" Esther shook her head. "But, Hannah, he sat across from me at the singing. He talked to me."

"He sat across from *me*! How could you do this, Esther? I thought you were my best friend!"

"You know I've been in love with"—she still shouldn't speak his name—"with my *he* since I was a little girl. You've only had a crush on him for a few months."

Hannah stood with her hands on her hips. "You think you know everything, Esther Lambright! Just because I didn't go yakking and yakking about him as you do, that doesn't mean that I haven't been in love with him for a long time. *In love!* Not a silly crush. Real and lasting love, and if you were my friend, you'd realize it was true because *he* sat across from *me*!"

"If you were *my* friend, you'd be happy for me."

"Esther." Hannah's voice softened. "How can I be happy

for you when you're going to be miserable after you see how wrong you are?"

"Wrong? You're the one who's wrong!" Esther's voice rose on every word. "You'll see that at the next singing, when he takes me home with him in his courting buggy."

"Maybe he'll ask *me* that night."

"Didn't you listen to what I said? He's already asked me!"

Hannah stared at her, hurt overtaking the anger on her face. Her mouth worked, but no sound came out. She turned and ran out of the farm stand.

Esther didn't move. Two *Englisch* women standing by the quilts stared at her, clearly curious about what had caused such a public argument. *Ach*, *Daed* and *Mamm* were going to be appalled when they learned that Esther had fought with Hannah instead of turning the other cheek. But how could she turn the other cheek when it would mean giving up everything she had ever wanted? To be Caleb Stutzman's girl, to be his betrothed, to be his wife.

But Hannah had always been her closest friend. She couldn't imagine her life without Hannah.

"Miss?" called one of the *Englischers*. "Can you help us?"

Esther fixed a smile on her face and rang up the two quilts and the bottles of chow-chow that the ladies wanted. She wrapped each item carefully while she kept an eye on the door, hoping Hannah would come back.

Esther was glad when the two women left with their purchases. There had to be a way for her to keep Hannah's friendship and still win Caleb's heart. An idea suddenly came to her. Hannah was desperately afraid she would be an old *maedel*. She had mentioned it a lot lately. All Esther

189

had to do was find Hannah another boy to fall in love with. A boy who would fall in love with Hannah, too. Once Esther succeeded in doing that, Caleb would be hers and hers alone. It was the perfect plan. She would get to work on it right away.

Fourteen

❧

On Saturday, Ruth stepped out of the Lambrights' family buggy and looked around. The day was perfect for the mud sale, sunny but not too hot. The trees wore glorious autumn colors, yet the brightest spot was Old Wayne's freshly painted red barn. It overshadowed the white farmhouse and the other outbuildings. Pens held the animals to be auctioned off, and every piece of equipment was surrounded by interested buyers.

A light breeze carried the scents of peppers and onions from where someone was grilling sausages. Tables were set up in rows, and potential customers were already admiring crafts and jars of jams, relishes, and apple butter.

"I didn't expect so many people here," Esther said as she jumped down to stand beside Ruth. "This is *wunderbaar.*"

Samuel handed the reins to one of the boys parking buggies and putting the horses out to graze. "Everyone knows Old Wayne took excellent care of his animals and equipment. The prices should be high today. Anyone thinking they're going to get a bargain may be sorely disappointed."

"But many people are here because they want to help him," Ruth guessed.

He nodded. "Old Wayne has been a *gut* friend and neighbor to many of us. Now, it's our turn."

"There are a lot of *Englischers* here," Esther said, glancing around.

"Who will be thirsty." Her brother grinned, then asked, "Where's Hannah? You two do everything together. Aren't you working at the table together?"

"She'll be along. I'd better get started."

Ruth watched as Esther picked up the canister that held lemonade then quickly vanished into the crowd that had gathered on the flat area leading to Old Wayne's big barn.

"I've never seen her that excited about selling lemonade," Samuel mused as he walked beside Ruth at a slower pace.

"I wonder if something has happened between her and Hannah."

"They've been best friends for years. If they've had a spat, it'll be over soon."

Ruth hoped Samuel was right. The two girls needed to work together at school, and if they didn't resolve their differences, there could be a problem. She would talk to them on Monday and make sure things were all right.

A group of beardless young men hurried past her, and Samuel then paused by the table where Esther was pouring lemonade into paper cups.

"Ach," Samuel said. "That explains it. She wants to flirt with boys before the auction starts. She's become quite the flirt. I've seen her speaking to several different boys in the last couple of days. It would seem like my little sister plans to enjoy every minute of her *rumspringa*."

"Odd, I thought she had set her heart on—" Ruth halted herself before she could break the promise she had made to keep Caleb's name a secret.

Samuel laughed. "She's told you something, hasn't she? Give me a clue—which boy does my sister like?"

"You know I can't do that, even if I knew the current state of her heart. At her age, her heart can change as fast as the sun sets and rises again."

Samuel put a friendly arm over her shoulders. "Cousin, I'm giving this problem to you, because you obviously know more about the state of a young girl's heart than I ever shall."

"No, no!" she teased back. "I've got enough to do without adding that drama to my life. She's your sister. That makes this your problem."

He clasped his hands together and gave her a pleading look. "I beg of you, Ruth . . ."

Before Ruth could tell him no, even though they both knew she would do all she could to ease Esther's way through the first year of her *rumspringa*, Levi said from behind her, "You'll never persuade Ruth to do something she thinks she shouldn't. She's stubborn that way." He smiled when she turned to face him. "Actually, she's stubborn in many ways."

Samuel laughed, but Ruth barely heard the joke. She drank in the sight of Levi in his best straw hat and a well-pressed, light-blue shirt that made his eyes appear as green as the grass in spring.

"You should know better than I," Samuel replied before he strolled away.

Ruth searched her mind for something to say. Since she had kissed Levi's cheek on that crazy impulse, she had avoided him. Earlier, it had been easy to imagine them working side by side to help David; instead, she spent time with the boy in the schoolroom working on the speech therapy exercises she'd found in the library materials. David sat and listened attentively, but never made a sound. Afterward, she sent him to the barn to see Levi and the animals.

All she could come up with was, "How's the fox?"

"*Gut.* He still has a long way to go, but he's eating better every day. He doesn't use his injured leg much, and spends most of his time in that den I made for him. I have hopes that one day he'll run free again."

"Is David helping you with the fox?"

He tilted back his hat slightly as they walked toward the rows of tables. "No, it's too dangerous for him, but he's been a great help with the birds and rabbits. And, before you ask, no, he hasn't uttered a word."

"I figured you would tell me right away if he had."

"*Ja.*"

"How is Graceless?"

"Gut."

"Is she getting housebroken?"

"Ja."

Ruth wanted to groan at his clipped answers. Frustration overwhelmed her common sense. "Are you angry with me?"

"Angry with you?" He stopped and stared at her as if she had said she wanted to grow a second head.

"You heard me." Now that the words had escaped, she wanted an answer. "Are you angry with me because of what happened in the barn?"

He didn't pretend not to understand. "I'm not angry, Ruth, but—" He turned as someone called his name.

But what? she wanted to ask, but she bit back that question when Paul and Micah came over to speak with Levi.

They were looking for an update on the schoolhouse repairs, and Paul looked very pleased to hear that they would be finished soon. Micah wore his customary frown. She had no idea what he was thinking, and she found that she truly didn't care. She couldn't think of anything but Levi's half-spoken comment. She was so lost in thought that she jumped when Micah spoke to her.

"I'm sorry," she said. "I didn't catch what you were saying."

Paul's mouth tightened. "This isn't the time, Micah."

"Delaying bad tidings doesn't make them go away."

"What is it?" Ruth asked.

"There has been a complaint about you sent to the school board," Micah began.

"Paul is right, Micah." Levi's voice was so calm he could have been speaking of the weather. "A mud sale isn't the time to talk about your wife's complaint."

Paul shook his head as he said, "I'm sorry, Teacher Ruth. This isn't how you should have found out about the complaint."

"It's all right," she said, copying Levi's serene tone. "I already know all about it."

Micah's eyes widened. Had he really intended to ruin her day by blindsiding her with the news of a complaint made by his own wife? She couldn't imagine why he was so angry that she had been hired instead of his niece. Nor did she understand why he was furious with her instead of his fellow school board members.

"I'm sorry that the scholars weren't in the classroom when your wife visited the school, Micah," she said as he stared at her. "As I told you and the rest of the school board members the night before school started, I take the *kinder* outside occasionally so I can teach them about the world around us. The school board gave me permission to have lessons outside. Don't you remember?"

His face turned red and he opened his mouth to retort, but Paul put his hand on Micah's shoulder.

Paul's voice remained calm. "Thank you for your time, Teacher Ruth. See you inside for the auction, Levi." He steered Micah away.

Once the men were out of earshot, Levi said, "The Bible teaches that a soft answer turns away wrath, but grievous words stir up anger."

"True," she replied. "But don't forget that Proverbs 15

goes on to say: 'The tongue of the wise used knowledge aright: but the mouth of fools pours out foolishness.'"

He laughed. "Don't let Micah hear you say that."

"I won't." She continued with him along the rows of tables. She halted when a familiar face by the animal pens caught her eye. "Levi, I'll be right back." She didn't give him a chance to answer as she wove through the crowd.

Ruth appreciated her height, because she could see over the heads of most of the women and some of the men. That kept her from losing sight of the man who was studying the cows.

The moment she broke free from the crowd, she called, *"Daed!"*

Her *daed* looked up from where he had been examining some heifers. Standing, he wiped his hands on his black trousers. "I knew I would see you here, Ruth. Sadie and Mervin wrote us that they were coming."

"How is *Mamm*? Is she doing well? And my sisters, are they being helpful? How are they? And you, how are you managing?" Words rushed out of her like a springtide as she grinned from ear to ear. She felt as happy to see her *daed* as she had when she was a toddler and he came in from chores to pick her up and toss her high in the air.

How things had changed! But one thing hadn't. She missed her family. Now that *Daed* was here, he could tell her all about how *Mamm* and the rest of the family were doing. She wanted to hug him and tell him how much she had missed all of them, but *Daed* frowned on such public displays. She restrained herself, but couldn't stop smiling.

He regarded her with puzzlement. "Why would all of

that be wondering you, Ruth, when you have your teaching and your scholars to think about? Don't you have as many lessons yet to learn as they do?"

Her joy at seeing *Daed* vanished. The old feeling of being in the wrong came back. Her thoughts immediately went to Ida Stutzman's complaint. She felt tears burning at the back of her eyes and tried to will them away. She heard a voice in her head crying, *Show me how to be what you want me to be!* She didn't know if those anguished words were a prayer to God or a request for *Daed*. Maybe both.

Someone called, "Hey, Zeb! C'mon over here and look at these calves."

He nodded to her and walked away.

Ruth couldn't move. *Daed* hadn't answered any of her questions. Didn't he realize how eager she was to hear that *Mamm* was well? And how much she wanted to please him? She knew it was wrong to want them to be proud of her, but she longed for *Daed* to understand she was trying to follow God's plan for her. She just didn't know how to reach him.

Esther poured the lemonade slowly. Very slowly. She looked up through her lashes at Andrew Miller, whom everyone called "Red" because of his vivid hair. He held the hand of his little sister, Abby, who was sipping the cup of lemonade Esther had already poured for her.

Red would be perfect for Hannah, because he doted on his little sister, and Hannah adored the girl. Esther did, too, but she wasn't looking for something she had in common with Red. This was all about finding the perfect boyfriend for her friend who had offered only a curt *"Gude mariye"* when she walked past to the table where she was selling whoopee pies and cookies with Miriam Brennemann.

"Are you looking for anything in particular at the auction today?" Esther asked. "Or are you just here for fun?"

"Ja, just for fun," Red said. "How about you?"

"Definitely here for the fun." Esther lowered the pitcher to the table and held out the cup to him. He took it, putting his wide fingers over her much smaller hand.

For a long moment he just smiled at her, then he said, "Maybe after you're done here, we can have some fun together."

Ach, this wasn't going as she'd planned. She didn't need a boyfriend. She had Caleb.

"Hannah and I were going to stroll around together." She slid her hand out from beneath his and refilled Abby's cup. She handed it to the little girl, who gave her a big smile. Looking back at Red, she said, "I can't disappoint Hannah. She's such a sweet girl, so funny and pretty."

"Ja, she is pretty. But so are you, Esther. I reckon you're about the prettiest girl here."

Esther blushed. Nobody had ever paid her such a compliment. Caleb had said she sang well, but it wasn't the same. That only made her glad he was paying attention to her. Red's compliment made her feel happy from her *kapp* to her toes.

"Can't Hannah find someone else to wander around with?" he asked.

"That wouldn't be right. Maybe if another boy went with us—"

"Now, that's a *gut* idea." He drained his lemonade in one gulp. "I'm sure I can find someone."

"I saw Caleb just a little while ago."

"So did I." Red's smile vanished then returned even wider. "Don't worry. I'll handle it, Esther. Where should we meet you?"

"I don't know when Hannah and I will be done." She hesitated then plunged ahead. "If we don't get to walk around here this afternoon, how about we sit together at the next singing? Then you won't have to worry about finding another boy."

"That's an even better idea, because my *daed* will probably buy a few head of cattle today. He'll need me to help him load and unload them, and I don't want to leave you waiting."

"*Gut.* It's all set then." He gave her another smile, seeming as happy about her plan as she was. Taking his little sister by the hand, he walked away.

Esther poured a half-dozen cups of lemonade and left them at the front of the table. People would have to pay on an honor system, because she couldn't wait to talk to Hannah.

Hurrying, Esther reached the table where Hannah and Miriam had only a few remaining quilted pot holders and carved farm animals left. "Can I borrow Hannah for a minute, Miriam?"

"Take all the time you want," Miriam said. "We'll be closing up soon, because the auction's about to start."

Hannah didn't protest when Esther seized her hand and pulled her away from the table. They walked closer to the parking lot where Amish buggies and wagons mingled with *Englisch* cars and trucks.

"Esther, if you're going to ask me to forgive you—"

"No. I came to tell you that I have a surprise for you."

"Really?" Hannah's stiff shoulders eased slightly. "What is it?"

Esther laughed. "How can it be a surprise if I tell you? You're going to have to wait until next Sunday evening. I promise that you'll love it."

Hannah hoisted herself up to sit on the back of the wagon. "I've got a surprise for you, too, but now I think I'll wait until next Sunday evening to tell you."

Esther pulled herself up next to Hannah and swung her feet in the air. "I hope this means we can be best friends again."

"It depends on how *gut* your surprise is." Hannah burst into giggles.

"It'll be better than yours."

"We'll see, won't we?"

Esther laughed with her friend, sure that Hannah's surprise was that her sister had agreed to marry Matthew Stutzman. Something that was probably no surprise for anyone, because Dorcas and Matthew had been keeping company for many months. It definitely wasn't a surprise for Esther, because Hannah had slipped and told her about Matthew courting Dorcas on the family's front porch. Esther's surprise for her friend was going to be better.

So much better.

Fifteen

❧

Excited voices filled the air. People hurried past where Ruth stood by a pen that held Old Wayne's mules. Everyone was getting ready for the auction, but she wished she could leave. One of the mules lowered its head to her, and she stroked it gently.

"I hope you go to a *gut* home," she said softly. "To someone who will love you and take care of you as well as Old Wayne did." Another mule butted her shoulder, wanting attention.

"They're lonely." Levi put his hand on the metal rail by her elbow. "They must miss Old Wayne. He always spoiled his animals."

"Like—" She halted herself, but not quickly enough.

"Like me? Is that what you meant to say?"

"*Ja.*"

Reaching past her, he rubbed the mule's face. "They'll be treated well, wherever they end up. I know all the farmers here, both Plain and *Englisch.*" He pushed away from the fence. "Come on. There's still some time before the auction begins. We could walk around and look at what's for sale."

"*Danki,* but no."

"Something to drink?"

"No."

He slanted toward her so she had to look at him. "Why are you sounding like me all of the sudden?"

She moved farther along the fence. "Levi, I know you mean well, but I'd like to be alone now. I need to sort out a few things."

"Can I help?" He closed the distance between them again.

"No."

He held up one finger. "Are you sure?"

"*Ja.*"

He arched his brows and held up the single finger again.

"Stop it," she said. "Why are you making a joke of this?"

"You needle me to talk when I don't feel like it."

"You're shy, so I'm trying to help you." She turned to fold her arms on the railing. "I'm not shy."

"I noticed that." His voice became tense. "Ruth, *was iss letz?*"

"Why do you think something is wrong?"

He touched her arm lightly and brought her back to face him. She couldn't meet his eyes as he asked, "Do we have to go through this all over again? You're not shy, but you're not talking, so something must be wrong."

"You're one to talk." She grimaced when he grinned. She hadn't meant to make a jest. "All right. You want to talk? Then why don't you start by explaining what you *almost* said to me before Paul and Micah interrupted. You told me you weren't angry. Then you said 'but' and nothing more."

He tipped his straw hat back slightly and sighed. "What I was going to say is that I'm confused, Ruth."

"About me?" She raised her eyes to meet his gaze. His green-brown eyes had lost their brightness, and lines of tension furrowed into his brow.

"About you, and about everything else. For a long time, I've known exactly what each day will be like. Now I'm not so sure." He squinted into the sunlight. "Isn't that your *daed* over there?"

"Ja." She didn't even try to keep her sorrow out of her voice. "Don't ask if I want to speak to him, because I already have."

"How's your *mamm* doing?"

She shoved herself back from the pens and walked away. When he matched her steps, she gave him a glower that Micah would envy. He kept walking beside her.

"Is your *mamm* all right?" he asked.

"I don't know. *Daed* told me to tend to my scholars because I had more to learn about being a teacher."

"Did he say exactly that?"

"Close enough. Maybe he's heard about Ida's complaint about me."

Levi glanced toward her *daed*, then back at her. "You

aren't a *kind*, Ruth. You must know you chose to come here. The rest is up to God."

"But knowing it here"—she pointed to her head—"is not the same as knowing it here." She pointed to her heart and gave an unhappy sigh. "I didn't expect to miss my family this much. Don't get me wrong. I'm happy teaching and being with the scholars and with the Lambrights, but I so wanted to hear news of my family."

He blinked once, then a second time before looking away. His hand gripped the rail.

She recognized his reaction. She had said something that hurt him, and he was trying to hide his feelings. What had she said? She replayed what she'd just said and knew instantly. She hadn't included him among the people who made her happy.

She wished she could put her arms around his broad shoulders and kiss him once again. Her dreams were filled with longings to have his arms close around her as he held her to his heart.

Ruth stopped and faced him. If she and Levi walked much farther, they would be among the mud sale crowd. More cars and buggies were coming up the farm lane, a sure sign that the auction would start soon.

"I'm sorry, Levi."

"For what?"

"You must think I'm silly. But I don't understand why *Daed* didn't tell me how *Mamm* is doing. Instead, he went off when someone called. He couldn't leave fast enough. Why—?"

He put his finger to her lips and held out his other hand. "Let's go where we can talk."

She nodded and put her hand in his. As they walked along the fence toward the road, she savored the warmth of his fingers, that held hers as tenderly as he did his injured animals.

When he stopped by a gate, she did, too. He didn't release her hand, but took her other as they stood face-to-face. "I know your *daed* hurt you, but maybe he didn't do it intentionally. He has shown that he loves you. After all, he came with you to the Lambrights' to make sure you had a *gut* place to live."

His kindness was shredding the last of her defenses, and she didn't want to collapse in tears as she told him that he was wrong. She was no longer sure that *Daed* loved her. He felt responsible for her and wanted her to have a *gut* and proper life within their Plain community. When she was a *kind*, he had shown her and *Mamm* and her sisters how much he loved them in so many ways. Then he had been chosen as the district's deacon, and since then he had only seemed concerned with correcting their behavior, especially hers.

"Let's talk about something else," she said, not wanting to dwell on those sad thoughts.

She thought Levi might protest, but he asked, "What?"

"Tell me about your parents, Levi. You've talked about your *mammi* and *dawdi*, but never about your parents."

His hands tightened on hers. "There's not much to tell. I was eight when they died."

"So young."

207

"*Ja*, and I regret that I never got to know them. I knew them as a *kind* would, but not as a teenager or an adult would."

Even though the sounds of people and animals surrounded them, she and Levi were a small island of silence amid the excitement of the auction. Her voice dropped to a whisper because it seemed wrong to speak louder. "What happened to them? If you don't mind telling me."

"It's no secret. Everyone in the district knows." He released her hands and looked past her as if the memory played out in the middle of the field. "*Mamm* had cancer. I don't know what kind, but one of the bad ones where there's not much chance of surviving. She was in and out of the hospital a lot, but she asked to come home from the hospital after the *Englisch* doctors said there was nothing more they could do for her. My *daed* understood she wanted to die at home. I was able to see her only a short time each day because she tired so quickly, and an eight-year-old boy doesn't sit still. On the day they died—"

"They?" she asked. "They died the same day?"

He continued as if she hadn't spoken. "—I was by my *mamm*'s bedside with my grandparents. *Daed* was determined to do as my *mamm* asked, and put in the corn so it could be harvested on time. We never knew exactly when it happened, but that night when he didn't come home, *Dawdi* went looking for him. He was dead beside his team. A heart attack." His hands fisted on the metal gate. "*Mamm* died never knowing that he had as well. I stood by their graves and saw *Mammi*'s and *Dawdi*'s tears. I vowed then never to do anything that would cause them such pain again."

"God must have loved your parents dearly."

"What do you mean?" He looked at her, startled.

"He must have known how both of them worried what life would be after the loss of the other. By taking them at the same time, He saved them from mourning each other. They entered heaven hand in hand, just as they lived their lives."

He swallowed hard before clearing his throat. *"Danki,"* he said quietly.

"For what?"

He took her hand and folded it between his. "For reminding me that God is *gut*, even when I don't understand His plan for our lives. It's been many years since my parents died, but you've opened my eyes today. I guess you can teach even me something, Teacher Ruth."

His smile warmed her to her soul, and she squeezed his hand gently. She imagined him drawing her close as he kissed her. It would be perfection, but by Old Wayne's fence during a mud sale was the wrong time and place. Even a hug would make tongues wag, so she had to be content with holding his hand.

"Levi, get over here!"

He dropped her hand as if it had grown briars. He turned to wave back to Mervin Lambright. "I'll be right there," he shouted back. Without looking at her, he said, "I've got to go."

"All right." She didn't know what else to say.

He took a step before facing her again. "Ruth, I need to get some things sorted out, too." He rushed away.

She folded her arms on the top of the gate. He hadn't given her a chance to ask the question that ached inside her:

When Levi finished sorting out what confused him, would there be any place in his heart for her?

"I told you so." Samuel grinned. "My little sister and her best friend had some sort of disagreement."

"You did tell me," Ruth said as they walked toward the barn where the auction would soon start. "But I just saw her sitting with Hannah on one of the wagons. It seems that whatever was bothering them has blown past."

"*Ja.*" Samuel's brow lowered. "Are you all right, Ruth?"

"*Ja,*" she answered automatically. It wasn't the truth, but she didn't want to talk about her jumbled thoughts in the wake of her conversation with Levi.

She thought he might ask another question, but he began talking about a nice wooden desk he had seen among the items to be auctioned. It would make a *gut* replacement for Ruth's ruined one at school.

"We'll keep an eye out for it," Samuel said, his easy grin returning. "Then we'll get Levi to bid, so the school board can pay for it. After all, if you don't have a desk, how can a student leave an apple on it for you?"

She laughed with him, but looked around as they entered the large hayloft where the auction was being held. Bleachers had been set up in an arc around an open area where the items and animals up for bid could be displayed. The men far outnumbered the women, and she saw plenty of faces she recognized from church Sundays. At the podium, the *Englisch* auctioneer was talking to a Plain man.

"That must be Old Wayne's cousin," Samuel said. "He looks enough like Old Wayne to be his twin."

"It's *gut* that someone is here to answer questions if the bidders have any." She looked around, but didn't see Levi among the crowd.

Samuel shrugged. "I doubt there'll be questions. Any farmer worth his salt will know what to look for in the animals, and any *fraa* knows what she wants in the furniture." He grabbed her hand. "C'mon. We need to find Levi and my *daed*."

She followed along, wondering why holding her cousin's hand was so different from holding Levi's. With Samuel, she didn't feel the waves of warmth that delighted her.

"There he is," Samuel crowed.

She smiled when she saw Levi sitting about halfway up the bleachers. He was talking to an *Englischer* behind him as easily as he did with Samuel. She recognized the *Englischer* as the farmer who often drove past the school with his tractor and wagon. He always had a friendly wave for her and the *kinder*.

"We can get up there over here." Samuel led her to steps at the end of the bleachers.

She hurried after him as she heard the auctioneer call for everyone's attention. He began reading the terms of the sale, so everyone understood.

Samuel motioned for her to precede him along the row. It was slow-going as everyone either shifted their feet or stood up to let her and her cousin pass. She kept her eyes on her own feet so she didn't step on someone's toes. Behind her, Samuel paused to speak with a friend. She kept going.

Her head jerked up when she heard a familiar voice ask, "You are Levi Yoder, aren't you?"

Daed!

She froze as she stared at her *daed* moving to stand next to Levi. Neither of them seemed to notice her standing only a few feet away.

"Ja," Levi replied.

"Do you remember me? I'm Zeb Schrock."

"Ja," Levi replied.

"You're a member of the school board, right?" Her *daed* put one foot on the seat beside Levi and rested his elbow casually on his knee, but Ruth knew that pose. His eyes would be drilling into Levi, measuring every motion he made.

"Ja."

"I assume you've heard about this complaint about Ruth's teaching," *Daed* said, his face becoming bright red.

Ruth bit her lower lip before she called out to Levi to explain to *Daed* that the complaint was silly because it had been made by a man and his wife who wanted their niece to have her job.

Tell him! she begged silently. *Tell him that, other than Micah, the school board is pleased with what I've been doing. Tell him that I'm not doing anything to shame him and the rest of the family.*

All Levi said was, *"Ja,* it is true there is a complaint, and—"

Her heart splintered in her chest, each shard slicing even more deeply into her soul.

"I was afraid this would happen," *Daed* interrupted him

with a deepening scowl. "Will you pass along to the other school board members that I will accept their judgment?"

"*Ja*, of course, but—"

"*Gut*." Her *daed* straightened and turned to go back to his seat at the far end of the row.

Levi looked down at his clasped hands. If he hadn't seen her, she still could leave without him knowing she'd overheard every word. Zeb Schrock could be intimidating, and Levi was shy. But, if he cared about her at all, why hadn't he come to her defense by telling *Daed* the truth about the complaint? She had thought, when he took her hands and spoke to her from the heart, that he might be the man she longed for him to be. A man who loved her.

"Why are you standing here?" Samuel asked from behind her. "Let's sit down before the auction starts."

"You go ahead. I'll—"

"C'mon. You don't want to miss a chance to bid on that desk." He put his hands on her shoulders and herded her toward Levi.

Ruth's feet were wooden, and pain rushed through her again when Levi looked up at them and smiled as if the conversation with her *daed* had never happened.

"We're just in time," Samuel said.

"Down in front," called a voice from higher on the bleachers as an early lot—a long kitchen table—was pushed to the center of the floor. It was the signal that the bidding was about to begin, and the bleachers became as silent as a church room on Sunday.

Levi took her hand and tugged her down to sit beside him. She yanked her hand away, angry at her own heart, which leaped at his touch. He gave her a baffled glance. She looked away as Samuel sat on her other side.

When he slanted past her to speak to Levi, she murmured, "I can move over so you can sit together."

Neither man acted as if he had heard her, so she folded her hands on her lap. She had no choice but to wait for a break in the auction. Then she would excuse herself and leave.

"The first lot today is the biggest," the *Englisch* auctioneer said, holding a microphone close to his mouth. "It's the farm and its buildings. A description of the land and the improvements were listed on the sheet you were given when you signed in."

Beside her, Samuel leaned forward, resting his elbows on his knees. There was an odd tension about him as he listened to the auctioneer drone on about the legal aspects of buying the land by auction. When Levi shoved a crumpled piece of paper at Ruth, she read along as the auctioneer went through each detail again. It was the perfect excuse not to have to look at Levi.

People grew restive on the bleachers. The auctioneer must have sensed that because he called for an opening bid.

An *Englisch* voice from close to the doors called out a bid for close to $25,000 an acre. That was, Ruth knew, a ridiculously low offer. The auctioneer knew it, too, because he began to exhort the rest of them to bid. The *Englischer* looked startled that nobody bid against him. He began to smile until the auctioneer announced that the bid didn't meet the reserve set by Old Wayne's cousin. Telling the *Englischer* to come and speak to him after the auction, the auctioneer turned his attention to the next lot.

"That's odd," said the *Englisch* farmer behind Levi. "I thought the farm would sell fast and for a lot of money. This is *gut* land, and the description says there are two natural springs on it for keeping crops and cattle watered."

Levi rested his elbows back against the bleacher behind him and smiled up at the *Englischer.* "You never know how things will go at an auction, Clarence. That's part of the fun."

"Ja," Samuel agreed. "You just never know."

Ruth looked from one to the other and felt as baffled as Clarence appeared. Then she asked herself why she cared what Levi said. He had shown his true colors today.

The kitchen table that sat in the middle of the open area was tilted by the auctioneer's assistants so everyone could see its polished walnut top.

"That looks just like the table in your *dawdi-haus,* Levi," Ruth said before she could halt herself.

"It should," Levi said, his eyes focused on the table as the bidding began among three *Englischers.* "Old Wayne built my grandparents' furniture. Before arthritis halted him, he was the best finish carpenter in Lancaster County." There was an odd disquiet in his voice.

Samuel must have noticed it, too, because he asked, "Are you all right, Levi?"

"Ja." He sat up straighter, his gaze never leaving the table.

One lot of household goods after another was brought up to bid and hammered sold. Levi's jaw worked. Did he want to say something, or was he fighting to keep from speaking? She had never seen such an expression on his face.

She asked herself again why she cared, why her foolish heart urged her to reach out to him. She wasn't going to listen to it any longer. Falling in love with a man who hadn't spoken up on her behalf was *dumm*.

The auctioneer kept up a rapid patter about the fine quality of the furniture. "Look closely. Many of the pieces have hardly been used. No marks from kids or pets. It's like having a new, quality antique used by an old man who lovingly built each piece himself." He pointed to a desk that was almost identical to the one Ruth had used at school. "What am I bid for this?"

"Go ahead, Ruth," Samuel said. When she didn't bid, he added, "Levi, that's the perfect desk to replace Ruth's at school. The school board needs to get it for her."

Levi turned, and Ruth caught his eye. She saw his eyes grow round, and she wondered what her face had revealed to him.

He abruptly stood. "Bid what you think is a fair price for the desk. Paul or Joseph will pay for it if you win it."

"Where are you going?" Samuel asked.

He ignored the shouts for him to sit down so he didn't block the people behind him. "I need a cup of *kaffi*." He edged past them and hurried down the steps.

Ruth stared after him, barely hearing Samuel bidding on the desk. Levi looked as if someone had hit him in the gut. Had he finally realized how he had hurt her?

Someone upped Samuel's bid.

"Thirty-five dollars for the desk for our school," Samuel called out.

That stopped any other bids, and Ruth knew that had been her cousin's intention. Nobody would bid against someone buying for the school. Even though the auctioneer tried to get more bids, no one raised Samuel's bid, so the hammer came down.

As soon as bidding started on the next lot, Samuel's shoulders sagged. He looked in the direction Levi had gone and sighed. "It's not easy when God gives us a glimpse of our future."

"I don't know what you're talking about."

"I'm talking about Levi. Didn't you see his face as things came up for bid? Aren't you curious about why he rushed out of here?" He frowned. "I thought you two were *gut* friends."

She ignored his comment. "Why did he rush out of here?"

"Because he couldn't stand seeing what life holds for him if he doesn't change. Old Wayne lived alone in his grandparents' house, just like Levi. He had furniture just like Levi's. Did you know that Levi donated your previous desk to the school? It had been his *dawdi*'s."

"I didn't know that." She looked at the furniture stacked to one side until the winning bidders came to collect it. "The other pieces?"

"You'll find a twin for most of them at Levi's house." Samuel sighed. "Guess it got him thinking. Old Wayne lost his wife and his *kinder* many, many years ago. I can't remember what happened, but they all died. Within two to three years, his parents passed away, too. He was all alone."

"Like Levi," Ruth said. She was still troubled by his conversation with *Daed*, but Samuel's words made her see Levi in a way she'd tried not to before.

"Old Wayne has always involved himself in the community."

"Like Levi does."

Samuel nodded. "Old Wayne cares deeply for his neighbors."

"As Levi does."

"And Old Wayne cares as much for beasts as he does people. Maybe more, because they don't require more from him than he can give."

She didn't need to say, "Like Levi." They both knew. He had lost so much. Now he lived by himself in that large house with only a puppy for company. Old Wayne Fisher's life was a mirror for Levi's, and the auction held it up so Levi could not fail to look in its reflection of all the empty years to come.

But wasn't that the way he wanted it? He didn't let anyone get too close to him. When he'd opened himself to her today, he'd clearly been glad for the excuse to flee from her as soon as her *onkel* called to him. He was planning to give Graceless, who loved him, to someone else. That should have warned her that he might treat a woman who was falling in love with him just the same.

Sixteen

◌

The scholars were as excited as Ruth when they returned to the schoolhouse on Monday morning. The fall sunshine made them eager for recess. Maybe today she would join them for a game of softball. They hadn't been able to play while school was held at Levi's *dawdi-haus*, because a stray ball could break a window. Now they again had the big yard, that was perfect for a few innings.

Levi hadn't been in the barn when Ruth left her buggy that morning. She had been relieved that she didn't have to face him.

Neither Esther nor Hannah had been able to help today. Once or twice, one of them hadn't come, but this was the first time both of them had to stay home. Ruth had asked Mary Beth to keep an eye on Abby and Gabe. Gabe was

Mary Beth's little brother, and the two *kinder* adored the eighth grader as much as they did Esther and Hannah, so Ruth had hopes that the day would go smoothly.

Ruth wasn't as sure about the other *kinder*, who all seemed to be in a state of excitement. From the moment she opened the door and rang the bell, the scholars had scurried around the room, examining everything to see what items were the same and what had been replaced. The older boys cheered for the new propane stove, because it meant that they wouldn't have to bring in wood on cold winter days.

She gave them some time to look around and then asked them to take their seats. As soon as they had, she said, "We need to give thanks to God for bringing us back to our school so soon." It had taken some of the materials almost a week to arrive, but the actual repairs took only two days.

"And thanks to Levi," Seth said loyally. The other *kinder* nodded.

"*Gut.*" She smiled. "Let's give thanks to God for bringing Levi to help us."

All the heads bowed in silent prayer. Ruth kept her own thanksgiving short, because she guessed the youngest ones would get antsy.

She began taking the roll. When she got to David's name she glanced up, looking for his raised hand. David's desk was empty! She hadn't even noticed because the *kinder* had been in constant motion since they arrived.

"Is David ill today?" Ruth asked his cousin Jimmy, who lived next door to the Zooks.

"No."

"Do you know if there is some reason he isn't here?"

Jimmy looked around then frowned. "He *should* be here. I saw him leave his house even before me and my brother and sister finished breakfast."

"I thought you walked to school with him."

"Naw, he never wants to walk with anybody else. That's why he always heads out earlier than we do. I guess he's afraid someone will forget he doesn't talk and ask him something."

Giggles came from both sides of the room, but stopped when Ruth said, "Scholars, that's enough."

While the *kinder* sang their morning songs, she went to the window and looked out. No sign of David in either direction. She hoped he was all right. He had never been late before, but maybe he'd gone to the *dawdi-haus* and wondered where the rest of them were. While the scholars began the deskwork listed on the blackboard, she took Seth aside.

"Go and check the *dawdi-haus* in case David's there," Ruth requested. "If he isn't, look in the outhouse."

Seth's nose wrinkled. "Why would anyone stay out there?"

"If he's sick—"

"I'll check, and I'll also see if he's behind the tree where he goes sometimes during recess."

"Gut." Ruth called the first graders to sit with her for their reading lesson.

She tried to keep her attention on the youngsters and help the one reading aloud if he or she stumbled over a new word. It wasn't easy because her gaze kept cutting between the main door and the side door. If David was at the *dawdi-haus*, the boys would return through the front door. The side door, however, was closer to the outhouse.

Seth came back alone. He raised his hands in the air and shrugged when Ruth looked at him. She motioned for him to go to his desk and get to work.

David still hadn't appeared an hour later when it was almost time for the mid-morning recess. Ruth's mild concern became stronger with every passing minute, but she didn't want to alarm the scholars. She wished Hannah or Esther were there; she could leave either girl in charge while she went to look for the boy.

Telling the *kinder* to continue on their workbook pages, Ruth went out on the porch and gazed to her right. If he had been delayed or returned home for some reason, David should be walking toward the school from that direction. The road was empty.

She went back inside. She looked at Nelson, an eighth grader, who was bent over his workbook. She could send him to the Zooks with a message. She needed to figure out exactly what to say so she didn't frighten Susan and Timothy. But she couldn't wait any longer.

It took her almost fifteen minutes to write two sentences that expressed her concern but didn't sound panicked. As she reread the note, she realized her choice of words really made no difference. David's parents would be horrified to know that their son had never shown up at school that morning.

Folding the note, she stapled it closed, just in case Nelson was curious to read what it said.

"Nelson, come with me." She walked past his desk and to the front door.

His face paled as he followed her, and she wondered what mischief he thought she had uncovered.

Ruth went out on the porch and was about to explain what she needed him to do. When she saw Levi loping across the road, she rushed down the steps. Her battered heart didn't matter when a *kind* was missing.

"Levi, David never came to school this morning. I was about to send Nelson with a note to alert Susan Zook, but now that you are here, could you go to the Zooks' house and find out if he's still at home? Don't alarm them. Maybe something distracted him on his way here. He—"

Levi put his finger to her lips to silence her. "He's in my barn," Levi said quietly. "I think you should come over, too, Ruth."

"Give me a minute." Running up the steps, she led a confused Nelson back into the schoolroom. The *kinder* craned their necks to see what was happening. "I need to leave for a few minutes. Mary Beth, please listen to the second graders read. The rest of you do your deskwork while I'm gone. I'll be right back. If you have any questions, Mary Beth will help you."

"*Ja*, Teacher Ruth," the eighth-grade girl said, clearly excited at her chance to prove she could handle the classroom on her own.

"Scholars?" asked Ruth.

"*Ja*, Teacher Ruth," all of them said except Jimmy.

He stood and asked, "What about recess, Teacher Ruth?"

She heard a muffled laugh beside her. She glanced at Levi, who stood in the doorway, and saw that he was trying to hide a grin but not too successfully. His mirth eased the fear clamped around her heart. He wouldn't be in such a *gut* mood if something bad had happened to David.

"Of course, you'll have recess," she said. "After I get back. Do your deskwork until I return. Is that understood?"

This time, all the *kinder* replied in unison, "*Ja*, Teacher Ruth."

Pausing only long enough to get her shawl to throw over her shoulders, Ruth left with Levi. She glanced back and saw the scholars bending over their desks. She would give them an extra ten minutes of recess as a reward when she returned.

"Is David all right?" she asked as she and Levi hurried toward his land.

"Better than all right," he said with the widest grin she'd ever seen on his face.

"Tell me," she pleaded as she added a silent prayer of thanks for the boy's safety.

He shook his head. "I've got to show you." He went up the lane at a pace that made her do a half-run to keep up.

Warning her to be quiet, Levi went to the barn's lower level. He motioned for her to bend down each time they passed one of the windows, so they wouldn't be visible to whoever was in the barn. So many questions filled her that she feared she would go crazy if she didn't get an answer to one.

The door was open, and Levi eased around it silently. Ruth took care where she put her feet, always trying to step where he had. When he put his hand on her shoulder, she compliantly squatted and walked like an awkward duck toward the stalls where he kept the animals he was nursing back to health.

The lightest pressure on her arm stopped her. She looked

at Levi, abruptly disconcerted to discover his face so close that not even her hand could have passed between them. Everything else receded as she gazed at his lips. If she shifted ever so slightly, she could press hers to his.

No! God had led her to see the truth about Levi. She must heed what He had helped her discover.

Her nails bit into her palms. Why was she thinking of Levi now? She should be focused on getting David and returning to her scholars.

She tried to peer past Levi. She wasn't able to see anything but the stall across the center aisle.

Then she heard a soft voice.

A *kind*'s voice. It was so low she couldn't make out any words.

Could that be David? She looked back at Levi with the question she couldn't have spoken even if she didn't want to give away where they were crouched. Her throat was clogged with so many joyous tears she could barely swallow.

He nodded.

She closed her eyes and strained to hear better. The young voice stuttered on almost every word, but it was the sweetest sound she had ever heard. She offered up a grateful prayer of praise for God's grace.

When she opened her eyes, Levi crooked his finger and inched around the end of the stall. She crept with him closer to another stall where the door was open. It was the one where Levi kept two bird cages.

"He's with the hawk that I rescued last week," Levi murmured in her ear.

It wasn't easy to ignore how his warm breath seeped

through her, but she did. Not sure if they should go closer, she sat back on her heels and listened to David's uneven voice.

"Y-y-you d-d-doing *g-g-g-gut*," the little boy said to the bird. "Y-y-your w-wing is b-b-bett-ter. I c-c-can s-s-s-see that, b-b-but a c-c-closer l-l-look—"

Levi surged to his feet to keep David from opening the cage. Ruth did, too, knowing a bird of prey like a hawk could hurt the boy badly, even if it was injured.

David whirled and faced them. His eyes widened, and he pressed his lips shut. He was silent as Levi put a hand on his shoulder and steered him out of the stall.

"Never," Levi said in a quiet but stern voice, "open a cage or stall door when I'm not with you. I thought you understood that, but do you really?"

David blinked back tears then nodded. For a moment, he resembled one of the animals looking for a way to escape. Then his shoulders sagged in what looked like defeat. Ruth guessed the boy thought Levi would ban him from the barn for not following the rules.

"You don't have to pretend with us any longer," Ruth said, smoothing David's hair back from his eyes. "We heard you talk."

He started to push past her, but paused when Levi took him by the arm. "Don't be angry at Teacher Ruth, David. You should tell her that you're sorry for being rude."

He frowned, then put his hand to his ear and tilted his head as if listening intently.

"David, I *heard* you," Levi said, "when I came into the milking parlor, so I went to get Teacher Ruth. She was very worried about you because you didn't come to school. Did you think about that?"

David hung his head again, then whispered, "S-s-sorry."

"You're forgiven," she replied as her heart danced. "But it must never happen again. Let's go back to school."

He shook his head more vehemently.

Ruth wasn't sure what he wanted, but Levi quickly said, "If you don't want us to tell anyone else what we heard, we won't." He glanced up at Ruth.

She faltered on her answer. Every instinct warned her to disagree; then she met David's pleading eyes. Pain burned in them. No *kind* should carry such a heavy burden alone. But he didn't need to carry it alone any longer. Both she and Levi would help him . . . if he'd allow them to.

"We won't tell anyone, except your parents."

David shook his head.

She knelt and put her hands on his thin arms. "David, your *mamm* and *daed* love you. You can trust them with your secret. And you can trust Levi and me. But working with you after school and letting you come to the barn like this has been . . . an experiment of sorts. Your parents only gave Levi and me one month to see if we could help you. That month will be over soon. Let us tell them that you've spoken. I've read of ways to help with stuttering." She had stumbled on the articles among the ones the librarians had found for her. At the time, she wasn't sure why those articles had been included, but now she understood how God had brought her what she needed. "Please, let us help you."

David was silent, but he didn't shake his head no. She tried to curb her impatience. She needed to get back to the schoolhouse. The other scholars were going to wonder when she was coming back to let them go out for recess.

"Listen to Teacher Ruth," Levi said. "She truly wants to help you. Haven't you seen that when she works with you after school?"

The boy nodded.

"We won't tell anyone other than your parents. We promise, don't we, Teacher Ruth?"

Again she hesitated, but this was a compromise she could accept. "I promise."

Relief and gratitude filled David's eyes.

"But you must continue to talk to us," she went on as she stood. "You and I will work on helping you speak without stuttering, and Levi will expect you to answer him out loud when you're here. If you can't agree to that, then I can't promise to say nothing." She held out her hand. "A deal?"

David shook her hand with the solemnity of a trader selling a fine horse.

"*Gut.*" She smiled. "Now, get back to school. No more skipping school if you want to spend more time here with Levi and the animals."

"*J-j-ja,*" he forced out. He walked away, but paused by another stall door. "L-L-Levi?"

As if there were nothing extraordinary about David initiating a conversation, Levi walked over to where the little boy pointed at the rabbit. "What is it, David?"

Ruth held her breath as the little boy struggled to get his question out. Levi was always patient with the animals in his care. He used that same patience now as David halted in frustration and began anew. When he realized that David had noticed that the rabbit had chewed through the bandaging on its hind leg, he clapped the *kind* lightly on the shoulder.

"I hadn't seen that," Levi said. "*Gut* job. I'll put a new bandage on it. When you come over after school, we can see if she's left the new one alone. If not, we'll have to figure out a way to keep her from gnawing it off. All right?"

David's grin was almost too big for his face. "All r-r-r-right!"

Ruth watched him run out of the barn, every inch of him radiating joy. "I hope we're doing the right thing by promising not to say anything to anyone but the Zooks."

Levi closed the stall door when the hawk began screeching out its annoyance at being caged. "I know it was your chance to show the others on the school board that you are a *gut* teacher."

"I never gave that a single thought." She was astounded he would think that. "*Danki* for coming to get me, but I have to get back to my scholars."

"Ruth," he said as she walked away. "Wait."

"I need to go."

He put his hands on her shoulders, and she stiffened. He didn't let her shrug off his fingers. Instead he slid his hands down to cup her elbows under her shawl as he turned her toward him. All happiness had vanished from his face. "Something has changed between us, Ruth."

"I need to go."

"Tell me why you haven't said two words in a row to me unless we're talking about your scholars."

She tried to hold the words back, but they burst out of

her. "Because you didn't defend me when *Daed* asked you about the complaint Ida Stutzman made to the school board."

"You heard that?" His face became ashen.

"What was there to hear? All you said was, *'Ja'* to every question he asked." She pulled away from him and went toward the door. As she reached to open it, a *kind*'s scream rang through the air.

She threw open the door and raced out as the *kind* shrieked again. She ran toward the school, pausing only long enough to take a quick glance in both directions when she reached the road. No cars. She rushed to where the scholars were gathered in the schoolyard. Many of them wore their coats. What were they doing outside? She had told them to wait inside; why hadn't they obeyed?

She pushed those questions aside when she saw, in the middle of their ragged circle, Irma Rose Knepp writhing and crying out in agony.

Ruth knelt and ran her hands gently along the girl's limbs. She winced when she felt an odd disconnection in Irma Rose's right forearm. The girl moaned when Ruth gently probed to make sure she wasn't mistaken.

She wasn't. Irma Rose's arm was broken. There was no doubt of that.

Levi arrived in her wake. "Is she all right?"

She was honestly glad that Levi had followed her. "She's broken her arm."

The other *kinder* backed away, horrified. Ruth gave quick instructions for Mary Beth to take them back into school. They went without protest.

"She needs to see the *Englisch* doctor," Ruth said.

"Let me get your buggy."

"Mine?"

"I only have the wagon, and she can't ride on that with a broken arm. I'll take her to Dr. Westcott's office. Send a scholar to alert her parents. They'll want to meet me there."

Ruth nodded then helped Irma Rose to sit, taking care not to jostle her arm, which hung at an odd angle. The girl became hysterical when she saw that, so Ruth slipped off her shawl and put it over the girl's shoulders to hide her broken arm.

As soon as Levi returned with the buggy, Ruth helped Irma Rose to her feet. Levi lifted her carefully and maneuvered her through the narrow buggy door. Once the little girl was sitting, he walked back to Ruth.

His voice was low and intense as he said, "It wonders me, Ruth, that you have so little faith in me. Did you ever ask yourself if there might be a *gut* reason why I didn't say anything else to your *daed*? He was so outraged about the complaint that he wouldn't have heeded a word I said. And to what purpose would it have been to argue with him when the complaint is petty?"

"I-I-I d-d-didn't know." She stuttered almost as badly as David did.

"Well, now you do." He stamped back to the buggy, climbed in, and drove away. She watched them go, then went into the school. She had never felt so lost.

Seventeen

❧

"A re you ready for my surprise?" Hannah asked as she adjusted her bonnet over her *kapp*. She stood beside Esther at the back of the line of women waiting to enter the Beilers' house for the Sunday service.

"Are *you* ready for mine?" Esther put her hand over her mouth so her giggle didn't escape. It wouldn't be polite to laugh now. All their thoughts were supposed to be focused on surrendering one's will to God and being ready to sing His praises. Usually Esther's were, but not today.

Tonight's singing couldn't come soon enough. She had seen Caleb when she arrived at the Beilers' farm with her family. When she waved shyly in his direction, he'd given her only the faintest nod before turning back to talk with his friends. It was all right, though, because tonight, when the singing was over, she was going to ride home in his buggy while Red Miller gave Hannah a ride.

As if she had called his name, Red looked over to where she and Hannah stood. He gave them a smile, and that strange quiver ripped through her middle. Red was her surprise for Hannah, so why was his smile having that odd effect on her? Maybe it was just the excitement of the day.

"I don't think I'm going to wait for other people to sit down tonight," Esther said.

Hannah stared at her, aghast. "But the couples usually sit first."

"I'm sixteen now, so it's time I was part of a couple."

"But I—" Hannah stopped and smiled. "You know, now that I think about it, that's a brilliant idea. We can sit, and then we can tell the surprises we have for each other."

Esther started to reply, but halted when Ruth walked back to where they stood. As a *maedel*, she had to sit with the younger girls.

"Have you seen the Knepps?" Ruth asked. "I want to tell them how sorry I am that Irma Rose broke her arm."

"I haven't seen them," Hannah said.

"Me, neither." Esther lightly touched Ruth's arm. "If I'd been there, this might not have happened."

Ruth shook her head. "Don't even think about blaming yourself."

"How did it happen?" Hannah asked.

Esther listened while Ruth shared the few facts she had. The scholars vowed they didn't know how Irma Rose broke her arm. Every *kind* seemed to have been busy somewhere else, either playing ball or swinging or playing tag. Not even Mary Beth, who had gone outside to try to bring them back inside, knew what had happened. She'd been tending to one of the second graders who had scraped her hand. Ruth had punished the scholars by taking away their recesses for last week and the coming one.

A family buggy pulled in late, and Esther saw Ruth whirl to see who had arrived. It wasn't the Knepps. The Millers and Barbara and Mary Beth Umble stepped out. Sela Miller held Abby's hand, but the little girl pulled away and ran over to hug Esther.

Sela and Mary Beth hurried over.

"Abby, you're supposed to stay with me," Sela said.

"Abby wants to stay with Esther," the little girl protested.

Ruth saw her cousin's happy smile. Esther had been in a joyful mood since the mud sale, but today her smile was even brighter than usual. While Sela tried to convince Abby to come with her, Ruth looked at Mary Beth. She had been absent from school the past few days, and Ruth suspected that it was because Irma Rose's fall had upset her.

"How are you doing?" she asked.

"Better," Mary Beth said.

"I'm glad to hear that. I've missed having you at school, and I know the other scholars have missed you, too." She put her hand on Mary Beth's shoulder but spoke to Barbara. "Mary Beth is a *wunderbaar* assistant. Your daughter will make an excellent teacher someday."

"You think so?" Mary Beth's eyes glowed.

"I do. You were calm during the crisis. That's the mark of an excellent teacher."

Barbara smiled and put her arm around her daughter's

thin shoulders. Beside her, Abby tugged on Sela's dress. "Not now, Abby. *Danki*, Teacher Ruth, for your kind words."

"Mamm," Abby said.

"Just a minute, Abby," she said with quiet patience. As the little girl rocked back and forth on her feet, obviously eager for her *mamm*'s attention, Sela stroked her younger daughter's hair. "Abby has missed coming to school, too, but I didn't want her going without her cousin. I know that Mary Beth always looks out for her and Gabe."

Ruth bent toward Abby. "I'll see you tomorrow then."

"Now?" asked Abby.

Sela nodded as the women lined up to enter the house for the service. "Go ahead, Abby. Then we must be quiet as little mice while Bishop John and the preachers talk."

"Irma Rose went outside," Abby said with a big grin. "Mary Beth said no. Irma Rose say *ja*. Mary Beth say no. Irma Rose say *ja*. Mary Beth say no. Irma Rose say *ja*."

With an indulgent smile, Ruth put her arm around Mary Beth and gave her a hug. "Mary Beth did her best, didn't she?"

Abby nodded enthusiastically. "Irma Rose fell boom."

"Ja," Sela said as the line of women began to move toward the open door, "and we need to pray that she'll get better again soon."

"So Irma Rose can walk on the fence again?"

Ruth halted, and everyone stared at her. She looked at Abby. "Did you see Irma Rose on the fence?"

"Ja. On the fence, and then boom she fell down."

"I didn't know that." Ruth chose her words carefully. "I've warned the *kinder* not to try to walk on it, and I thought they understood how dangerous it was." She was shocked that the girl had disobeyed her so blatantly. "I'll have to have another talk with the scholars."

"*Kinder* sometimes need a lot of warnings before they see the wisdom of doing as they're told," Sela said, patting Ruth's arm and smiling. "They take risks far too often, but taking those risks are part of growing up."

Ruth nodded, but she was disturbed by Irma Rose's disobedience. She thanked Abby for telling her what had happened and took the little girl's hand as they continued into the house.

Fannie Beiler rushed from the kitchen to join the other women, and asked if anyone had heard who bought Old Wayne's farm.

"Has it been sold?" asked Sela. "I thought the bids were too low at the auction so it wasn't sold."

"Someone bought it afterward," Fannie said.

"Who?" The question came from someone standing behind Ruth.

"That's what I was hoping one of you would know." Fannie raised her work-worn hands and shrugged. "I guess we'll find out soon enough. I hope it's not an *Englischer*. After one of them bought that farm out on Little Bridge Road, he built dozens of houses for other *Englischers*. Such a shame to lose *gut* farmland."

Questions buzzed around Ruth, who was relieved that Fannie had changed the subject with her tidbit of gossip. Nobody asked about Irma Rose again as quiet was called while the women filed into the house and took their places on the backless benches facing the men.

Even though she kept her eyes lowered as the service

began, the only time Ruth had looked up, her gaze was snagged by Levi's. She saw the hurt that she had caused when she accused him of not standing up for her with her *daed*. Her heart ached, but she couldn't take back words she'd already said.

She lowered her eyes and opened her *Ausbund* as the first hymn was announced. *You always follow your heart and leap before you look. Maybe once in a while you should look?* Her *mamm*'s advice was sound, but Ruth hadn't heeded it. She hadn't given Levi a minute to explain his reason. And because of that, she had deeply hurt Levi, the man she loved. *Loved!* It was ludicrous that she could admit that now after she had ruined any chance to win a place in his heart.

Where was Ruth? Esther looked around the Beilers' barn as the singing came to an end. How could Ruth disappear *now*? She was getting too much like Levi, going off by herself and never around when someone needed her.

Esther murmured a quick prayer of forgiveness. Ruth was a *gut* friend to her, almost as dear as Hannah. She always listened to Esther's questions and tried to answer them. And she never made Esther feel stupid or immature. Esther should be grateful instead of complaining.

But she needed to speak to Ruth. There wasn't anyone else she could talk to now.

She almost cheered when she saw Ruth sitting in the far corner of the barn, where she could keep an eye on all the teens. During each break, Ruth had stood by the door with some of the other chaperones. As far as Esther knew, none of the singers had slipped past them to go outside to kiss in the dark.

Esther hurried over and dropped into the empty chair beside her. "Ruth, I need some advice."

"About what?"

She quickly told her cousin how she had arranged for Hannah to spend time with Red Miller tonight. "Did I do the right thing? What if Hannah is angry with me?"

"Why don't you ask her yourself? She's coming over here."

Esther jumped to her feet. Her hands suddenly felt clammy as Hannah rushed toward her. Esther glanced over her shoulder. Ruth was no longer sitting in the chair, but had gone to the treats table to start stacking the dirty dishes. Esther opened her mouth to call her cousin to come back, but before she could speak, Hannah said, "Esther, I think it's time for my surprise for you."

"All right."

"Then you can give me my surprise." Hannah's eyes twinkled.

Rubbing her sweaty hands on her apron, Esther said, "I know what your surprise is."

"You do?" Hannah's face fell.

"It's all right." Esther grabbed her friend's hand. "I think it's wonderful that Matthew Stutzman asked your sister to marry him."

"Do you think *that's* my surprise for you?" Hannah's laugh was so loud that heads turned all around the barn. "Nobody will be surprised when that happens because everyone has been expecting they will marry before Christmas. But it hasn't happened yet."

"So that's not your surprise for me?"

Hannah shook her head, her *kapp* strings bouncing on her shoulders. "I've had this planned since before the mud sale, but I'm glad the surprise is here tonight." She looked down at her shoes. "Especially after what Caleb did tonight."

"Caleb? What did he do?"

Hannah rolled her eyes. "You didn't see him try to sneak past Mose during the first break? I thought everyone saw."

"I was . . ." Esther blushed, not wanting to reveal that she'd been busy talking with Red, setting up what would be a surprise for both Hannah and him.

"You should have seen Mose holding Caleb up by the back of his suspenders, so high that Caleb was on tiptoe. Mose took him outside and told him not to come back until he learned some respect."

Esther was confused. "Respect for whom?"

"All of us," Hannah explained. "Haven't you heard? Caleb invites one girl to ride in his buggy then flirts with another and kisses a third. He doesn't care about anyone's feelings except his own. You know, now I feel pretty silly getting angry with you because of *him*."

Esther thought about how at her very first singing Caleb had sat across from her and then ignored her. How he'd invited her to ride home with him tonight and then never even sat across from her; she'd barely seen him all evening. And how Ruth had tried to warn her not to get all caught up in Caleb. Then she thought of something else, and gasped. "Oh no!"

"What?"

"I told Samuel that I had a ride home tonight." She felt embarrassed as she added, "With Caleb. What am I going to do now?"

"Can I help?" asked Red as he swept out his arm in a clumsy bow and almost struck Peter Hooley in the nose. "My buggy has room for two, and your *daed*'s farm is on my way home."

"Surprise!" Hannah clapped her hands in delight.

Esther was stunned. For a few seconds, she couldn't even speak, though she tried. Finally, she said, "But Red is my surprise for *you*, Hannah."

"What?" Hannah spun to face Red. "You didn't tell me that, Red!"

Red shot Peter a look, and the two boys grinned.

Hannah glanced at Esther who looked confused.

Finally, Peter said, "Red told me about you trying to match him with Hannah, Esther. He knew I was trying to get my courage up to ask Hannah to let me take her home."

"You were?" Hannah's voice softened. "Really?"

"*Ja*. Would you let me take you home?"

Hannah said, "*Ja*." Then her smile vanished. "But, Esther—"

"Will make me very happy," Red said, "if she'll let me take her home. Will you, Esther?"

How could she have ever thought she loved Caleb? He'd been nice to her years ago, true, but nothing he'd ever said or done sent such happiness through her as the way Red was looking at her now.

"*Ja*," she said. "I would like that."

Looping their arms together, the four of them went out

of the barn. Red kept them laughing with his jokes. Esther fired back some of her own. She gave Hannah a hug before her friend went with Peter to his buggy. Hannah's face glowed in the golden moonlight, showing how happy she was to be taken home by him.

"Aren't they cute together?" Esther asked.

"Cute?" Red helped her up into his buggy. "Hannah may be cute, but Peter? Nope!" He smiled. "And neither of them are as cute as you, Esther."

She looked back toward the barn and saw two girls flirting with Caleb. He must have sensed her gaze, because he looked back at her, over the girls' heads. When he saw Red getting in the buggy with Esther, Caleb's eyes widened in astonishment. Esther just laughed.

"You're really all right with this?" Red asked as he picked up the reins.

"I think," Esther replied, "that I'm happier than I've ever been."

"Me, too." He slapped the reins, and the horse began to follow Peter's buggy down the farm lane. Red began talking about getting everyone together for a volleyball game on the next church Sunday, and they laughed together as they picked out who should play on each side.

When she saw Ruth carrying plates to the Beilers' house, Esther waved. Her cousin had given her the perfect advice when she said that when Esther was with the right boy, she wouldn't have any trouble talking to him.

Eighteen

❧

Ruth watched Red Miller's buggy drive down the lane. Esther looked so excited to have a boy take her home. Red was a boy whom Sadie and Mervin would approve of, as long as neither Red nor Esther got too serious too fast. She was happy for her cousin.

She carried some of the dishes into the kitchen then went back for the rest. Fannie Beiler was washing the dishes almost as quickly as Ruth brought them. Her two younger daughters dried them and put the dishes away, so none of them would be delayed getting to bed after the long day. Her husband and his three brothers sat in the living room, where they could keep an eye on the young people as they hitched up buggies.

"Let us know if anyone is without a ride," Paul said

when Ruth brought another armload of plates into the house. "We'll make sure they get home."

"Danki." She remembered her own *daed* doing the same. She put the stack of plates on the table. "That's the last of them, Fannie."

"I appreciate your help." She turned from the sink and, with a wave, she said, "Go on now. I can't believe there isn't a fine, young man out there eager to take you home."

Ruth didn't want to spoil kindhearted Fannie's illusions, so she just said, *"Gut nacht."* Stepping onto the porch, she watched more courting buggies leaving in a parade down the straight farm lane.

She recognized Samuel's buggy at the lead, and she guessed he had Lizzie Hartzler with him. Ruth wouldn't be surprised to hear their wedding announcement published soon. Lizzie was a sweet girl, quiet and demure, the *dochder* Ruth's *daed* wanted.

"But he's stuck with me, so he'd better get used to it," she murmured as she walked down the steps and onto the dew-drenched grass.

She paused, astonished at her own words. She wondered what *Daed* would say if she repeated them within his earshot. She suspected *Mamm* might laugh. Homesickness swelled over her. Had it been a mistake to come to this district to teach? So much *gut* had happened, like making new friends and hearing David speak and seeing the joy on his parents' faces when she told them and getting their permission to continue to work with him. David never spoke to her unless Levi was there, but she prayed he would one day soon.

So much *gut*, but also things that were harder. Now Irma

Rose had a broken arm, and Ruth couldn't rid herself of the ache in her heart that brought her to her knees night after night as she prayed for God to help her understand why she had cast Levi's friendship away. She saw him each morning and afternoon when she left her buggy and horse at his barn, but only from a distance and only to exchange a *"Wie geht's?"* or a "Have a *gut nacht.*"

Except for glimpsing him on the other side of the room during the service, she hadn't seen Levi all day.

Maybe she had been as foolish to fall in love with Levi as Esther had been to have a crush on Caleb. It was a heart-wrenching thought.

One by one, the kerosene lamps in the barn were being extinguished. It was time for her to leave, too. None of the young men had shown any interest in taking her home tonight. Though the night was growing chilly, it wasn't a long walk to the Lambrights' farm, and the moonlight was so bright that she wouldn't need to bother the Beilers to borrow a flashlight.

She started down the farm lane, edging to the side each time a buggy approached. When she reached the end of the lane, she faltered. She'd forgotten that the Beilers' farm was on a main road. Cars whizzed by in both directions, their headlights blinding her before they sped past. Would they be able to see her in her dark dress? Maybe that flashlight wouldn't be such a bad idea, after all.

As she turned to go back up the lane, she heard the heavy *clip-clop* of hooves. "Need a ride home?" asked Levi as he stepped out of the darkness, leading his horse and an open buggy. He had changed from his black *mutza* coat and

245

trousers he'd worn to the morning service. Instead of his black felt hat, he wore his familiar straw one.

Her heart urged her to shout that she would love to ride with him. But how could she accept a ride when she had been so heartless in her accusations?

To cover her hesitation, she asked, "Where did you get that buggy?"

"It was in the small barn out behind the *dawdi-haus*. I'm not sure if my grandparents used it last or if my parents did. There was a lot of dust on it as well as enough acorn shells to show that some squirrels had claimed it as a *gut* winter home." He smiled. "It cleaned up nicely, didn't it?"

"*Ja.*" Sudden shyness overwhelmed her, and she understood what Levi must feel. Not that he'd been shy in her company for a while now, so why was *she* suddenly acting bashful? "I thought you left after the service."

"I did. I took the wagon home so I could get the buggy. I didn't think it would take so long to get it back here, but several of the animals needed my attention."

"Are they all right?"

"They are now, but the fox took a turn for the worse. His fever was climbing, and I had to make sure I got some liquids into him. Once his fever broke and he was asleep, I came back here because I haven't been able to forget what you told me at the mud sale." He leaned one arm on the open buggy. "You said you had a lot of things to sort out, and I do, too. I can't think of any *gut* reason why we can't sort them out together. Can you?"

"No." Joy soared through her, and she put her hand on his while she stepped up into the buggy.

Coming around the other side, he climbed in and picked up the reins. "You never gave me an answer, Ruth." He smiled. "Can I take you home?"

"*Ja.*"

He picked up a folded blanket and draped it over her knees and his. She appreciated his thoughtfulness, and she was glad for an excuse to sit closer to him so they could share the blanket.

He flipped the switch to activate the signal lights the state required for buggies. Then he slapped the reins on the horse, and the buggy bounced out onto the asphalt. When he turned in the opposite direction of the Lambrights' farm, she knew he was planning to take the long way there so they would have time alone.

Suddenly she was too aware of her quivering hands, her knee so close to his, and how any movement she made might give him the wrong message.

"Cold?" he asked as a car whipped around the buggy and vanished over the rise ahead of them.

"No."

"Was there a large crowd for the singing?"

"*Ja.*"

He laughed, startling her. "Are you trying to give me a taste of my own medicine?"

"What?" She looked at him for the first time since he'd climbed up beside her. The moonlight left his face in shadow, but she could re-create every inch in her mind as she had done so often in her dreams.

"You're giving me one-word answers."

Ruth let her stiff shoulders relax. "I'm sorry."

"*Ach*, a two-word answer." He held up two fingers as Samuel did when he was teasing Levi for being terse.

"I'm sorry, and not just about my short answers. I'm sorry for what I said in your barn last Monday. I never gave you a chance to explain."

"No, you didn't."

"I've been furious with *Daed* for judging me without listening to all the facts." She looked down at her hands. "That first night at the Lambrights', I was annoyed with you because I thought you were being judgmental."

"I noticed that." A hint of humor slipped into his voice. "Samuel did, too."

"Probably everyone did, but they were too polite to say so." She took a steadying breath. "But, Levi, I judged your conversation with my *daed* without knowing the whole truth. It's wrong for anyone to do that, but doubly wrong for me to do that because I know what it's like to be misjudged. I'm so sorry, Levi. I hope you can forgive me."

Levi flipped the turn signal again as he turned the buggy off the main road. She didn't recognize this road, but surely Levi knew every byway in the district. They passed farms where no lights showed and others lit brightly, marking them as *Englisch*.

"I already have." He shifted so he could look at her. "You probably think I should have told him what a *gut* job you were doing and how grateful the district is to have such a skilled teacher. Especially since all of that is true." Ruth's heart warmed at his praise. "But I have to be honest. Even if I'd known you were there, Ruth, I probably would have done and said exactly the same things, because I doubt many people have changed Zeb Schrock's mind for him."

"That's also true." A smile teased her lips. "I never have, but I keep hoping I can."

"Who knows? Maybe you will someday. As my *daed* said several times in his sermons, 'God works in mysterious ways, His wonders to perform.'"

"Your *daed* was a preacher?"

Levi held the reins lightly as the horse clip-clopped along the deserted road. "He was chosen before I began school, but I remember my *mamm*'s dismay. She knew his ministerial duties in addition to his work on the farm would be difficult for him. It was only years later that I discovered my *daed* had a lung weakness. I suspect it was asthma, but nobody ever confirmed that. It may have led to the heart attack that killed him when he was so young."

"I remember when my *daed* became the new deacon," she said. "*Mamm* was happy for him, because she knew he longed to give back to the community. Yet, I remember how pale her face got when he opened the Bible to reveal the card that meant he had been chosen. She knew their lives would never be the same. Or ours." She raised her gaze to the moon, which was changing from bright orange to ghostly white. "Sometimes, I wonder how different *Daed*'s expectations of his *kinder* would have been if he hadn't become the deacon. He takes his obligation to maintain exemplary behavior very seriously."

"And God gave him a daughter who would challenge him."

"*Ja*. It wonders me sometimes how God puts people in our lives who force us to face our greatest weaknesses. And He also gives us people who allow us to show our strengths."

Looping the reins around one hand, Levi put his other arm around her shoulders. He let the horse find its own way as he bent to whisper against her *kapp*, "Ruth, please listen to me. Really listen to me."

"I'm listening," she replied, though she knew it wouldn't be easy, because her heart was beating so loud and fast that she could barely hear his voice.

"I know you and your *daed* have butted heads, but you don't know that I used to do the same with my *daed*."

"You? Everyone says you were a *gut* boy."

"I was a boy just like any other boy before my *mamm* got sick and my folks died. Mischievous, sometimes naughty, always curious." He leaned his head against hers. She drew in the rich scents of soap and laundry detergent mixed with smells from the barn. It was a delicious and incomparable aroma that was uniquely his. "Let me tell you something else my *daed* used to say: 'Preachers' sons and deacons' daughters never do what they oughtta.' "

Ruth laughed softly. "I've never heard that."

"*Mammi* told me that it's a saying among the *Englischers*, but my *daed* repeated it whenever I got into trouble. Then he'd laugh, and say what else could he expect from a preacher's son?"

She put her hand on his. "I can't imagine you ever being naughty."

"I was. But when my grandparents gave me a home and all their love after my parents died, I was so grateful to them that I vowed never to give them a moment's grief." He smiled quickly. "Other than doctoring wounded animals I found."

"My *daed* would be so happy if I vowed to do the same, but I can't."

She looked up into his shadowed eyes. "When I told you that I overheard your conversation with *Daed*, you turned pale. Why?"

"Because I realized how hurt you were and that I was partly to blame."

"You did what you thought was best."

"Sometimes what we think is best isn't God's will. What we need to seek is what is best in His eyes."

Levi's words resonated within Ruth as she thought of her struggle to find her way to acceptance of how God wanted her to live her life, even if Levi wasn't a part of it.

"I hope you are right," she said.

"Do you want to know what is truly right?"

"What?"

He curved his hand around her nape. He brought his mouth down gently on hers. His lips were as warm and delicious as she had dreamed—even more so, because no dream could be as *wunderbaar* as his kiss. She wrapped her arms around his shoulders and melted into him.

When he lifted his lips from hers, she ran a single fingertip along his jaw, delighting in its strong, firm line.

"I've wanted to do that since the first moment I saw you," he whispered.

"You did not," she retorted, her voice as breathless as if she had run from the schoolhouse to the Lambrights' farm. "You barely talked to me that night."

He chuckled. "True, but that doesn't mean I wasn't thinking how pretty you are and wondering how it would be to kiss you."

Before she could reply, he captured her mouth again. She quivered as his hands moved along her back. She softened against him, sharing kisses as the horses pulled the buggy through the moonlight.

Nineteen

❧

A single lamp was lit in the Lambrights' house when Ruth hurried up the walk an hour later. As she turned toward the back door, she heard a laugh then Esther called out, "You don't think you're going to slip in that easily, do you?"

A tall form rose from one of the rocking chairs on the front porch. Samuel. "You may as well come and join us, cousin," he said. "Esther has been talking my ears off, and I'm sure she would love to start all over and tell you about her evening."

Ruth yearned to take her own memories of the evening and hold them close to her. But those memories of Levi's kisses and his invitation to go for another ride soon were hers to enjoy forever. Spending some quiet time with her cousins seemed like a special gift.

"Shall I bring out lemonade and some of those ginger molasses cookies we made yesterday?" she asked.

"Bring lots," Esther said with a giggle. "My brother hasn't said much, but I can tell he's got something to share, too."

"How could I say anything, pipsqueak?" Samuel retorted. "I haven't been able to slip a word in edgewise with my *blabbermaul* sister."

"I'm not a chatterbox," Esther protested.

"No, you're more like a parrot. Saying the same things over and over and getting even more excited about it each time." He pressed the heels of his palms to his forehead and gave a groan. "See if there's something in *Mamm*'s medicine cabinet for a man whose ears have been about talked off by his little sister."

"We could sew them back on for you," Esther offered.

Ruth left her cousins to their teasing and went into the kitchen. She lit the lamp over the table before going to the cupboard to take out a tray and three glasses. Her fingers paused on the last glass as she imagined having a kitchen of her own, with dishes of her own and a husband waiting on the porch for something cool to drink after a long day's work in the fields.

A husband of her own. How *wunderbaar* that sounded! In her mind, she saw a simple kitchen with the big, black, woodstove in the back corner. Levi's kitchen. The kitchen where she would cook his meals if he asked her to be his *fraa*.

But she mustn't get carried away. Levi and she had spoken of the past. Neither of them had said anything about the future. Maybe that was for the best now, because when she thought of spending her life with him, she remembered, with a pulse of sorrow, how he intended to give Graceless away. The puppy had touched his heart, and even that simple love made him shy away.

Ruth set the glass on the tray with the others and filled a plate with moist, fragrant cookies. Using her hip to open the door, she carried the tray around the house to the front porch.

Esther jumped up to take the plate and set it on the low, wood table. By the time Ruth had poured lemonade for them, Samuel was reaching for his third cookie.

"Save some for Ruth," his sister scolded.

"Just remember whoever eats the most has to wash the dishes when we're done." Ruth handed her cousins their glasses then sat in a rocking chair facing them, which gave her a wonderful view of the moon over the barn.

"You're in a happy mood," Samuel observed.

"No more than you and Esther." She turned to her younger cousin. "Tell me how you ended up riding home with Red Miller."

Her cousin's blush was so bright that it was visible in the dim light. "You know we aren't supposed to talk about those things."

Samuel snorted, and Ruth wondered how long he and his sister had been out here talking.

"That rule," Ruth said, trying to keep her voice serious,

"has more to do with seriously courting couples. You aren't seriously courting already, are you?" she asked in mock horror.

"Of course not! I'm only sixteen!" Esther's outrage lessened when both Ruth and Samuel burst out laughing. "*Ach,* now I've got both of you teasing me!"

Ruth took a sip of her lemonade and picked up a cookie. "So tell me, how did you end up riding with Red instead of Caleb?"

"Caleb?" Samuel halted his rocker. "Not Caleb Stutzman. I wouldn't want my little sister in his courting buggy. His reputation is that he kisses and tells. I thought you were smarter than getting involved with someone like him."

Esther took a deep breath to answer back, but Ruth said quietly, "Let's not ruin the evening with gossip."

Esther frowned at Samuel then explained how her surprise for Hannah, and Hannah's for her, had turned out. "I'm so happy how it worked out for me. I hope Hannah is, too." Esther took another bite of cookie. "Do you think I'm fickle, Ruth?" she asked. "I thought Caleb was the one for me since we were little, but once Red drove me home, all I've been able to think of is how much he makes me laugh with his silly stories about training horses."

Ruth patted her cousin's arm. "I think you're sixteen, and you should use your running-around time to find out more about what your heart truly wants."

"But you didn't."

"I did. I needed that time to know that I truly wanted to be baptized."

"But you did it without getting married."

Ruth leaned back in her rocker and stared up at the pattern of stars scattered across the night sky. "I used my *rumspringa* to learn more about myself and what I wanted for my life. For me, it wasn't a simple decision to be baptized, because, as you know, I sometimes have trouble with not bending the rules."

"No!" gasped Samuel with false horror.

"Ignore him," Esther said. "So tell me. What made you ask for baptism when you could have waited until you wanted to marry?"

"Because I realized that even though sometimes the rules have been a bit too constricting for me, I like living under the *Ordnung*. Among the *Englischers*, I wouldn't have rules to bend." She looked from one cousin to the other. "But the most important thing was that I wanted a closer relationship with God, so maybe He would guide me to answers about why I am the way I am. I wanted to discover that answer while I walked more closely with Him. That's what I learned during my *rumspringa*."

Esther groaned. "You make it sound so easy. I still have too many questions."

"We all do." Samuel grinned at his sister. "I have one right now. Are you going to eat that last cookie, or can I have it?"

His jesting shattered the serious mood. Ruth picked up the cookie and tossed it to him, and he caught it with a laugh.

"You're in a very *gut* mood, too, cousin," Ruth observed.

"It's been a *gut* day." He stretched past her and tugged on his sister's *kapp* strings. "Right, pipsqueak?"

257

"Don't you dare call me that when Red Miller is here!" Esther snapped.

"Hush!" Samuel warned. "Or are you *trying* to wake up everyone in the house?"

Ruth sat back and slowly rocked while Samuel and Esther continued their teasing. She missed her little sisters and how they joked with each other. The few letters they'd sent were full of the things they'd done, but it wasn't the same as sharing their lives each day.

"Did you hear that Old Wayne's farm has been sold?" Esther asked.

"I heard that before today's service, but nobody seems to know who bought the farm," Ruth answered.

"Gut." Samuel's grin reminded her of one of the barn cats after it had cornered a mouse.

Ruth waited for him to go on, but Esther didn't have that much patience. "What do you know, Samuel?" she demanded. "Is this what you've been grinning about all evening?"

"Well, let's see what I know. I know the farm has been sold."

"We know that. Tell us something we haven't heard."

"I know who bought it."

"Who?" His sister's voice squeaked so loudly that both Samuel and Ruth hushed her. More quietly, she repeated, "Who?"

"Me."

"You?"

Even in the dark, Ruth could see Samuel's broad grin, which told her all she needed to know.

"A little over a month ago, I decided to ask Lizzie Hartzler to be my *fraa*," Samuel confessed. "The deacon spoke to her parents last week, and her *daed* gave his permission for us to marry. I asked her the next day when we went riding down by the creek. We plan to publish in late October. She wants to have the first wedding of the wedding season in November."

"She deserves that," Esther said. "She's been so patient!"

Samuel looked at Ruth. His voice was suddenly serious as he said, "She knew I wanted to have a home for us before I asked her to marry, but it's difficult to find *gut* land in Lancaster County, especially in this district. I didn't want to travel west to get land, though a lot of my friends are considering that. I like our ways and my family and friends are here. So I kept praying that God would show me a way to have both. He answered my prayer when Old Wayne's farm was put up for auction. I spread the word quietly that someone in our community wanted to buy it but didn't want to buy it at the mud sale. That's created a lot of speculation about who's getting married and who will be living there."

"So that's why nobody but that *Englischer* bid on it at the auction," Ruth said.

"I feared he would offer more than the reserve Old Wayne put on it."

"And that's why you looked like you were sitting on pins and needles during the bidding."

"*Ja.* I don't know when another fine farm like Old Wayne's will be for sale. The last one was almost two years ago."

"Why didn't you just buy it ahead of time?" asked Esther.

"Then everyone would have known I intended to ask Lizzie to marry me before I could speak to the deacon and ask him to be my *Schteckliman*."

Ruth understood. Her *daed* had often, as a deacon, acted in the traditional role of intermediary between the groom and the bride's family. *Daed* always enjoyed it, because such a happy task was a nice change from raising money for the district's poor and sick or from reprimanding church members who violated one of the unwritten rules of their *Ordnung*.

"So who else knows?" Esther sat back in her chair, rocking as if she wanted to speed it down the road. "*Daed* and *Mamm*?"

"Yes."

"Anyone else?"

"Other than you two, only Levi knows. I asked him to be one of my *Newehockers*." He chuckled. "I guess that means that Lizzie can't ask you, Ruth."

Ruth felt her face redden. She knew that courting couples could not serve as *Newehockers*, the bride and groom's special attendants, at the same wedding.

Not looking at her cousin, because she wanted to keep tonight's lovely memories to herself, she said, "I'm sure I'll find plenty to do. Brides always need as many women as they can find to help in the kitchen."

"*Danki,* Ruth. I'll let Lizzie know you're willing to help." He stood and yawned widely. "I guess I don't have to ask *you* to keep this a secret." He smiled at his sister. "How about you, pipsqueak? Can you keep quiet about this until it's published?"

"*Ja*, but now you're going to owe me a big favor."

He grimaced. "I knew I was letting myself in for trouble by telling you." When Esther stood, he gave her a big hug. "But I'm also glad you know. Lizzie needs someone other than me to talk to about wedding plans."

"I'll be happy to do that!" Esther's smile almost glowed as she picked up the plate and set it on the tray. "I don't know if I'll be able to sleep tonight."

"Time to try."

When Esther hurried down the steps, Samuel looked at Ruth.

"I'll be in soon," Ruth said, still rocking.

He put his hand on her shoulder and squeezed gently. "I know I shouldn't say anything about you and Levi, but you have to know that I'm very happy for both of you."

She didn't reply. To admit that she and Levi were courting was something she must not do, even with her cousins. They weren't a young couple like Esther and Red Miller. The *Leit* would assume that she and Levi were serious.

But was that possible?

That question ricocheted through her mind as Samuel went in, closing the screen door behind him. She pulled her shawl more closely around her and wished Levi's arms were around her instead. In Levi's arms, she felt both safe and free. What she had talked to him about tonight, she had never spoken of to anyone, not even to God in her prayers. Then Levi had kissed her. As she rocked and gazed up at the stars, she wondered if she had ever been so happy.

Twenty

Ruth's happiness lasted less than a day. The next afternoon, Paul Beiler arrived at the school while Ruth was calling the *kinder* in from recess.

"Ruth, the school board members wish to meet with you at the schoolhouse after the scholars go home," he began. "They want to talk about Irma Rose's accident."

"I was expecting that," she replied, her voice far calmer than her emotions as despair sank like a rock in her stomach. Since the school board had hired her, Paul always called her "Teacher Ruth." Had the school board already made up their mind to send her home in disgrace?

"I'm glad you understand." He didn't meet her eyes. "When a single complaint has been made, we try to settle the matter quietly, but . . ."

She stiffened. She hadn't realized there was a complaint. She had assumed the school board simply wanted her to explain what had occurred.

Her voice was brittle as she said, "But this isn't the first complaint against my teaching, and a *kind* was hurt. This is far more serious than a disgruntled parent."

"*Ja.*"

"I've got some papers to grade after school, so whenever it's convenient, I'll be available to talk with the school board."

"Thank you, Ruth."

She kept from flinching until he turned to walk down the steps.

"Teacher Ruth," called one of the scholars, "are we supposed to do page 15 or 16 of our workbook?"

Ruth fixed a smile on her face, closed the door, and turned to face her beloved scholars. She doubted she'd ever again hear "Teacher Ruth" once the meeting with the school board was over, so she was going to enjoy it as long as she could.

"Put your workbooks away," she announced as she walked briskly to her desk. "You've worked hard today, so what do you think about having a spelling bee?"

The scholars cheered as they shoved their books into their desks. She pretended not to see how careless they were. What did it matter if their desks were as neat as she requested or not?

Shaking those dreary thoughts from her head, Ruth sent several of the *kinder* back to their desks to make sure their books weren't bent or torn. She was still their teacher. Until she was fired, she would act as she always had.

She waited until the scholars had lined up and selected a boy and a girl, to be team captains. They picked their teams, and she opened her book where she kept the lists of spelling words. "Nelson, spell authority."

As his teammates waited, holding their breaths, to see if he could spell it correctly, Ruth thanked God that He had given her time with these *kinder*. And the chance to know Levi. Just the thought of his name lifted her spirits. Surely he would speak up on her behalf at the school board meeting. She wouldn't be alone with both God and Levi on her side.

Darkness was falling, and Ruth paced the schoolroom. She had finished grading the papers. In spite of her resolve not to pay any attention to the state of the scholars' desks, she had checked them, making note of which ones needed to be tidier. She had written out the next day's lessons on the blackboard. She had refilled all the kerosene lamps and re-arranged the few reading books that had been donated after the storm. She'd mopped the floor and dusted the window-sills.

Now all she had left to do was pace from her desk to the front windows to look out and wait for the school board to arrive.

Paul had said they would speak with her after school today, hadn't he? Was it possible that she had misunderstood him because she'd been upset?

No, she was certain that he said the school board would meet with her after school today.

But where were they? The scholars had headed home more than two hours ago. Some of them might be eating their evening meal by now, while others would be finishing up chores.

She couldn't leave until she was certain that the men weren't coming today. She had looked across the road before it got dark. Levi's buggy hadn't been in his yard. Maybe the school board had decided to meet first without her before they came to fire her.

No! Levi wouldn't let her—or anyone else—be fired without a fair hearing. She had hoped he would arrive before the other members of the school board, but that hope had faded as the minutes slipped by.

Wrapping her arms around herself, she leaned back against the wall and stared at her classroom. She couldn't think only of herself. One of the worst parts of all of this was that, if the decision of the school board went against her, Levi was compelled to be one of the people who fired her. She knew that would break his heart as much as hers, because he knew how much she loved teaching and how hard she had worked to be a *gut* teacher.

That thought brought new tears to her eyes. She hastily wiped them away when she heard footsteps on the porch.

Be with me, God. If it's Your will that I remain here as the teacher, put the right words in my mouth. If it's Your will that I don't stay here as the teacher, please put compassion and forgiveness in the hearts of the school board members.

The door opened, and she walked forward to greet the board members.

"We're sorry to keep you waiting, Ruth," Paul said as he took off his straw hat and put it on a peg. This time, she couldn't hide her despair at how he addressed her, and sympathy filled his compassionate eyes.

"It's no problem. I'm always available for the school board."

Three men—Joseph, Simon, and Micah—followed Paul into the school. She stepped aside as they entered her schoolhouse.

None of them looked in her direction. From the expressions on their taut faces, she guessed it wouldn't be *her* schoolhouse much longer.

Where was Levi? She looked across the road again and saw that his house was dark. If he wasn't home and he wasn't with the school board, where was he?

Paul walked to the replacement desk from Old Wayne's auction. The other men gathered on either side of him. None of them smiled as they faced her while she walked to the front of the room. She wasn't in a hurry to hear her punishment announced, but she wondered how much longer she could endure the suspense of not knowing.

Leaning his hands on the desk, Paul said, "Again I want to apologize for keeping you waiting so long." He glanced at the other school board members. "We'd planned to have a short meeting to discuss this matter before we sat down with you. One of our members wasn't there, however, so we decided to wait for him. When he sent a message to come here without him, we hurried over so you wouldn't have to keep waiting here."

Ruth started to wrap her arms protectively around herself as she had earlier, then stopped. She must remain professional, even if it was obvious that the school board had already decided to send her home in disgrace. But that didn't explain why Levi was nowhere in sight. He hadn't even bothered to attend the first meeting with just the board members. But surely, he could have found a way to be here now to help her explain what had happened. There must be some way they could tell the truth and still not break their promise to David.

How could he leave me here like this? she wondered. *How could he not be here to help me?*

She couldn't imagine a more bitter betrayal, and the pain of it almost took her breath away. She tried to remind herself that she didn't have all the facts. She had judged him unfairly once before. She didn't want to do so again; but why wasn't he here?

Paul sat at her desk and gestured for her to sit, too. She shook her head, preferring to stand rather than to look silly with her knees up high in front of her at one of the small desks.

He glanced at the other men, but they stared straight ahead. Not at Ruth, but at the windows behind her. She wondered if they wished she would disappear so this would be over.

Clearing his throat, Paul said, "The school board has received a complaint about you, Ruth."

"A second one," Micah interjected.

Paul frowned at Micah. "The first one has been dealt with and dismissed. This complaint is far more serious.

Thaddeus and Laureen Knepp have questioned your wisdom in leaving the scholars under the eye of a girl who is only in eighth grade herself. We know you were concerned that David Zook hadn't come to school that day, but when you left, you already knew that David was safe. We need to know why you made the decision to leave the scholars here by themselves?"

It would be simple to explain the truth if she hadn't promised David not to reveal to anyone but his parents that he could talk. Without that one fact, anything she said would sound ridiculous. But she had to try. She couldn't just give up. The way Levi seemed to have given up on her.

She could tell them that Levi, a board member, had asked her to come with him, and so she had had to go. But even in her own mind that sounded like a cowardly excuse. She couldn't blame Levi for what had happened.

Trying not to let the sob in her throat escape, Ruth said, "David had been missing for more than two hours. I needed to see for myself that he was all right. The *kinder* were about to go outside for recess, but I told them to remain inside until I returned."

"They didn't, and Irma Rose broke her arm," Micah pointed out.

"Yes, and I feel terrible about that."

"You haven't mentioned," Simon said quietly, "that you told the *kinder* not to try to walk on the fence. You told them that it was too dangerous and someone could get hurt."

"I did tell them. Many times." Was he offering her a way to keep her job? Even if he was, she didn't want to remain as their teacher on some sort of—what did the *Englischers* call it?—loophole. "But I should have kept a closer eye on the *kinder* to make sure that my warnings were heeded."

Simon sighed, but nodded. She appreciated his attempt to help her, and she would tell him so once this meeting was finished. It shouldn't take much longer.

Micah opened his mouth again, and she hurried to speak before he did. If she heard more of his mean-spirited remarks, she might lose the courage to say what she must. "I care deeply about my . . . about the scholars." She corrected herself when Micah's frown grew even more forbidding. "I love teaching, and you've said I've done a *gut* job."

"Otherwise," Micah said coldly.

"*Ja, ja,*" she hurried to agree. "Other than a lapse in judgment, which ended with Irma Rose Knepp breaking her arm."

"Because you left to check on a *kind* you knew was all right."

"*Ja.*" She clasped her hands more tightly. *Lord, help me find a way to make the school board understand and still let me keep my promise to David unbroken. A vow is more important than my job or even my foolish belief that Levi might love me as I love him.*

Micah asked impatiently, "How much longer is this going to take, Paul? I need to be home to make sure my *kinder* finish their barn chores."

"We want to be fair."

"We've been more than fair! Tell her what we've decided."

Ruth's stomach twisted as she realized that she had been

270

right all along. The school board had met to make their decision before coming to speak with her.

"May I make a suggestion before you announce your decision?" she asked.

"*Ja*," Paul said. Everyone but Micah nodded. Then, with a glance at the other men, he did, too.

"I'm going to assume your decision is to ask me to leave." She felt sorry for the men, who looked so uncomfortable. They hadn't asked for this when they volunteered to serve on the school board. Because she couldn't tell them the truth, she was making the situation more difficult for them. Maybe there was something she could do to make it easier. "As we all know, the scholars are already behind on their school year because they didn't start on time. Without a teacher, they'll fall even further behind, and they won't have completed their minimum number of school days before the planting season begins."

"My niece could take over," Micah said.

"We discussed that already." Paul's voice grew hard, and Micah quieted, grumbling.

"My brother's *fraa* used to teach," Joseph began.

"Your *brother's fraa* is going to have their *boppli* any day now," Paul said.

"There must be someone else," Micah insisted.

"I'm sure there's someone else you can find," Ruth said, "but while you're looking for that person, why not allow me to continue here?"

"That makes sense." Paul smiled for the first time.

"If we want more lapses in judgment," grumbled Micah.

"This is something we should discuss in private," Paul

said. He looked toward Ruth. "If you don't mind stepping outside . . ."

"Of course." She went out the side door.

Before she closed it behind her, she heard Micah begin to press his case to have her fired immediately, no matter what effect it would have on the scholars and their parents. She looked up at a single star gleaming through the dusk.

From her memory came her *daed*'s voice, reading from Psalm 27:

The Lord is my light and my salvation; whom shall I fear? The Lord is the strength of my life; of whom shall I be afraid?

That lone star wasn't afraid of shining in the dark as a reflection of God's light. She must be as unflinching and hold on to the light of knowing that whatever happened was God's will. How many times had someone talked to her about God's will? How many times had she said those words herself? But now, for the first time, she understood what those words truly meant. Even in her darkest hour, God was walking beside her on the path that He had created especially for her.

The door opened beside her, and Simon looked out. "You may *komm* in, Ruth."

There was only a slight quaver in her voice as she said, "You made the decision quickly."

"Ja." He couldn't hide the sadness in his voice, and she knew that they had decided not to accept her offer.

Even though she wasn't surprised, having the moment finally arrive was horrible. She prayed her deepening faith could withstand the trials ahead of her. Not only with the school board but with her family and her friends . . . and Levi.

Pain pierced her. Once she was fired, *Daed* would insist that she return home. More than fifteen miles from where Levi lived. Would she ever see him again? She might, at a mud sale or some event that involved both of their districts. But it wouldn't be the same. Their first buggy ride might have also been their last.

Help me understand, Lord, why he isn't here with me, she prayed as she went into the schoolroom and back to the spot where she had stood before. She saw the regret on Paul's face and on Joseph's as well. She couldn't help wondering what Micah had said to convince them to turn down her offer.

Not that it mattered any longer.

"Ruth," Paul began, "I'm sorry to—" He looked past her as the front door opened.

"About time you got here, Levi," Simon said.

Levi?

Ruth spun to see Levi holding the door for David Zook and his parents. Timothy and Susan Zook waited at the back of the room while Levi and David walked hand in hand toward the front.

"I'm sorry I'm late," Levi said in the same calm voice he used to comfort the *kinder* during the storm. "As I was getting ready to come to this meeting, the Zooks arrived at my door. Their son wanted to speak with me."

"Speak?" Paul's brows rose in surprise as Micah's face turned white above his full beard. "But David never speaks."

"That's no longer true." Levi smiled down at the towheaded boy, then raised his eyes to the other men. "That you don't know the truth means Ruth kept her promise to David, even though it will cost her the teaching job she loves. David asked us not to tell anyone except his parents. I would have kept my promise to the boy, too, if David hadn't released me from it."

"Are you saying the boy has talked to you? Both of you?" Hope brightened Joseph's face. "Can you really talk, David?"

"Before he answers that, Joseph," Levi said, "let me explain that David told me he wanted to come and address the school board. It's because he doesn't want his beloved teacher to pay the price she will if he keeps the silence that hides his painful secret."

"What's his secret?" Paul asked.

"It's better if David tells you himself."

"T-T-Teacher R-R . . . Teacher Ruth." He smiled at her then continued in his uneven speech. "L-l-let h-her s-s-stay. She helps me t-t-talk. She b-b-believes in me. She b-b-believes I can t-t-talk *g-g-gut*. She is a *g-g-gut* teacher. *I-I-Ich l-l-liebe d-dich*."

Ruth drew the little boy into her arms and hugged him. No matter what happened now, she thanked God that He had brought this little boy into her life.

For a long moment, nobody spoke. Sobs came from the back of the room, and Ruth looked over David's head to see Susan weeping openly. Beside her, Timothy dabbed a handkerchief at his eyes as he nodded to Ruth. No other words were necessary. Even though she had told them about their son's progress, this must be the first time they had heard him speak.

A throat was cleared at the front of the room, and Ruth turned her attention back to the school board. Levi had gone to stand with them, and Paul was lowering himself into the chair behind the teacher's desk. Neither he nor Joseph looked in her direction. Simon fumbled in his pocket and pulled out a handkerchief and blew his nose. Beside him, for the first time, Micah wasn't frowning. He'd lowered his face into his hands, and his shoulders shook.

Ruth said nothing as David sat at a desk in the front row. She gasped when he called a greeting to his *Onkel* Micah, who embraced the boy. Micah and Susan Zook must be brother and sister.

"I never thought . . ." Micah began, then said, "You've brought a miracle into our lives, Teacher Ruth."

"Only God can make a miracle," said a smiling Joseph, but Ruth could only marvel that Micah had called her Teacher Ruth.

"*Ja*, Joseph." Micah was smiling now, too. "But, when He cannot be with us to make that miracle happen, He sometimes sends someone else to do His work." Micah hugged David again. "Someone like you, Teacher Ruth."

Tears clogged her throat as the proud man broke down. She looked past him to Levi. The distance between them vanished as their gazes connected. How she wanted to ask his forgiveness for doubting him! He hadn't left her to defend herself after all.

With difficulty, because she had to keep blinking back

the happy tears that gave a jeweled gleam to everything, she answered the school board's questions about the day Irma Rose broke her arm. Now she could explain why she'd gone to the barn and what had happened there.

"What she is telling you is true," Levi said when she had finished. "I told her to come with me. It was very important that she see that David was speaking."

"I agree," Micah said softly.

The school board asked for time to deliberate, asking Ruth and David to go to where his parents stood. Both the Zooks hugged their son and then her as they thanked her over and over.

"David's the one who has done all the hard work," she told them.

"But you didn't give up on him, as other teachers have," Susan said.

"And like we had." Timothy bent so his eyes were level with his son's. "David, I'm sorry I didn't believe right from the start that Teacher Ruth could help you."

"That's o-o-okay, *D-d-daed.*"

At the name he must have longed to hear for years, tears rolled down Timothy's face. He pulled David to him and praised God for helping his son. Susan dropped to her knees and put her arms around both of them. She openly sobbed when David called her *Mamm.*

A finger tapped Ruth's arm, and she turned. Paul motioned for her to follow him toward the teacher's desk. She wasn't the only one who looked back at the Zooks, and she heard Paul sniff. They were all moved by what had happened here tonight.

As soon as Paul sat behind her desk, he said, "I'll make this quick. We agree that we should give you two weeks' probation. If, during that time, there are no further complaints against you . . ." He glanced at Micah and corrected himself. "If there are no legitimate complaints against you, this matter will be forgiven and forgotten. Is that understood, Teacher Ruth?"

"Ja." She hadn't guessed she could put so much happiness into that small word. Then she looked at Levi's smile, and she knew she would never have guessed she could squeeze so much happiness inside herself.

Twenty-One

❧

As soon as she returned to the Lambrights' house and explained the school board meeting and their decision, Ruth was congratulated by the whole family, even the younger *kinder* who really didn't understand what was going on. She offered to help Sadie with supper, but Sadie shooed her out of the kitchen and told her to rest.

"You must be exhausted after such a day," Sadie said. "Go upstairs. I'll send someone for you when supper is ready."

Ruth nodded, glad for the excuse to escape the cheerful chaos of the Lambrights' kitchen. A headache had followed her home from the schoolhouse, and every bone in her body ached as if she had spent hours working in the garden. She went up to the room she shared with Esther. Without lighting the lamp, she stretched out on her bed.

A tentative rap came on the doorjamb.

Ruth pushed herself up to her elbows as Esther and Hannah came into the room. "Why are you knocking?"

"We didn't want to disturb you," Hannah said, sitting on Esther's bed.

"Ruth," her cousin began, "Hannah and I need to thank you."

"For what?" Her brain was too exhausted for guessing games.

"For helping us see what life is really all about," Esther replied. "If you hadn't come to stay with us, Hannah and I might have thought the only important thing in life was Caleb Stutzman."

Hannah's nose wrinkled. "Like it says in the Book of John, 'One thing I know, that, whereas I was blind, now I see.' You opened our eyes, Ruth. We can make good choices—whether it's choosing boys who don't flirt with all the other girls, or whether it's having a job, like teaching or working in a shop, before we settle down and marry."

"We didn't even think about that before you showed us it's possible," Esther hurried to add.

Ruth gave a little laugh. She wasn't sure what the girls' parents would think if they heard them now. Maybe Sadie and Mervin would be happier about Esther being a teacher than her own *daed* had been. Hannah's *daed* was on the school board, so he probably would be pleased.

"And," Esther went on, "your advice about boys is so *gut*. It's silly for us, when we're only sixteen, to tie ourselves down."

"Or into knots over a boy," Hannah added. "We should

take advantage of our *rumspringa* to enjoy all the boys' company. There will come the time when we'll pick our special ones."

Esther giggled. "Or he'll pick us, like Levi has you because he loves you so much. Anyone can see that!"

Ruth let them chatter on, not wanting to disillusion them. She loved Levi, but she wasn't sure he loved her the same way. Even if he did, would he take the risk of opening his life to her? He might deny his love because he could not face another loss. It was a decision only he could make. Only he and God. This was one time when she must wait with patience and accept God's will without question.

School had ended for the day, and Ruth stood in the empty classroom, writing the next day's lessons on the blackboard.

All during the past week, as she had waited for the school board to act on Irma Rose's accident, the scholars were on their best behavior. Each of them, including David, answered promptly when she called roll. When she told them to pull out their books or cautioned them to be quiet, they obeyed instantly. It eased her heart's grief because she knew that they were doing their best to make sure she didn't lose her job. Several *kinder* had spoken with her privately to ask what they could do to make sure the school board didn't fire her. It was so sweet, and she appreciated their wanting to help. She hadn't realized that they'd come to love her as she loved them.

The door crashed open, and Ruth whirled as Esther ran in, calling, "Ruth, Ruth!"

"What is it, Esther?"

The girl put her hands on her thighs and leaned forward as she struggled to catch her breath. "Ruth, your *daed* called the phone in the barn. Your *mamm* is in labor, and he wants you to come home NOW!"

"Is she having trouble?" Ruth asked, fearing the worst.

"I only know what Samuel told me. He took the call. He said that your *daed* said it was an emergency."

"*Ach*, no!" Ruth knew it was too soon for the *boppli* to be born. Her mother must be having complications. "Esther, I don't know how long I'll be gone. Can you and Hannah take over for me tomorrow and possibly a few days more?"

"*Ja. Mamm* told me to do whatever you needed. And I'm sure Hannah will help, too."

"You know the schedule. The lessons are on the board, and my book with the work for the coming week is on my desk."

Ruth paused only long enough to grab her bag, her shawl, and pull on her bonnet. She tied it under her chin as she rushed out the door. Her fingers fumbled on her bonnet strings as she hurried toward Levi's barn. She ran into the pasture to get Jess. The horse came docilely and waited by the buggy, but Ruth's fingers fumbled on the reins.

"Ruth!" called Levi as he came up from the lower level. "I thought I heard someone up here."

"Levi, please let the school board know that I got a call from *Daed*. There's an emergency at home. I've got to go." She continued to try to hitch Jess to the buggy.

Levi put his hand on hers, stopping her. "What emergency?"

"*Mamm* is in labor and it's too soon!" The words exploded from her.

He drew her back from the buggy. "Wait here."

But Ruth couldn't wait. She darted back to Jess's side and reached for the horse's reins. "Levi, I've got to go now!"

"I know." He grasped her shoulders and spun her to face him. "I'm going to call Esau. He's the best Mennonite driver. If he's available, he'll get you home far faster than a buggy will. If he's busy, he'll give me the name and number of another driver who can take us."

"Us?" she asked.

He didn't answer as he raced down the stairs. Moments later, she heard him talking on the phone. There was a pause, and then he began speaking again. She wondered if he was calling a different driver. That conversation was short, and he hurried back to her.

"Esau is on his way. I asked him to hurry." He reached to unhook the one buckle she had managed to close. Leading Jess out of the barn, he walked the horse down the hill. He put her in the pasture before he came back to where Ruth stood on the driveway in front of his house.

"How long will it take for him to get here?" she asked.

"Not long. Maybe five minutes. He doesn't live far from here. I know you're anxious."

"I am." She paused, then added, "You said, 'Us.' You don't need to go home with me. In fact, it'd be *gut* for you to be here in case Esther and Hannah need help."

"Ruth, the *kinder* will do as the girls tell them, because they want to keep you as their teacher. You don't have to feel guilty about leaving them. You've got enough guilt weighing you down as it is."

"True." She couldn't stand still. She walked over to the porch, peered down the farm lane, then went back to the barn. "I can't help thinking that if I'd only stayed with her—"

"But you came here."

"I wish I could be in two places. Here with my scholars and home with my *mamm*."

"That's impossible." A hint of a smile eased his mouth. "Even for you, Ruth."

"I know, but . . ." Her voice trailed off as he stopped her pacing by taking her hands and folding them between his. She hadn't realized how her fingers were shaking until his strong hands held them.

"You know what your biggest fault is, Ruth Schrock?" he asked.

She yanked her hands away, hurt anew that just when she dared to open herself to him again, he said something like that. She started for the porch again. "The driver must be coming any minute now. This isn't the time for such silliness."

"No?" He followed her to the porch and stepped in front of her when she would have paced back toward the barn. "You are impatient."

"Really? It's taken you this long to find that out?"

He put his finger under her chin and tilted her head back gently. His green-brown eyes darkened with strong emotion. "No," he said in barely more than a whisper. "I noticed that from the moment I first saw you, but since then, I've learned that what makes you impatient is that you want so badly to be able to help others."

"You're wrong. I'm impatient about everything. That's why I came here. Because I prayed for an adventure, and when one was offered, I took it. I didn't wait and consider if it was the right thing."

"*Ja*, and that has been God's gift to all of us." He kissed her, a quick, deep kiss.

"It has?" she whispered when he raised his mouth from hers.

"*Ja.*" He leaned his forehead against hers. "You are impatient about everything, and you are impatient for everyone. You can't wait to set things right. You want to help all of us so much that you sometimes forget that our lives must unfold on God's time, that it is only He who sets things right."

"I know." She lowered her eyes. "I can't argue with any of that."

Levi shook his head. "No, please, I'm not trying to reproach or correct you. I think you are"—he hesitated—"extraordinary. It's only because *you* wouldn't give up on David that he can talk now, that he has a chance at a normal life. God gave you a warm heart, which allows you to touch so many other hearts and change them." He took her hand and pressed it to the center of his chest. "Even mine."

Ruth's breath caught in her throat, and again she found herself blinking back tears. "You helped David as much as I did. If it weren't for you and the animals—"

"Hush." Levi bent his head to kiss her again, his hand slipping around her waist to draw her closer.

A car horn beeped, and Ruth reluctantly stepped back and tore her gaze from Levi's. A large black car turned onto the farm lane. The sight brought her fears slamming back into her. She quickly prayed that she would get home in time to help her *mamm*.

When Levi held out her shawl, she took it. She hadn't even noticed it slipping from her shoulders when he kissed her.

"Danki." She pulled her shawl around her. "And, *danki*, Levi, for calling Esau. But, really, you don't need to go with me. I know it will soon be time to milk."

"After I called Esau, I phoned the Lambrights. Samuel was in the barn, because he guessed that you or I would call. He's coming over to handle the milking tonight and let Graceless out so she doesn't piddle on the floor." He brushed her cheek with the back of his hand. "She's pretty much housebroken, and I don't want my dog to get into bad habits."

"Your dog?" Hope surged in her heart. "You're keeping her?"

"Ja."

"I'm so glad. She adores you, and you'd both be miserable without each other." She paused as the car turned around in the barnyard. "I've got to go."

"I'm going with you. You need someone beside you, someone who loves you."

"You love me?" she whispered.

"Ja. How could I not? When I look into my heart, I find you there."

286

She wondered if any man had ever said anything more beautiful to a woman. She held his words close to her heart while he took her hand and led her to the car, that had rolled to a stop a few yards away.

Opening the back door, he motioned for her to get in. He shut the door and came around the other side. "Esau, as I told you, Ruth needs to get home as soon as possible."

The chubby man smiled over his shoulder. "Give me the address, and I'll get you there as fast as I legally can."

Ruth did and watched as he pushed the screen of a small device hanging from the windshield. When a map appeared, she guessed it was a way to help him find her family's farm. She buckled her seat belt, and Esau steered the car toward the main road at a speed that seemed astounding.

She would get home in minutes instead of hours. She hoped it would be soon enough.

Twenty-Two

When Esau stopped the car in front of the Schrock house, everything looked almost as it had when Ruth left. The maples and oaks had red and gold leaves instead of green, and the flowers had dried with the first frost. The mules looked up, curious, but the horse and the pony continued grazing. Inside, the house glowed with lamplight, even though it wasn't yet dark.

Ruth stepped out of the car, and her sister's goat stood on its hind legs to peek over the chicken wire on its pen. She saw Levi hand Esau some money.

She hadn't even thought about that. "I can—"

"Save it for later," Levi said, taking her arm and leading her up the walk, as if he had been to the house a hundred times. "The money isn't important."

She couldn't argue with that. Dread solidified into an invisible wall in front of her, and she had to force her feet forward. When Levi put his arm around her shoulders, she hoped she could draw on his strength.

The back door opened just as they reached the small porch that separated the main house from the empty *dawdihaus*. Her little sister Naomi burst out and flung her arms around Ruth.

"I'm so glad you're here. *Komm* in!" She glanced at Levi, but didn't ask any questions as she ran through the kitchen to the living room.

"*Daed!* Ruth is here, *Daed*."

Ruth entered the kitchen where she had spent so many hours working alongside her *mamm*. The ordinary room didn't look any different from any other kitchen in the district, but here special memories were layered as deeply as a winter quilt.

Levi took off his straw hat and put it on the peg beside her *daed*'s. It looked odd to see two straw hats hanging there. Ruth met his anxious eyes, then turned and went into the living room.

Daed sat on his favorite chair, his Bible open on his knees as he held his face in his hands.

"*Daed?*" she called quietly as she glanced at her sisters who stood on the stairs, watching him with uncertain expressions. She understood. Their *daed*, who dominated every room he walked into with his powerful presence, looked fragile.

He lowered his hands and raised his eyes. "Thank God you're finally here."

"I came as quickly as I could. *Daed*, what's wrong?"

He stood. "It's your *mamm*. She's having a difficult labor, and she needs help."

"The midwife—"

"Is on the other side of the county delivering twins. It may be a while before she's here." He hung his head. "I pray she won't be too late."

"So do I, *Daedi*." She hadn't called him that since she was a youngster, but he was so vulnerable in his fear. She had never seen him this way.

"Zeb," Levi said, "I can call 911, and the ambulance will be here fast."

Daed shook his head. "Deborah said she won't go to the hospital. She says she's always given birth in our home, and this *boppli* will be born here, too. Usually everything goes well, but twice . . ."

Ruth looked quickly away as her *daed*'s voice trailed off. He didn't have to explain further. Even though she had been little more than a *boppli* herself when her *mamm* lost Ruth's only brother, she had heard of how difficult that labor was. Her brother had been born feet first, the umbilical cord wrapped around his neck, already dead. She wasn't sure why the other *boppli* had miscarried, but it was obvious that *Daed* feared this *boppli* wouldn't survive, either.

"Help her, Ruth," her *daed* pleaded. "Help her and the *boppli*."

"Martha—"

"She's barely more than a *kind*, and she's too cautious. She isn't one to take a chance like you are, Ruth. You're willing to look for different ways to help." He rubbed his palms together nervously. "I've heard how God worked through you and that you helped a mute boy talk. Help your *mamm* now. Please."

She knew how hard it was for him to say that last word, for he was more used to giving orders than asking for help. Now he was asking.

"I'll try, *Daed*." She looked toward the room beyond the kitchen, where *Mamm* always gave birth. "But I'm not a midwife. If she needs more help than I can give . . ." She glanced at Levi, and he nodded. Without either of them saying a word, she knew he understood that he shouldn't hesitate to call the paramedics to the house, even if her *mamm* didn't want that.

"Do what you can, Ruth," *Daed* said. "It's always been more than enough."

She blinked back tears at his faith in her and nodded, unable to speak.

Levi walked with her to the closed door to *Mamm*'s birthing room, which was used as a storage room the rest of the time. In a whisper, he asked, "Why isn't your *daed* with your *mamm*?"

Ruth put her hand on the doorknob, a faint smile on her face. "I know a husband is usually with his *fraa* when she's in labor, but not mine. *Mamm* told me that when she was in labor with me, *Daed* was so overwhelmed that he fainted. He vowed he'd never make a fool of himself like that again."

Levi grinned and squeezed her hand. "I'll be here, praying with your *daed* and your sisters that all goes well."

"Danki." She opened the door and went inside, closing it behind her.

The big bed had been pulled to the center of the room. The crib was next to it, already made with soft sheets and with small clothes waiting. The blanket chest had been moved away from the foot of the bed and against a wall, so it wouldn't be in the way. On the other side of the bed, her seventeen-year-old sister, Martha, looked up.

"*Mamm*, Ruth is here."

Her *mamm* lay in a nest of pillows, a sheen of sweat across her face.

"Ruth, my dear daughter." She smiled and held out her hand, and Ruth rushed forward to take it. "I'm so glad you're here. Your younger sister or brother is in a big hurry to join us."

"But it shouldn't be coming for another month."

"*Bopplin* come when they and God wish them to." She winced with another contraction.

Ruth put her hand on her *mamm*'s belly and waited for the muscles to relax again. "How close are the contractions?"

Mamm looked at Martha, who said, "About two minutes."

Silently, Ruth groaned in dismay. If the contractions were spaced farther apart, they might subside until the *boppli* was nearer its due date. Now . . .

She smiled though she felt like crying. "It looks like you're right, *Mamm*. This *boppli* is coming soon."

For the first time, her *mamm*'s serenity cracked. "Nothing feels as it should, Ruth. I'm laboring, but it doesn't feel right."

"What do you mean?"

"I can't explain it other than to say that the *boppli*

293

doesn't seem to be moving toward being born. It's as stubborn as you, Ruth." She tried to smile again. "I pray it has a *gut* reason, like you always do, for being mulish."

Ruth guessed this was the reason *Daed* had sent for her. She had no idea what to do, but prayed that God would guide her, giving her inspiration to help her *mamm*. As if she had no doubts, she sent her sister to get some warm cloths to put on *Mamm*'s forehead and to bathe her sweaty limbs. *Mamm* smiled, and Ruth wished she had as much faith in herself now as her parents had in her.

Hour after hour, she stayed beside her *mamm* and prayed that the *boppli* would be born alive. When each contraction began, she massaged *Mamm*'s back as she'd seen the midwife do last time. She had Martha bring in some broth so *Mamm* could have something to eat and keep up her strength. She kept up a steady, mostly one-sided conversation. She told *Mamm* about her scholars and how David was speaking more and more. She shared Esther's and Hannah's plan to surprise each other and how they both had been surprised more than they could have guessed. She related how she and the scholars outran the storm in Levi's wagon. She made both her sister and *Mamm* laugh with stories about Graceless and how Levi thought she was going to teach with the scholars' desks all pushed into the middle of the room.

"Who is this Levi?" *Mamm* asked. "You mention his name over and over."

How did she explain Levi? He was the man who exasperated and thrilled her. The man she had doubted would defend her, but who had stood by her during her darkest moments. The man who had brightened her life beyond anything she could have imagined. The man she loved . . . and the man who loved her.

"Look, *Mamm*!" Martha teased. "Ruth is blushing. This Levi must be pretty important to her."

"Then I need to meet him," *Mamm* said with mock sternness.

Ruth grinned. "Now?"

They all began to laugh.

The door opened and Naomi looked in, her eyes wide because the ten-year-old had never seen *Mamm* in labor.

"*Daed* wants to know why you're all weeping," she said.

"We're not weeping. We're laughing." Ruth shooed her little sister out of the room. "Tell *Daed* that laughter is the best thing for *Mamm* now." She closed the door.

That set off a new round of laughter until another contraction began.

But their high spirits disappeared. *Mamm* became more and more exhausted as the labor took its toll on her. She fell asleep between contractions and woke with a groan. Even back rubs and warm cloths no longer helped.

Ruth saw the growing panic in her sister's eyes. She fought to be calm herself, but it was harder with every passing minute. Where was the midwife?

Lord, how much longer should I let this go on before I send Levi to call the ambulance to take her to the hospital? Show me the future You see, so I make the right decision. Don't let me decide wrong. Don't let my mamm suffer for my pride in believing I know best. I know that I don't know best. You do. Show me, Lord, that I'm not alone.

The answer came from a memory she treasured. It was

of her sitting at her *daed*'s feet while *Mamm* rocked one of her younger sisters. *Daed* held the Bible, opening it to a special verse, as he did each night. He began to read aloud from Chapter 28 of Matthew: *All power is given unto me in heaven and in earth. Go ye therefore, and teach all nations, baptizing them in the name of the Father, and of the Son, and of the Holy Ghost: teaching them to observe all things whatsoever I have commanded you: and, lo, I am with you always, even unto the end of the world.*

She was humbled by the words Jesus had spoken to His disciples. The ones *Daed* had shared with her and the ones God now used to remind her—as He had often—that there was no challenge that she couldn't overcome if she turned to Him and submerged her will to His.

Ruth glanced up as the door opened again. Was it the midwife?

Naomi slipped into the room, her eyes wide with fear. She edged around the bed and grasped Ruth's hand. "Is she . . . ?" She gulped, unable to put her fright in words.

"She's resting," Ruth quickly reassured her little sister. "The labor is still moving slowly."

Naomi hugged her. "I'm glad you're here."

"Me, too," said Martha from the other side of the bed. "*Daed* said you would know what to do."

Ruth didn't want to tell them how little she knew. Instead she said, "When she's awake, *Mamm* is helping me help her."

"Maybe, but *Daed*'s right. He said you are the one God made to help others. Levi told us how you helped that little boy talk when nobody else could. *Daed* and *Mamm* thanked God for putting you in the right place to help him."

She slowly sat on the blanket chest, unable to speak. She was filled with joy that her parents had so much faith in her, but she wished she'd known before now. Then, as she thought back to the day before she left for the Lambrights', she recalled how both of her parents had said they depended on her to help her sisters and others. Why hadn't she realized until now that they meant their words as praise?

A groan came from the bed, and they all turned. Ruth stood and hurried to the bed. She took *Mamm*'s right hand while she motioned for Naomi to leave. As soon as Naomi had shut the door behind her, Ruth told Martha to take *Mamm*'s other hand. Martha clasped *Mamm*'s left hand, grimacing when *Mamm*'s fingers crushed theirs as the contraction rose to its peak and then faded.

Ruth sent Martha for a cup of apple juice for *Mamm*, whose face now had an alarming gray sheen.

Mamm continued to hold Ruth's hand. *"Danki."*

"I'm glad to be here with you. I wish I could do more to help."

"You are here. That is more than enough."

Ruth wouldn't argue with her mother now, but she feared that *Mamm* was wrong. What if they couldn't bring this *boppli* safely into the world? What if her help wasn't enough?

Where was the midwife?

Ruth stood by her *mamm*'s bed with tears rolling down her face. *Mamm* looked so peaceful now, her golden eyelashes lying on her pale cheeks. It was over. At last, it was over. Ruth knew it was God's will that her *mamm* had endured so much suffering, but it was over now. Ruth must accept what had happened instead of railing against it.

She lightly touched her *mamm*'s cool arm, wishing *Mamm* could give her a giant hug as she had when Ruth was a little girl. Drawing back her fingers, she wiped away her tears.

"Ruth?"

Turning, she saw Diana, the *Englisch* midwife. Diana placed a bundle in Ruth's arms. "You caught this one, so you should be the one to introduce your *daed* to his newest *kind*."

"*Danki*—I mean, thank you for all you did, Diana."

"I didn't do much but watch." She curved her hand around the *boppli*'s head. "You go to your anxious papa while I get your mom cleaned up." She sighed and looked back toward the bed. "I'm so sorry I wasn't here earlier."

"I'm just so grateful that you got here when you did. So very, very grateful to you and to God." Tears filled Ruth's eyes again. How many more could she cry?

Taking a deep breath, Ruth went to the door. She wished someone else could tell *Daed* the news, but it was up to her.

Silence came from the living room as she walked to the wide doorway. Levi was on his knees beside *Daed*, his arm over her *daed*'s quaking shoulders. Around them, her sisters also prayed.

She drew in another deep breath before she said, *"Daed?"*

He jumped to his feet, his face ashen above his graying beard. When he saw the bundle she carried, he asked, "Your *mamm*?"

She blinked back even more tears. That *Daed*'s first question was about his *fraa* showed, yet again, the deep and abiding love they had shared for so many years.

Walking toward her *daed*, she said, "It was a very bad labor, even for a strong woman like *Mamm*." The tears refused to stay in her eyes, but she smiled weakly. "*Mamm* is sleeping. Diana says that healing sleep is what she needs now."

"The *boppli*?" His hands shook as he looked at the bundle she cradled next to her heart.

"Healthy and perfect. Ten toes and ten fingers and a headful of hair. Diana believes that *Mamm* miscounted, and the *boppli* is close to full term." She hesitated before asking, "*Daed*, would you like to hold your newest daughter?"

She held her breath, fearing his disappointment at learning he had his eighth daughter. She knew how hard he had prayed for a son after so many girls, a son to carry on his name and help him in the fields and take over the farm when he and *Mamm* retired to the *dawdi-haus*.

His grin was broader than any she'd ever seen on his face. "*Ja!*" He held out his arms. "It's time for little Deborah to meet her *daedi*."

Ruth placed the tiny *boppli* in his arms. Her *daed*'s forbidding face softened as he carried his new daughter to his favorite chair and sat down so Ruth's sisters could look over his shoulders to admire little Deborah. How had she forgotten the expression *Daed* wore each time God blessed their family with another, healthy *boppli*?

Daed looked at her and smiled. The love on his face wasn't just for little Deborah—it was for her as well as all her sisters.

When Levi drew Ruth up against his chest, he pressed his face to the side of her *kapp* and whispered, "I knew you could do it, Ruth."

"I had help." She took his face between her hands and gazed into his eyes. "I was never alone. God was with us, and I knew whatever He had planned for us was because He loves us."

"As *ich liebe dich*. Is it possible that you love me, too?"

"With all my heart."

He stepped back and winked, startling her. She was even more shocked when he turned to her *daed* and said, "Zeb, I want to marry your daughter Ruth."

She stared at Levi in amazement. Asking her *daed* for his permission to wed her wasn't the way it was done among the Plain people. Her *daed* and sisters stared at him as if they couldn't believe what they had heard. She was even more astounded.

Levi was always the *gut* boy . . . until now.

Levi never bent a rule . . . until now.

But what would her father say to such a break with tradition?

Levi broke the silence when no one else spoke. "I know I should go to my own deacon and ask him to serve as my *Schteckliman*," Levi said. "But I can't wait the week it would take him to come over here to talk to you. The wedding season is nearly here, and I don't want to wait another year to marry your daughter. If you believe my behavior is wrong, I will accept your chastisement, as I would from my own deacon. But I wanted you to know the truth of how much I love your daughter."

For once, her *daed* was speechless . . . and so was Ruth. She could hardly believe that the man standing before her, so handsome and yet so humble in his request, was the same Levi who hadn't been able to say more than a few words in a row to her when they first met.

Her *daed* looked down at little Deborah, as if she were a great treasure. He raised his eyes to meet Ruth's, and his expression was the same. In his gaze, she saw the truth he had hidden so well that she only now dared to believe it. Her *daed* did love her. But what would he say to Levi's surprising question?

A smile tickled her lips as she wondered what he would think of Levi's saying about preachers' sons and deacons' daughters. One of these days, she would mention it to him. She suspected he might laugh.

Finally, *Daed* spoke. "I never expected this day to turn out as it has. Not only have I been blessed today with a beautiful new daughter, but with a son." He smiled at Levi and gave a slight nod toward Ruth.

As her sisters giggled, Levi grasped Ruth's hands. "So will you marry me, Ruth?"

"Ja." She ran her hand along his cheek. *"Ich liebe dich*, and I'd be so happy to marry you, if you're willing to put up with such a wayward *fraa.*"

"You aren't wayward, Ruth. You are simply filled with . . ." His eyes twinkled. "Filled with zest."

"Zest?"

"It means—"

"I know what it means," she said. "Joyful, filled with a love of life and everything around you."

"To me, it means Ruth Schrock, the woman I love." He laughed in the moment before he sealed their promise with a kiss.

Glossary

ab in kopp crazy

ach oh

aenti aunt

Ausbund hymn book

blabbermaul chatterbox; blabbermouth

boppli (plural: bopplin) baby

daed, daedi dad, daddy

danki thank you

dawdi-haus grandparents' house attached to main house

Deitsch Pennsylvania German

dochder (plural: dochdern) daughter

doctorfraa a woman healer

dumm dumb; stupid

Englisch non-Amish
Englischer non-Amish person
fraa wife
gennuk enough
graabhof graveyard
gross-mammi grandma
gude mariye good morning
gut good
gut nacht good night
ich liebe dich I love you
ja yes
kaffi coffee
kapp prayer head covering for females
kind (plural: kinder) child
komm come
Leit the people, the district
maedel (plural: maedels) girl; young unmarried woman
mamm mom
mei kinder my children
mutza coat worn by a man to Sunday services
onkel uncle
Ordnung district's rules of behavior and worship
rumspringa running-around time before baptism
schatzi little treasure (an endearment)
Schteckliman intermediary between groom's and bride's
 parents
snitz pie dried apple pie
sohn (plural: söhne) son
vorsinger lead singer at services or singings

was iss letz?   what's wrong?
wie geht's?   hello, how are you doing?
wilkomm   welcome
wunderbaar   wonderful
yunga   young one

Ready to find
your next great read?

Let us help.

Visit prh.com/nextread

Penguin
Random
House